I0773143

Orcs Do It Better

ORCS LOVE CURVY GIRLS
BOOK ONE

MICHELE MILLS

Copyright © 2025 by Michele Mills

All rights reserved.

No part of this book may be reproduced in any form or by any electronic or mechanical means, including information storage and retrieval systems, without written permission from the author, except for the use of brief quotations in a book review.

Cover Artist: Mayhem Cover Creations

Editor: Aquila Editing

Thank you for taking a chance on my body-positive, quirky romance about hulking orcs who love their females exactly as they are. I appreciate you more than you'll ever know!

CHAPTER 1
Ellie

THE CELL PHONE vibrates again for the third time in the last two minutes. I'm finally able to pick it up and look at the screen. My stomach sours because it's Marcus. Calling again and again and again.

Ugh. I drop the phone like I've been bitten by a snake. Why is my ex trying to contact me on a Friday morning before work and school? Nothing good will come from this. Why can't he text, or leave a voicemail like a normal person? If he needs something, he's supposed to contact my lawyer.

Doesn't this man remember we don't talk anymore and haven't for years?

I stare down at the phone, bad memories of a relationship gone wrong flooding back into my head. Once upon a time Marcus Adams, whom I originally met in college, was a charming man, and I thought we had a lot in common. Looking back, he was much *too* charming. But I married him, thinking he was the right guy for me. We had a daughter together, and afterwards, everything went to hell in a handbasket.

My ex is a narcissist whose social drinking morphed into the disease of alcoholism and I'm ninety-nine percent certain he's now living a life of interstate crime that will eventually land him in federal prison.

Hence our divorce.

And the subsequent restraining order.

This was all finalized long ago, and I haven't seen or heard from him since. Hell, prior to that we hadn't shared a bed together in years, due to his cheating. I'm now at a stage in life where our marriage is a fuzzy, distant memory that seems like it happened to someone else.

Zoe and I moved far away to start a brand-new life together in Northern California.

I put the phone on silent and shove the small screen under a throw pillow. How can Marcus have anything important to say? If he wants to get his act together and regain the right to see his daughter, this would be great. He can contact my lawyer and get the ball rolling.

My nonresponse might seem rude, but I've been burned so many times, this "planned ignoring" is really the best route. It's in fact the response I'd planned out with my therapist, in case he ever came back.

This reminds me of what my next step should be... I pick up the phone, block and delete him. And then note the time and day so I can later alert my lawyer or the local authorities, if needed.

I take a deep, calming breath.

We're not in the same part of the state anymore. He's far, far away living his own life. I can do this. Boundaries are a good thing.

"Grandma, can I have another waffle?"

I smile at the sound of my six-year-old daughter's lovely voice. *My baby girl.*

"Sure honey, just a sec," my mom answers from the kitchen.

There's a clatter of dishes. The opening of a cabinet and a drawer.

When I accepted this new teaching position, my mom, Laurie Willis, offered to come along, which has been wonderful. This relocation from Southern to Northern California has been difficult for three sun-loving gals, who only viewed snow as something to visit but not actually live amongst. But all three of us are pleasantly surprised at how much we love this ski resort town we've moved to.

We're even contemplating taking ski lessons.

My mom wakes up early each morning and gets Zoe bathed, dressed, fed and monitors that she gets off to school. And when Zoe returns at the end of the day and steps off the school bus, my mom feeds her, makes sure her homework gets done and keeps her entertained until I can get home from work. My mother even tidies up around the house, does most of the laundry and all the dishes.

I feel spoiled.

For the last six months I've been able to focus on my demanding job as the head of the social studies department at Black Oak Academy—a fancy, brand new private K-12 school that just opened this year. I remain grateful to have snagged such an amazing position at the relatively young age of thirty-two years old.

My daughter now has a life as drama-free as I can make it, with two people in her home who love her unconditionally.

I open my MacBook and refocus on the job at hand. These student essays aren't going to grade themselves. This assignment for AP history seemed so promising but has now turned into a total disaster. I'm tired of pretending I'm an expert in ancient orc history. I did not teach this lesson very well, hence the lack of credible responses. The good news is that I've already turned in the grades for this semester and this essay can be extra credit for next term. No harm, no foul.

"Still regretting the 'orc communal economy before human contact' essay question?" my mom questions as she strolls into the living room with another steaming drink.

I smile in gratitude and take the offered mug of coffee. "Yeah, lots of regrets…and thanks." Then I rub at my temples where a headache has threatened since the moment I opened this laptop earlier this morning. "If one more student claims that orcs traded exclusively in virgin sacrifices, I'm going to fail the entire class."

"No, you won't," my big-hearted mother laughs. "You're too nice for that." Mom flashes me a wide smile and sits primly in a nearby chair.

I give her a warm smile in return. She's right, of course I won't.

My dad passed away a few years ago (much too young) from a sudden stroke, leaving my mother, me and our whole family heartbroken and in a state of shock we've all never fully recovered from.

My mother took an early retirement package offered by the company she'd worked for. After losing her husband and an all-consuming thirty-year career, Mom stated she wanted to start a new life with her only grandchild nearby, so we moved in together.

We were both going through tough times. For her, the death of a husband and a huge life change. And for me, my beloved father passing away and my nasty divorce proceedings.

We needed each other.

Mom sold the home I'd grown up in and we pooled our money and bought a much nicer house than we would've gotten individually. We now live in a nice neighborhood and the school I work at, and where Zoe attends, isn't all that far away.

It's a wonderful situation.

At first, I wasn't sure how us living together again would work out, because it'd been over a decade since I'd lived with my mother, but it turns out we get along great. Zoe loves having her grandmother in the house and I'm grateful for all my mom's help.

The only negative about living here, in Truckee, California, would be all the snow. The snow, snow, snow.

"I'll make this assignment extra credit and have it count towards next semester. It's not the students' fault that I'm not the right teacher for this subject." I glance over, checking out what she's wearing today. "Nice outfit, mom. I love it. That looks great on you."

"Thanks," she grins. "I got this on sale."

Today, her slender form is highlighted in a navy blue athleisure outfit and a very expensive pair of white sneakers. She's ready for her daily powerwalk in the neighborhood, which always starts right after I leave for work and Zoe leaves for school. Because it's December and there's snow outside, she's ready to layer up, with her jacket, gloves and hat ready in the hallway closet to walk along snowplowed streets, because nothing will stop "the walk." There's even a backup treadmill in her bedroom, for those days when a storm hits and going out is impossible.

My mother dresses better and more stylishly than I can ever dream of. At fifty-six years old, I consider her to be fantastically beautiful. There's never a hair out of place, or a nail that's not perfectly manicured. I want to grow up to be my mom.

The main difference between the two of us is that she's always been slender, and I've always been overweight. I'm reasonably certain I get this tendency from Dad's side of the family. Despite this difference between us, she's never said a single negative comment about my weight. Instead, she's my greatest ally and always makes positive remarks about my appearance.

I love this woman so much. She's not only my mother but my best friend too.

"You should've hired that orc professor you were talking about," she comments, while sipping at a vitamin-packed green smoothie through a glass straw. "He could've taught this lesson instead of you and be the one assigning these essays. It just makes sense."

"Oh, I did hire that professor. He couldn't start the school year with us in August, for reasons which I still don't entirely understand, which sucks. But he's starting when winter break ends and will be with us for the second half of the school year."

"Oh, how did I not know this? I guess I assumed since he didn't start the year with you, he wasn't hired. Does that mean my daughter has hired the first orc to ever teach at a human high school?"

I sit up straight. "Well...yes. I did. This is the whole point of Black Oak Academy. We're going to be the first school to integrate orc teachers. Schools near orc communes have been allowing young orcs to be taught alongside humans for decades now, but we're the first in the nation to also have orc teachers who will be teaching not just orcs but humans too."

She sets down her green smoothie and claps her hands. "Ellie, that's wonderful. I have to tell my friends and followers that this is finally happening. Ooh, I can make a video of this and maybe it will go viral..." She wanders away, tapping on her phone.

I roll my eyes. "He sounds pretty wonderful," I say, mainly to myself. "Three books published on orc history, tenure at that new orc university in Maine, and recommendation letters that made the school board swoon. He and I are going to be co-teaching together. The only weird part was that we conducted the final interview via video call, with his camera conveniently malfunctioning. I've never actually seen what Professor Garlen Irontree truly looks like. But the hiring committee loved him, and I was convinced."

Mom wanders back and opens her mouth to respond but is interrupted by the sound of tires crunching on the snow outside. She turns toward the front window. "Who is that?"

I put down my laptop. "Huh. I don't know. Why would someone be visiting this early?"

We're both on our feet, curious, peering through the curtains.

And unfortunately, I immediately recognize the man stepping out of the backseat of the car parked in the driveway and let out a groan of disappointment. "Oh hell no. Tell me this isn't happening."

"It's happening."

Thankfully, Zoe has left the kitchen and I can hear that she's using the hallway bathroom. I don't want her to see this. I'm ninety-nine percent certain her father is up to no good. "I moved away to start over and now he's followed me?" I hiss.

"Because he's an asshole and he's probably drinking again and not making good decisions."

I wince. While my mom might be speaking the plain truth, I've always considered Marcus's alcohol addiction a disease. The underlying narcissism would probably have led to divorce anyways, but I really believe the inciting incident was that damn addiction that I suspect he still can't beat. I attended weekly Al-Anon meetings for two whole years, which helped me to learn how to remain supportive and retain my own sanity during his many trips to rehab. Those people were my consistent support system, and I still miss them.

But Marcus's subsequent verbal abuse, cheating and possible criminal behavior dissolved any feelings for my former husband.

"He used to always say he was trying to come around because he wants to see Zoe."

My mom purses her lips. "Lies, all lies."

"I can't figure out what he really wants. Why is he following me like this when he knows it can mean jail?"

I watch as he kicks snow onto the walkway that was just cleared. He makes wild gestures, making me wonder if he's indeed been drinking again, which makes me sad. Marcus Adams has changed so drastically from the man I originally met ten years ago as to be unrecognizable. He doesn't even look the same. His normally meticulous appearance has turned scraggy. Even from this distance his dark hair looks dirty and not even brushed. He wears an open coat, a T-shirt, jeans and black boots.

Marcus lost a cushy, high-paying job his father had helped him to get. He stole from his family and mistreated them so much, they've also had to cut him off, even while holding out hope that one day he'd overcome his disease. But for me, it's not simply the alcohol disease that I'm concerned about.

I can't have this man back in our lives.

And suddenly it becomes important that I confront him. "Stay inside with Zoe," I grit, grabbing my coat and phone. "I'll take care of this."

"Ellie, don't… there's no use in trying to talk to him. Let's just call the…"

But I'm already out the door, slamming it behind me.

CHAPTER 2
Ellie

THE DECEMBER AIR bites at my cheeks as I march toward Marcus, phone ready to call the police. The planned ignoring has flown out the window, and my anger has now gotten the best of me.

Rage boils deep in my veins. How dare he show up like this, as if the restraining order means nothing?

I was lucky enough to grow up in a loving family and I'd always wanted that for my own children one day. The last two years have been about me remaining single, attending lots of therapy sessions, and moving beyond what happened between us. Rearranging my life so I could give Zoe something better. I will not allow this man to blow up the peace I've built.

I stop at a safe distance and glance over at the car. A wide-eyed Uber driver is parked in my driveway. He must be freaking out with indecision. Poor guy.

"Ellie," Marcus snorts, looking me up and down with a sneer of disgust. "You haven't changed. Still as huge as I remember, not even trying to lose any of that extra fat you're always carrying around."

Ugh, I forgot how much I hated his verbal abuse. When we were first together he claimed that I was beautiful and sexy just the way I was, and after we exchanged vows those claims quickly devolved into cruel remarks.

"Well, you look worse than I remember," I respond, trying my best to remain calm and not escalate the situation.

A muscle ticks on his jaw. "So this is where you took our daughter."

"Yes. You found me," I answer, trying my best to curb the worst of my rage and give my daughter's father a modicum of respect. "As you can see, this is where we live now. And you know you shouldn't be here. I'll give you one chance. Your driver is waiting. If you get back in that car and leave right now and never come back again, we can pretend this law-breaking never happened."

"Hell, no," he rages. "Do you know how much it cost me to get here? I have to talk to you about something."

I throw my hands up. "Marcus, that doesn't make any sense. If you need something, you can talk to my lawyer. There's a restraining order. I took a new job and moved across the state so we could both have a fresh start. Get in that car and leave."

"I'm here because I also want to see my daughter." He steps a little too close and I swear I can smell a hint of alcohol on his breath and his clothes. "It…it's my right."

This declaration doesn't move me in the least. Marcus wanting to see "his daughter" is always code for him needing money. "Your *right*? Marcus, you lost that right when you emptied our bank accounts and disappeared for six months. You lost that right when you kept missing your visitation appointments and then showed up drunk at her preschool. You lost that right when the judge signed that order saying you had to stay at least one hundred feet away from us."

His features darken, and he clenches his fists.

I lift my chin and stand my ground.

"You think you're so much better than me now, with your fancy job and your fancy house."

My finger hovers over the emergency call button. "You've got thirty seconds to leave before I call the police."

"You fat bitch. You paid for this house with my money. All those years supporting you while you played college, and this is how you—"

"*Your* money? You mean the money you stole? The money the feds are investigating you for?" I cut him off, retreating a step. Ugh. Why am I even outside? Mom was right. This was dumb of me. Trying to reason with someone in the throes of addiction is like trying to talk to a brick wall. I should've stayed in the house and called the police from there.

Words spill out of my mouth because I suppose I've still got a lot I wanted to say but never had the chance.

"It's not my fault you dropped out of school. I stayed and got my degree and teaching credential, while raising our daughter basically alone because you were 'too busy' to help. And I didn't buy anything with any of your money. I've got a good job and did all of this myself. My mom lives with me now and we went in together on this house. Zoe is happy here, but she'd be happier if she had a dad she could count on."

His face contorts with rage, and he lunges forward unexpectedly.

A gasp of fear flies out of my mouth, and I stumble backward, nearly falling in the snow. My finger jabs at my phone screen so I can alert 911, but I keep missing the button. Before the call connects, something massive and green barrels into my peripheral vision.

No, not something. Someone.

A hulking orc, at least seven feet tall with curved horns and elongated tusks that protrude from his lower jaw, slams into Marcus, sending him sprawling across my snowy front lawn. Behind him, four more orcs appear, spreading out to surround him.

I freeze. The phone is forgotten in my hand.

I've never seen orcs in real life, and I must admit these guys are amazing. They are all dressed in boots, jeans and unbuttoned flannel shirts Where did they come from? The lead orc, clearly the largest, plants one massive black boot on Marcus's chest, pinning him to the ground.

"What the hell?" Marcus sputters, squirming on his back, face red with a mixture of rage and terror.

The main orc ignores him and turns slightly to bark orders at the others. "Secure the van. Check for weapons and lock the handcuffs. Standard procedure. Oh, and pay off the driver."

Standard procedure? Do these orcs regularly arrest people? They don't look like the police, but there is a shiny black van nearby with the side door open. And they do have very heavy handcuffs in their hands.

Marcus shouts obscenities, spittle flying out of his mouth as he struggles. His free arm swings wildly, connecting with the orc's shin.

Big mistake.

The huge orc hauls Marcus up by his jacket collar and delivers a punch to his face that makes me wince. My ex drops like a stone, blood trickling from his nose, moaning pitifully on the snow.

"What are you guys doing?" I blurt out, finally finding my voice.

Five heads swivel toward me, blinking in surprise as if they've only just noticed I'm standing there.

The orc who punched Marcus gives me an intense gaze. "We're making a citizen's arrest of this unworthy human," he announces with an impossibly deep voice, as if this explains everything. "We're transporting him to the police station and passing him off to the local authorities."

"A citizen's arrest of an unworthy human?" I repeat and glance down at Marcus who is indeed behaving in a way that can easily be described as unworthy. In the past, no matter how much he drank, Marcus never physically hurt me, or hurt Zoe for that matter, and yet when he took that menacing step towards me, there was something dangerous in his gaze. Something I'd never seen before. This new version of Marcus Adams is a stranger I simply don't recognize.

"Thanks for the help," I finally respond as the other orcs lift my ex off the ground and shove him into the nearby van. What else can you say when monstrous strangers arrive and behave heroically? I hold up my phone. "I guess I don't have to call the police then?"

The orc's eyes widen slightly, as if my easy acceptance has caught him off guard. His heated gaze slowly travels from my face downward, taking in my thick curves with an unexpected intensity that makes my body heat up.

Oh wow. I literally can't remember the last time a man looked at me with appreciation in his gaze, and I felt a feeling of reciprocation. I suppose this is because I've been in the midst of a very long "working on myself" phase, coupled with a deep mistrust of relationships in general that I haven't been able to shake off.

Thankfully, I'm neatly dressed for work. My strawberry-blonde hair is blown out, makeup applied, and I happen to be wearing my favorite outfit. And for reasons I can't explain...I lick my lips and smile back at him in a highly suggestive manner.

Oh wow. Am I flirting with this orc? No, this can't be. We don't even know each other. And we're standing in front of my house, with my ex-husband screaming obscenities in the background. Awkward. And not exactly romantic.

Movement catches my attention. A ball of black and white fur darts between the orc's massive legs. I gasp with surprise when I spy the cutest corgi I've ever seen in my entire life, with an impossibly fluffy rear end, wearing little blue snow boots and a matching blue sweater.

He is so adorable I cry out with joy and clap my hands. I want to take this sweet animal home and make him mine.

The dog must like me too, because he wags that comical

behind and races toward me through the snow, jumping up against my legs.

Without thinking, I bend down and gather the excited animal into my arms. "Well, hello there," I coo, momentarily forgetting the chaos surrounding us. I had no idea I liked dogs so much, but this one is simply darling. "Do you belong to these big, scary orcs?" I question.

The corgi licks my face enthusiastically.

I can't help but laugh, planting a kiss on its wet nose.

The lead orc now stands much closer while the others remain busy behind him. He's so very tall and continues to silently watch me with that dark, heated gaze.

And I realize he's probably the sexiest man I've ever encountered. I've always known that orcs were big and muscular, but I guess I thought if I ever met one in person I'd be turned off by the horns, tusks and the green skin. This isn't true at all. Mainly, I'm enthralled with the fact that he's not even wearing a coat or gloves on this cold, snowy morning.

His muscular chest expands with a deep breath, nostrils flaring as if he's scenting me.

Strangely, I feel comfortable next to this fierce orc, while holding his dog. In fact, I'm giddy with delight that all of them are dealing with Marcus so I don't have to.

The van door closes and the vehicle pulls away from the curb. Another orc waves goodbye to the Uber driver as he backs out of the driveway.

I'm about to make introductions and even invite them all inside for coffee, when the sexy orc says something I don't understand.

"You need to leave," he suddenly growls, his voice sounding deeper than before.

My brow furrows. "Huh? You...you want me to leave for work? I mean, I could...I was going to leave soon anyways, but..."

Another growl rumbles in his chest. "Orcs historically kidnap their brides in the dark of winter with or without their consent. If you don't leave immediately, I *will* impregnate you with my orc son."

My mouth drops open. What the heck? Did I hear him right?

Did this orc say he wants me pregnant?

I'm frozen in place, stunned in amazement. I should be terrified, wanting to run into my house, lock the door and call the police, because I know he's not joking. This is not an idle threat. Orcs kidnapped and impregnated human women for thousands of years, hence the former hatred between our two species.

But these are modern times, and the past is the past. Nowadays orcs are citizens with equal rights, and modern orcs do not kidnap women off the street.

My gaze catches on the defined muscles of his bare chest and the glint of that silver belt buckle. His green skin looks so smooth and touchable. His dark hair is cut very short. And there's something familiar about his smooth, deep voice. Have I met this orc before? It seems impossible considering I've never met any orc in real life until today.

Instead of following his direct instructions, I instinctively snuggle his dog and take a step closer. "What do you mean, dark of winter?" I question, as if we're having a perfectly normal conversation.

The beastly orc inhales again, and this time something feral flashes in his gorgeous, dark eyes. The tall black horns on his forehead and those white tusks that jut out from his lower lips appear more menacing.

I bite at my lips and hold the dog closer.

"Female, you need to get away from me, *now*," he bellows.

"But..."

He throws his head back and lets out a thunderous roar that seems to echo down the street. His green neck is corded, and his massive chest and arms grow wider and thicker. His crotch is obscenely tented with something bigger than I've ever seen on a human male.

This time I take a step back. Uh oh. He tried to warn me.

The corgi leaps from my arms, barking frantically.

The three remaining orcs stop their conversations and exchange alarmed glances. "Garlen, no!" one of them shouts, lunging forward.

What happens next is utter chaos.

"My bride," the orc snarls as he reaches for me. I stumble back, trying to deflect the second time a man tries to grab for me this morning. This time I fully land on my ass in the snow.

Three orcs converge on their leader, swiftly tackling him to the ground with surprising force.

Mom rushes outside, her face pale. "Ellie? What on earth… are you okay?" In moments she's beside me, helping me up from the snow and pulling me farther away from the warring orcs. I stand with her and swipe at my ass, hoping it's not too wet.

The orcs struggle with their violent, thrashing companion. It's basically like *Clash of the Titans*, but with lots of green muscle and black horns. Fists fly, legs kick and a set of chains appears out of nowhere. Working together, the three of them manage to subdue the snarling orc, binding his wrists and ankles with heavy black chains.

All the while Garlen repeatedly continues to shout, "my bride."

And each time something within me takes notice, thinking it somehow sounds right.

Meanwhile, Zoe innocently hops down the front steps, her pink backpack bouncing, ready to wait for the school bus. My daughter takes in the scene before her, lets out a squeak of dismay and runs right for me. "Mommy?" she whispers, clutching at my hand. "What's happening to that orc?"

Before I can answer, I notice that one of them breaks away from the others and stomps over to us. There is a smear of blood on his cheek, from a cut lip. He glances over at Mom and then down at Zoe and gives them smiles of greeting. Then he meets my gaze. "I know this looks bad, but don't worry. We will throw him into the pit in the basement and try to keep him caged all winter," he explains breathlessly. "Garlen Irontree will not be able to act reasonably until spring." And then he returns to help drag him away.

They're going to *try* to keep him caged? And did they say that orc's name is Garlen Irontree? The same Garlen from…?

"Who are those guys?" Zoe questions.

"I *think*," I say slowly, recognizing the address they're heading toward, "the one they've chained is our new neighbor. In fact, all of those orcs are our new neighbors."

"Why is he chained?"

"Because he likes your mom too much and lost his mind when he got too close to her beauty," Mom comments, shaking her head. "He instantly turned into a savage and had to be restrained."

"He tried to warn me," I say. "He must've known it was happening and told me to get away from him. But I didn't leave quick enough, and they had to do…that."

I should be terrified. Disgusted. Maybe still contemplating a call to the police. But I feel none of these things. Instead, I'm strangely hot and bothered, wishing I could follow behind them and hold Garlen's hand and try to calm him down.

What is wrong with me? Of course I don't *really* want that orc to kidnap me, but I wouldn't mind at all getting to know him better.

Mom, Zoe and I continue to stand side by side and watch open-mouthed as the group of orcs drag their snarling companion all the away to the front portico of the mansion next door. The orc's gaze continues to remain locked onto mine with an intensity that sends shivers down my spine. The corgi follows alongside the group, bouncing in the snow.

They pause and engage in some sort of intense conversation. The same orc as before, who seems to be the youngest, breaks away and returns to us to speak again. He nods apologetically. "We just moved in yesterday. Sorry about…" He gestures vaguely at the entire situation. "Winter is especially difficult for wild orcs like Garlen. You have nothing to worry about as long as you stay away from him until the spring. We will take care of this." And then he rushes back.

He pitches in to help them finish their job—dragging Garlen over the threshold. The corgi rushes in behind them, and the front door slams shut.

It's suddenly very quiet outside.

"Well…" my mom muses. "That was certainly an interesting way to meet our new neighbors. A group of mysterious orcs arrive and perform a citizen's arrest on Marcus, which I very much appreciate. And then one of their own loses his mind and is now chained and caged in their basement? That's odd. I always wondered who was going to move into that McMansion next door. Now I know." She takes out her cell phone, captures a quick picture and starts tapping on the screen. "I've got to tell your aunt about this; she was always curious about who was going to move in next door."

Meanwhile, a horrible realization dawns on me.

Garlen.

That orc is Professor Garlen Irontree. The male we hired to teach at Black Oak. And he's also the same orc who threatened to kidnap and impregnate me. And two weeks from now, when school starts again after winter break, I'll be his boss at Black Oak Academy, co-teaching with him in the same classroom.

Oh hell. How is this going to work out?

CHAPTER 3
Garlen

I SCENTED MY FUTURE BRIDE.

And turned into a wild, feral Irontree from days of old.

My three cousins tackled me to the ground and chained me before I could do something stupid, like throw that female over my shoulder and carry her off into the mountains.

The heavy metal cuffs and links around my wrists and ankles are specially forged by a blacksmith on the commune to withstand an orc's winter strength.

They've done this for my own good.

For *her* good.

Ellie Willis is out of sight and her scent is distant. That insistent need to bellow her name like a wild animal dissipates. The dark need, forcing me to instinctively snarl and claw, trying to grab, sprint and take her away to my lair, has finally decreased.

My shaft is no longer hard and leaking in my pants, and my tusks have mainly retreated.

My family drags me down the basement stairs, one sharp step at a time, digging into my spine. I blink at the overhead lights and try to regain my composure. I know I met my bride, lost control and they had to tackle me, but the specifics of exactly what I said and how she acted in return are fuzzy.

Luckily, when the five of us moved in yesterday, we'd immediately built a cage in the basement, in case one of us happened to meet a bride in the dark of winter and turn feral.

Which is exactly what happened to me.

The worst part is I'd bragged, on and on, to anyone who would listen, that I was beyond those primitive instincts. Claiming I'd never kidnap a human female. The building of this cage was supposed to be an extreme measure all of us did to silence the worried elders, so they would feel more comfortable allowing Irontrees to lead this integration, despite our barbaric history.

It would never be needed, and if it was, it would be for one of the others, never for me. And yet here I am, barely twenty-four hours into this new mission, feral with need.

The worst part is that there were many other orcs who also wanted this position, two of whom were already mated, therefore safe bets. When the humans reached out, wanting the name of an orc who would be a good match to teach at Black Oak Academy, the three of us were the finalists. I managed to convince the elders to choose me. My qualifications were better and my speaking skills amongst humans were already noted. I was the only one who had the experience and cool temperament for this experimental job at a human school. A good role model for human-orc workplace integration.

I like the idea of being hired to teach at different human universities and private high schools. This way I can better inform humans of orc history. And now I've secured a temporary teaching position at Black Oak Academy, the first orc ever hired there. It's only for the second half of the school year and then a summer session, but it's a start—an opportunity to prove that orcs can integrate into prestigious human educational institutions.

And this is all in jeopardy because I met my mate at the worst possible time—during the dark of winter.

They took a chance with me. I was sent with the other Irontrees in my commune as backup. Due to our arrival at the start of winter, we are meant to live quietly, remain isolated and have no contact with any humans beyond the ones I must teach or speak with at the school. In the spring, these restrictions would be eased.

But this morning, Dane sighted a human behaving badly next door, threatening a female. This is unacceptable. Irontrees are well-known for our timely citizen's arrests, helping law enforcement to keep the peace. We hadn't planned on continuing this practice while on this mission in Truckee, California. But the moment we saw a male, who we could scent was inebriated, behaving in a threatening manner toward that female, we all swiftly moved into position.

"Ugh," I groan, as my head hits the stone floor. I grunt and lick my lips, feeling the jut of my sensitive tusks.

They continue to drag me toward the cage, talking as if I'm not even here.

"I'd forgotten how big Garlen is," Aldar grunts as he pulls on my arm and shoulder. "Did he gain weight?"

"Open the damn door to the cage," another voice barks.

A lock clicks and an iron door creaks open.

"At least he's calming down."

"Good. I think he broke my nose."

"I can stand and walk into the cage," I rasp. "You don't have to drag me anymore."

They ignore me and toss me inside. My body hits the floor in a painful clatter of chains. The door bangs shut.

Everything that happened outside flashes in full color, like images on a cell phone. We tackled the unworthy human male to the ground. I easily brought him to submission, with my boot on his chest. And then the female spoke to me, and I got my first good look at her. That was the moment my entire life changed.

Loki ran up and introduced himself to the fantastically beautiful female.

I heard her voice and knew who she was.

Ellie Willis, head of the social studies department at Black Oak Academy. This is my future bride. I had no idea I'd purchased the domicile next door to my boss at Black Oak. A strange fluke of orc-luck? Or maybe bad luck since this has occurred in the dark of winter. The moment I inhaled her pheromones, every cell in my body went on high alert and I recognized her as mine. She is the sexiest female I've ever seen. My normally dormant cock sprang to life. Underneath her open coat I caught glimpses of a thick, curvy shape that could easily withstand my orc lust.

I close my eyes and take deep breaths, willing down all my mating urges. Then I push myself up, stand and look around. The cage measures ten feet by ten feet, with reinforced steel bars embedded into quick-drying concrete. A heavy steel door with three separate locks created by our blacksmith. A simple cot, a composting toilet, sink, and a stack of books.

The large safe that holds all of our cash, gold and jewels is in a corner of the basement.

All three of my cousins look disheveled, as if they've been through battle. Cut lips and heavy breathing. They limp over and drop, groaning into available chairs outside the cage.

"Is it really necessary to leave me chained?" I question.

"Finally, he can talk like a civilized orc," Keric rasps. "Where was this Garlen thirty minutes ago?"

"Yes, it's necessary to keep you chained, and locked in that cage too," Aldar growls in response. "I've never seen a male turn that wild, that fast for a bride. I didn't even know that was possible."

"What if we hadn't been there when it happened?" Jonus adds.

"What if I'd left with Dane and there'd only been the two of you?" Aldar answers. "It took the three of us to get him down here."

"I've heard stories of other orcs and especially Irontrees behaving this way, during tales elders told in front of the fire at night," Keric remarks. "But no one has seen anything like that in modern times."

I'm stunned into silence because I knew it was bad but not that bad. Have I scared away my bride with my behavior?

"Are all Irontrees this wild?" Jonus questions. "Is this my future?"

Aldar rubs at his short hair. "I hope not. Garlen is the first of us to find his mate, and this behavior does not bode well for the rest of us."

Keric leans forward and braces his forearms on his thighs. "We always knew it was possible. It's why we have the cage and chains in the first place. It sometimes skips generations, but… Most of the worst aspects of kidnapping come from the wildest communes in Siberia and from…"

"From the Irontree line in northern Maine. Our line."

All three of them grow quiet.

And I continue to wonder how the hell this happened to me. I sit heavily on my cot. Why couldn't I have met Ellie Willis at any time of the year other than winter? At thirty-five years old, I'd begun to assume I'd never meet my bride. Never did I expect to arrive for this temporary position and meet the female who would birth my orc sons.

"Every time I step foot amongst humans," I say quietly, "there is always the possibility I might meet a female I would find compatible, but only in the dark of winter is this danger-ous. During the rest of the year, all adult, unmated orcs can behave reasonably and follow all the human laws. But in the dark of winter this is impossible. Hence the reason I did not arrive alone and the five of us brought along chains and a mobile cage. We had to be ready, just in case, because Irontrees are historically known to be prone to kidnapping. But I am a modern orc, and a citizen who follows all human laws. I didn't think this could…"

"I didn't think it could happen either," Jonus responds.

Aldar meets my gaze. "None of us thought this could

happen, but now that it has, you need to give this job up and return to the commune."

I let his words settle in my mind. For a moment I think he's right, but then I remember why I'm here in the first place. "No, no. I can't leave. I must complete this mission. I am meant to be the first orc teacher at the first integrated school in the nation. The humans need to learn that they can trust us."

"How can we build trust with humans when they see you having to be kept caged to refrain from kidnapping your next-door neighbor?" Keric barks.

I fist both of my hands and bare my tusks at my cousin.

"There is no need to fight," Aldar responds. "The elders can tell the humans that you were…sick…and they can put one of the other orcs in this position instead."

"No," I growl. "We need to teach our kind that Irontrees can be trusted. I said that I can do this—I can do this."

"You cannot do this," Keric shouts. "The three of us had to tackle you to the ground. How can you do this when you can become that version of yourself again?"

"All of you will stay here with me and make sure that I don't escape and go over there and try to kidnap her."

"For the entire spring?"

Jonus shrugs. "Well, that's what I told that female. I just assumed we'd remain in Truckee until this job is completed. I warned her to stay away and that we'd keep him caged until the spring."

Keric slumps back in his chair and shakes his head. "You'll try to escape."

I look down at the ropes of chains binding my arms and legs. "It's true. I estimate I'll lose my mind at least once more this season, with her so close. But don't let me. All of you are going to stay here with me. And if you do this for me, one day I will do this for you."

Keric snorts. "You won't need to do this for me. I would never lose control in that manner."

"You don't know that," Jonus comments. "I thought this Iron-tree nonsense was a tale told to scare young orcs into remaining on the commune." He looks at me. "But now I see that the precautions were correct."

"It won't happen to me because I'll never meet a female who is right for me," Keric shrugs.

I secretly agree he has the longest chance of any of us. Keric is the most glaringly wild. His nose is large, his horns are twisted. He's so tall he has to crouch to get into human doorways. And his bouts of rage and anger are legendary.

"I am the one who humans feel the most comfortable around, which is why I can teach the young humans as well as young orcs," I remind them.

"You just broke that unblemished record."

I cross my arms. "Tell me more about what happened out there. I don't remember all the details. How did I behave?"

Keric snorts. "Your pupils dilated, your tusks extended further, and you literally told her you'd impregnate her with your orc son. In front of everyone."

"You kept staring at her," Jonus adds, "shouting that she was your bride. You tried to grab her, and we had to tackle and chain you, right in front of her. Then drag you back into our domicile."

I sink back into the cot, shame washing over me as I remember every minute of how I behaved. "I wasn't thinking clearly."

"Obviously," says Aldar, looking up from the screen in his hand. "That's why we're here. We purchased this large house, with the pit constructed in the basement just in case. But there's a bigger problem," he says, pulling his chair closer. "I looked up the names of those females living next door. Do you realize who that female is that you say is your bride?"

"Of course I do," I growl. "My bride is Ellie Willis," I say out loud for the benefit of everyone in the room, "the department head of social studies at Black Oak Academy. My new boss."

Silence falls as my words sink in.

CHAPTER 4
Garlen

"FUCK," Keric snarls. "The human who hired you sight unseen is the same one you threatened to kidnap and breed? This is worse than I thought."

"I knew right away who she was, because I recognized her voice, but I also knew she didn't know who I was. I was trying to decide if I should introduce myself or wait until a better circumstance, and then she stepped forward. I inhaled her pheromones."

"And everything went to hell," Jonus mutters. "Did you know she was our new neighbor, yesterday, when we first moved in?"

"No, I hadn't seen her or heard her voice. I had no idea we'd moved next door to the female who interviewed me for this position."

A whining noise draws our attention to the basement stairs. Loki, my brave and loyal corgi hates being left behind. They must've accidentally closed the door on him and he finally pried it open. My dog pads down each step with exaggerated care, his stubby legs navigating the descent. He still wears his blue snow boots. Once at the bottom, he races over to the cage, excited to see me.

"At least someone's on my side," I mutter.

"We're all on your side," Aldar responds, crouching to pet the small dog. "Which is why we're here making sure you don't kidnap the department head."

Keric looks up from his cell phone. "Dane says that the human we performed the citizen's arrest on is with the police. That male is Ellie Willis' ex-husband. He broke a restraining order and is in custody."

My jaw clenches and fists tighten. The thought of that male treating my bride poorly fills me with blinding rage. She is now mine and nothing will harm her.

Loki wiggles through the bars and jumps onto the cot, turning in three tight circles before settling down on my lap. I lay my hands on his soft, thick, fur, instantly calming at his bright presence. I've had this dog for three years now and he's become my best friend, my companion and possibly even my therapist. Not that orcs even have therapists…hence the need for a dog with a happy demeanor.

"I can't lose this position," I quietly declare. "I need your help with this. The Black Oak job is the first time an orc has been hired as a teacher for humans. The elders want this to work, but I want it too, beyond the fact that I'll be working with my future bride. This will be another step forward in healing the wounds of the past and bringing our two species together. I am here to teach orc history for the first time to humans from an actual orc, not through the history that was rewritten by humans. They will begin to learn our true history, told from our original voices and through our primary source material. This is important. I don't have a proper credential yet and this is only temporary, but I must be a good example so that other orcs will be hired in the future. And if this works, then credentialing programs across the country will allow orcs to enter and become fully credentialed teachers. Humans need to feel safe around us."

They all nod in agreement.

"I could care less about becoming a teacher, but I do want the freedom to eventually work or live anywhere I want, with no pushback," Keric responds. "So, I'm still in."

"This job is now ten thousand times more difficult than before, but I'm still in too," Jonus agrees.

"I think it's much safer to go back to the commune and try again for this position next year, but I agree with what you've said. I'm still in," Aldar grumbles. "We've all made a vow to work together, to break the Irontree curse. We will be the first generation to not kidnap."

"All for one and one for all?" I question, mimicking a line I learned from a human fiction story I like.

"All for one and one for all," they laugh and agree in unison.

"But how is this going to work out exactly?" Jonus questions. "Yes, we all want this, and we can see that Garlen has finally calmed down and is acting like himself again, but even he admits that he can easily be triggered and revert into an Irontree beast of old. If we stay, how does a male in the throes of a dark of winter mating call teach, in public, alongside the exact same female he wants to kidnap?"

Aldar exchanges glances with the others. "We could… manage it. Keep him locked up except for teaching hours. Guard Garlen during classes."

"You want to escort me to work in chains?" I snarl.

"Better than the alternative," Keric points out. "Total confinement until spring, or…well, you know what traditionally happens when a wild orc meets his mate in winter."

I do know. Orcs would kidnap and carry off human females in the dark of winter, claiming them without consent, keeping them captive until spring thaw when the mating urge calms enough for rationality to return. It was barbaric and primitive and was exactly why a human mob with torches and pitchforks would arrive, wanting their female returned. And it's exactly what every cell in my body is screaming for me to do.

"I can do this," I insist. "I've never lost control like this before. You don't need to escort me anywhere in chains."

"You'd never met your mate either," Aldar counters. "It took three of us to knock you down, chain you and drag you away. What if we hadn't been there?"

Loki whimpers, sensing my distress. I stroke his fur, focusing on the feel of his soft fur to calm myself at the thought of me mistreating Ellie in any way. Usually Loki likes only me, but today he did leap into Ellie's arms, which was unusual.

Smart dog, actually. Recognizing my mate before even I fully acknowledged it. "I refuse to harm Ellie. She must be kept away from me until the spring."

"We are here. We'll make sure no harms come to your bride."

"And we need to find out more about her," I say finally. "Because we need to know more about the male we arrested and learn if she's in danger because of his arrival. Her life used to consist of an unworthy male who treated her improperly. But she is now mine and this will no longer continue. We will all keep her safe. She is going to be an Irontree."

"Of course."

"And Loki," I add, scratching behind the dog's ears. "While I am in this cage he will still need his walks, feeding…"

"We'll take care of him," Jonus promises. "But you saw how he took to Ellie Willis. Maybe he'd like to visit your mate occasionally."

A growl builds in my chest at the thought of Loki interacting with Ellie without me there. The thought of Jonus taking Loki to visit Ellie. This is ridiculous jealousy over a dog and my cousin, but winter makes me irrational. "Fine," I concede. "But don't let her keep him."

They exchange glances, and I can read their thoughts. I'm already possessive, already seeing her as mine to control. This is the winter madness setting in.

"What about my position at Black Oak?" I ask, sitting back against the wall, lifting the chains to a more comfortable position. "The new semester starts after winter break."

"When is winter break over?" Keric asks.

"Two weeks from now," I reply, mentally calculating.

Aldar sits forward. "I've been thinking about this. You're right that you can't simply step down, especially not after Black Oak took the unprecedented step of hiring an orc teacher."

"Exactly." I look up. "Maybe I should have disclosed my… condition ahead of time. Irontrees like me experience winter cravings more intensely than modern orcs."

"No, the elders did not want this to be exposed. We were allowed to come here, with precautions. No human institution would understand what happened here," Aldar says. "And it's never been relevant until now. We've always had a backup plan if something did happen, and now we're working the plan. All humans remain safe. But we can't let the local humans know of what is happening to you and how we are keeping you caged until spring. They will not understand and they will overreact."

We all nod in agreement.

"What about remote teaching?" Jonus suggests suddenly. "Humans do that now, right? Teaching through screens?"

I sit up straight, the chains clinking. "Online teaching? It could work. I'd need a computer, camera, stable internet…"

"We can get all that," Keric says. "Set it up down here where you can't break free."

"But Ellie would have to approve it. She's my boss."

"Well," Jonus points out, "she did see you lose your mind and have to be dragged away in chains."

"Does she know that Garlen is the orc she hired to teach with her? There's the possibility that she doesn't know that you're the orc who will be at Black Oak Academy."

"I told her his full name. She has to know."

"You did?" Aldar growls.

"Well, yes, I had to tell her something. All three of those females in that house were watching us knock him down and drag him away. They know. I couldn't lie. And I said she had to wait until spring to see him again."

I nod slowly. "She must be surprised to find out that I'm the orc who will be in the classroom with her. In order for this to work, I'll need to be able to communicate with the school administration and with Ellie about the curriculum and expectations."

"We could get you a burner cell phone," Aldar suggests. "Just for professional communication."

"That would help."

"With restrictions," Aldar clarifies, giving me a knowing look. "Professional contact only. No late-night texting about your irrational feelings. You will not be allowed to talk her into coming down here to visit you."

I bare my tusks at him but don't argue. The opportunity to communicate with my future bride, even in a limited capacity, is better than nothing. "I'd still need to prepare for classes. I'll need my books, notes, laptop…"

"We'll bring everything you need down from your bedroom," Keric agrees.

I rise, pacing the confines of my cage. Loki jumps off my lap and paces with me. "And if I…slip? If I can't control myself when I see her on video and hear her voice again?"

"That's why we'll be monitoring every interaction," Keric says, flexing his considerable muscles. "Dane will be with us, and winter or not, the four of us can handle you if needed."

I nod in agreement. The physical restraint is humiliating but necessary. Without my cousins' intervention today, I might have slung Ellie over my shoulder and carried her off to a cave in the wilderness. The thought both disgusts and excites me. This is the true struggle of a wild orc in the modern world. I refuse to take her without consent. I'd never forgive myself. And yet there's a primitive side of me that wants exactly that. "What about Ellie?" I ask. "She saw everything. Is my female still upset?"

"Actually," Jonus says with a slight smile, "she took it remarkably well. Didn't seem afraid at all."

I suddenly remember the expression on her face when I made my declaration. There was surprise on her beautiful features, but not terror. And she stepped closer, not away, and asked about the "dark of winter" as if genuinely curious.

This is good news.

"She's probably in shock," Aldar suggests. "Once it wears off, she'll likely file a complaint."

"Or a restraining order," Keric adds.

I wince at the thought. I've become yet another male she needs protection from. "I need to apologize," I say. "To explain."

"Absolutely not," all three cousins chorus together.

"Not until spring," Aldar clarifies. "No private contact."

A frustrated roar builds in my chest, but I swallow it down. They're right. I know they're right. But every instinct I possess screams to get to her, to protect her, to claim her. I sit back down, and Loki jumps again, back into my lap. "What about her ex-husband? He was violating a restraining order. The humans will eventually let him out of that jail and she could be in danger."

"We'll keep an eye on her house," Keric promises.

"And we'll look into this Marcus person," Aldar adds. "I have contacts in the human legal system."

I nod, grateful for their support. Loki snores softly in my lap, completely relaxed now that the tension has eased. "There's something else. When we were subduing the human male, I caught a scent on him. It reminded me of..."

"Crimson Tusk," Keric finishes, referring to a notorious orc gang that specializes in various criminal enterprises throughout California. Not all orcs were raised on tribal communes, some were instead raised in criminal fortresses. Crimson Tusk has ancestry in the Alaskan communes, but their largest modern fortress is deep in the Sierra Nevada mountains. "I caught that scent too. Could be coincidence. Many humans use synthetic orc scent as a sort of cologne; it's popular lately. But if he's connected to the Tusk..."

"She could be in real danger," Keric says, his expression darkening.

"He seemed like a standard abusive ex," Aldar observes.

"But we'll investigate. She was standing there with her daughter and I assume the grandmother. We will protect all three of them."

I close my eyes, imagining Ellie, her mother and small daughter in their neat house, potentially targeted by one of the most dangerous criminal organizations in the world, second only to the Russian orc Bratva. My protective instincts surge, rattling against the chains that bind me. "I need my laptop," I say abruptly. "Books. Paper. If I'm to be confined, I might as well work."

"We'll bring your things down," Adlar agrees. "And set up internet access."

"And that phone. For professional communication only. I'll need to coordinate with Ellie about the online teaching arrangement."

My brothers exchange skeptical glances, but Aldar eventually nods. "Fine. But we'll be monitoring your communications. And you're not to contact her directly until she reaches out first about the teaching arrangement."

"I understand." My mind already envisions ways to extend our professional conversations into something more personal. Not to approach her physically, but to learn more about her.

"Well, at least you've got two weeks until winter break ends," Aldar points out. "Time to prepare and…adjust to your situation."

I look around at the bars of my cell and down at the chains around my wrists and ankles. Two weeks of confinement, with my only connection to Ellie being whatever professional communication she might initiate about my teaching arrangement. Two weeks to regain my control before attempting to teach hormonal human teenagers through a screen while chained in a basement.

And then three more months until spring.

"It'll work," I say with more confidence than I feel. "It has to."

CHAPTER 5
Ellie

MY HANDS still shake slightly from this morning's confrontation with my ex and then the surprise meeting with my sexy co-teacher, Garlen Irontree. The image of that muscular orc with the black horns and tusks, being dragged away in chains by his orc relatives, continues to flash through my mind. And the way he looked at me, inhaling my scent...and the way I felt when his gaze moved along my body.

Stop it. Don't think about that right now.

I take a deep breath of the crisp mountain air as I drive to work, focusing on the freshly snowplowed roads. The heat in my veins needs to decrease. I have that buzzing, high feeling like I'm back in high school with a crush on a guy, but worse. My body is also enflamed, like I could run back there and jump his body, strip him bare and beg him to fuck me.

I've got it bad.

I'm beginning to understand how women have been enthralled with orcs for millennia.

And I've got to ignore all of this, stuff it down as if it never happened because now, I'm at work and need to get my head on straight.

This is the last day before winter break, which is always

nutty with a million fires to put out before I'll be off for the next two weeks. Yes, I met my orc coworker in person and realized he's hot as hell and right now caged in his basement, but I need to keep it together.

Plus, my ex-husband arrived despite his restraining order and behaved in a threatening manner, which normally I'd be either livid or crying about, bouncing back and forth between the two sets of emotions, busy calling the police and my lawyer. But the good news is that encounter barely registers in my mind. All I can think of is Garlen. And his darling corgi.

Black Oak Academy looms ahead of me like something out of a fairy tale. I pull into the parking lot, still in awe at the imposing stone façade and those gleaming windows, each of which probably cost more than my monthly mortgage. The morning sun catches on the tall glass panes, making them shimmer against the crisp, snowy mountain backdrop. Even after six months working here, I still feel a flutter of disbelief every time I arrive.

I teach here. Me. Head of the social studies department at the first school in the country to intentionally integrate orc faculty.

I park my practical, small Honda SUV between a Range Rover and another enormous and highly expensive red truck. The faculty parking lot at Black Oak Academy is like a luxury showroom for rugged vehicles. I've joked with Mom that I need to upgrade my car just to avoid embarrassing myself, but she reminds me that paying off my credit cards is probably the smarter financial choice.

"One battle at a time, Ellie," I mutter to myself, grabbing my tote bag from the passenger seat. I pause to double-check that I'm properly bundled with my coat, scarf and gloves because it's cold as hell outside. Our state is so huge that this move involved entirely new topography and climate. The heavy winter clothes are bizzarro to me, but I'm getting used to it. Luckily the drive over is only a short distance, along roads that the snowplows pass through regularly.

I've already decided to tell no one about what happened this morning on my front lawn. Not a single soul. I'm going to get through work today pretending like nothing untoward happened, and during our two-week winter break I'll talk with those orcs next door and see if we can work something out prior to school starting again. I owe them that much, considering they came to my rescue, and now Marcus is jailed without me having to lift a finger.

Also, I want this orc integration at our school to work out so badly that maybe I am giving this more grace than someone else would.

And there's the fact that Garlen called me his bride and mainly all I've felt ever since is a giddy happiness.

I'm a mess and I'll need more coffee if I'm going to pull this off.

At least Zoe is safely on the bus to school already. She took what happened this morning in stride and then waved goodbye to me as I left. Mainly, I think it's because she didn't see the part where her dad was tackled by the orcs. She only caught the tail end, where Garlen was dragged away.

My six-year-old insists she's "big enough" to ride with the other elementary level kids, and with Mom at home to meet her after school, I couldn't argue. She's ridden the school bus every day for this whole school year so far with zero incident.

I enter the high school wing and wave good morning to students in expensive outfits. Black Oak Academy bustles with pre-break energy this morning. I can overhear them chatting excitedly about vacation plans to Hawaii or Europe while rushing past with their MacBooks. My heels click against the polished floors as I continue to make my way through the soaring main hallway. Those massive windows frame the snow-covered mountains. The founders of Black Oak spared no expense when building this unprecedented educational experiment in Truckee.

This job is still a little intimidating. I was recruited from my position teaching at a successful public magnet school in southern California. I've never taught somewhere so elite, and the pressure of helping launch this massive experimental school feels enormous.

Especially now that I've met my orc co-teacher and learned he wants to kidnap me and fill me with his orc son.

An embarrassed snort-laugh escapes my lips.

I look around, glad no one noticed.

I reach my classroom, happy for the blissful quiet. My desk is its usual mess. It's always impossible to remain organized before the break. There's a stack of curriculum I was going to give to Garlen Irontree, so that we could easily start lesson planning. The thought sends a warm flush through me that has nothing to do with the excellent heating system.

That muscular chest. His lips. The rumble of his deep voice. What would it really feel like to be fucked by a wild orc in the dark of winter?

Ugh. My mind is full of filthy thoughts about my new co-teacher.

Focus, Ellie. Work first, complicated orc feelings later.

After stashing my coat and purse and arranging my desk materials for the day, I glance at my watch. The faculty meeting starts in twenty-five minutes, which gives me just enough time to get my favorite coffee and swing by Anna's classroom.

I'm lucky to have found a close friend here at Black Oak.

I like and respect the other amazing teachers in my department, but they're all men who can't exactly hide the fact that they're annoyed that I'm the youngest by far and yet was made the department head. They are all originally from a variety of fancy private schools across the country and I'm the only one who'd taught public school. All of them are professional, and wonderful teachers in their own right. We get along well and are all focused on student achievement, but we don't have much in common and I can't find true friendship with any of them.

Anna, who teaches college-level English literature to the seniors, is my best friend on campus. We're both about the same age and have a similar sense of humor. She's easy to talk to and I love having lunch with her most days.

I haven't told her all the details about my ex-husband, mainly because I was truly in a frame of mind of wanting to move on, but she does know that I'm divorced and I live with my daughter and my mom, who moved with me. Anna is really the only one I talk to about personal details.

Anna remains very private and doesn't say much about her own family or personal life, present or past. I get the sense sometimes that she's about to open up to me, but then changes the subject. I can't help but feel there's something big and mysterious she's keeping to herself. I figure at some point she'll feel comfortable sharing more with me. Meanwhile, we've got lots of other stuff to share.

Also, she's a formidable teacher who remains a pure-hearted sweetheart, and I'm lucky to have earned her friendship.

The English department is housed in the east wing. As I pass through the student commons, already festooned with tasteful winter decorations, I spot a few high schoolers sipping what smells suspiciously like real espresso, my favorite drink. The student cafe here serves better coffee than most actual cafes in town. I sweep by to get one for myself and another for Anna.

Finally, I pause at Anna's classroom door, which is slightly ajar, and knock gently.

"Come in," a soft voice calls.

I push the door open.

Anna Kim hastily shoves something under a stack of papers. Her cheeks flush pink as she adjusts her glasses and sits up straighter. "Oh, Ellie, it's you. Good morning. Is it time already?"

I pretend not to notice the glossy corner of a magazine that peeks out from beneath her lesson plans and hand her a coffee. "Yep, almost time for the faculty meeting. Thought we could walk together."

Today Anna wears her signature cardigan in a muted beige. Her shiny black hair is cut into a severe bob, and her face is again makeup-free. She's shorter than I am and probably wears the same size in clothes that I do. Anna likes to wear thick, tortoiseshell glasses that block blue light.

I think she's gorgeous, with perfect skin and teeth that I'm jealous of on a daily basis. Her fingernails are also perfectly short and painted a nice ballet slipper pink. I always feel too busy to get my nails done, and my strawberry-blonde hair is always one step removed from wild. I admire Anna so much. She's my role model in how to be "fluffy" and yet remain a gorgeous class act.

"Oh, thank you. One sec. Let me grab my notepad."

This is when I notice that what she's hiding is the latest issue of *People* magazine. I can't resist. "So, what's the celebrity news this week?"

Anna freezes, then sighs dramatically and pushes her glasses higher up on her cute button nose. "Was I that obvious?"

"Only to someone who's found you reading *People* three times already this month. Also, you know I love celebrity news. Come on, Kim. Let's walk and talk."

She grabs the magazine and takes it along with us. Anna's professional facade cracks into a girlish smile and her black eyes sparkle with delight as we step out of her classroom together. "Did you see what Jason Momoa wore to the premiere? I nearly died."

This is the side of Anna that only I get to see—the brilliant teacher who can quote Shakespeare from memory but also knows every detail about the latest in Hollywood fashion. When we first met at the new faculty orientation last July, she barely spoke two words. It took nearly a month before I discovered her secret passion for celebrity news and fashion. She follows it on various social media but still prefers the feel of a glossy magazine in her hands.

This works out great because I love the same thing.

"Let me see," I say, taking her coffee cup and leaning closer as she flips to the page so I can see the picture. "Oh my gosh, is that actually a pink velvet tuxedo?"

"With matching boots," Anna squeals, then immediately glances around like she's afraid someone heard her being unprofessional. "It should be a crime to look that good," she whispers.

"Right? That man could make anything look good. Speaking of looking good while committing crimes," I say, lowering my voice conspiratorially, "any updates on the DiCaprio arrest rumor?"

"Total fabrication," Anna says with the authority of someone who's cross-referenced multiple sources. "But did you see his new girlfriend?"

"Oh, I did. I'm giving that relationship two months max before that girl dumps him for someone younger."

We both snort-laugh, and for a moment, I forget about restraining orders and chained orcs. It's a nice break from all the pressure at the end of a semester. Good thing I already finished all the grades and turned them in yesterday.

"We should probably walk faster," Anna says, reluctantly closing the magazine and tucking it into her tote bag. "Principal VanWagoner hates it when anyone arrives after him."

I hand back her coffee cup and roll my eyes. "Gawd forbid we disrupt the delicate ecosystem of faculty hierarchy."

We both chuckle as we walk faster.

Anna smooths her cardigan and adjusts her glasses, physically transforming back into the serious academic everyone else sees. It's like watching Clark Kent become Superman, only in reverse. "So," she says, her voice shifting to a more professional tone as a math teacher passes us with a nod, "your new co-teacher is starting after break?"

I mentally pull out my pre-planned excuse for Garlen not showing up on our first day back. Because how could he, considering he's chained and caged until the first day of spring. I haven't run this news by the principal yet, but it needs to be done. I'll email VanWagoner with this slight change before I leave for break. I suspect he won't care much. If everything goes smoothly and there are no student, parents or staff complaints that he must deal with, he'll be fine.

I lift my chin and tell my friend only the little bit I can. "Yes, he was supposed to start in person when we get back after break, but I just learned he can't be here yet and needs to teach remotely at first."

"That's unusual, isn't it? Mid-year, remote start?"

I choose my words carefully. I want so badly to confide in her and tell her the entire story, but it will have to wait until I come back from break and know that the coast is clear. "His email said he has some logistical challenges that make remote work necessary initially."

"Because he's an orc?" Anna asks directly but keeps her voice low.

"I literally don't know. He was being vague. It's a little odd, but I'm sure we can work it out together. I'm just happy he's still going to start when we'd planned, even if it's remote teaching. I was sad he couldn't start at the first of the year like the rest of us and had to wait until the middle of the year."

Anna nods thoughtfully. "I've never actually met an orc in person. Read about them, of course. Their literary traditions are fascinating. They had nothing but oral histories until relatively recently, when Alden Overlook helped to invent their written language."

This is why I like Anna. Where others might judge, she approaches everything with sincere intellectual curiosity.

"Garlen is brilliant," I say, perhaps too quickly. "Did you know that he was part of the team of orcs that negotiated with the government on orc citizenry?"

"Did he tell you that when you met him at the interview?"

"Oh, I didn't get to talk to him personally then, and I didn't even see him because there was only audio and not video. I learned that information from his résumé… But, um, I did learn that he moved into my neighborhood."

"Convenient," Anna says with a small smile. "This will make

it easier during winter break to find out why he needs to start remotely, considering he's so close. Knowing he's already here in town makes me wonder more why he has to do that. Is he sick?"

"Maybe?" I answer. "I'll find out."

Before Anna can respond, we reach the faculty mailboxes outside the lounge. I stop short when I see a printed flyer taped to the bulletin board. In bold red letters it declares:

ORC INFILTRATION: THE HIDDEN AGENDA BEHIND BLACK OAK ACADEMY

Beneath are crude illustrations of orcs looming menacingly over human children.

"What the hell?" I whisper, instinctively ripping it down.

Anna peers over my shoulder, her expression darkening. "There was another one of those in the workroom yesterday too. I took it down before anyone could see it."

I crumple the paper in my fist. "Who would put this up? Only teachers or staff are allowed back here. How can this come from the people who work at Black Oak? It's literally in the school charter that this academy was founded to integrate orc faculty and eventually students. That's the whole point of this place."

"Well, I've been meaning to tell you this, but I was waiting because I knew it would upset you, considering you're the first one of us to be working with another orc teacher," Anna says, glancing around first before speaking. "But yesterday I over-heard some of the faculty grouped together, expressing concerns about working with orcs."

"Concerns?" I snort. "Like what? That they'll learn they can work with and maybe become friends with an orc?"

"More like worries about 'winter behaviors' and 'biological instincts,'" Anna says, making air quotes. "Singh from biology had quite a lot to say about orc mating habits around the copy machine this morning."

My cheeks heat as I think about Garlen being dragged away by his relatives, warning me about orcs taking brides in winter.

"Modern orcs don't kidnap," I mutter, shoving the crumpled flyer into my bag to show the principal later. "And those teachers are working at the wrong school if they're anti-orc integration. It's what we're here to do. Part of the hiring process involves asking if you can work with orcs. The parents all consider this orc integration a major part of why they pay to have their children here. They think it's a good thing."

"I suppose it's just that people fear the unknown. I've learned all about that over the years. They have no problem with letting you know they don't like how you look or dismissing you outright." Anna wraps her cardigan over her thick midsection. "It's why I spend my time trying to blend in." She gestures to her baggy, neutral outfit of white and beige. "I'm an overweight single woman without a pedigree family background, trying to prove that I belong here at this fancy school. I don't need to draw more attention."

I've never heard her speak so negatively about her appearance before. And I suddenly feel annoyed that this smart, beautiful woman minimizes herself. Words come out of my mouth that are partly for her and partly for me too. "Anna, neither you nor I should have to hide ourselves. I used to believe when people, or really my ex, would say that if I lost weight, I'd finally be beautiful, meaning I'm not that way right now? I admit it took a lot of therapy to excise that verbal damage from my head, but I'm done with all of that. I'm in a new headspace now. I show up with the expectation that I'm hot, and if people don't like how I look they can avert their gaze."

Anna rolls her eyes. "Says the tall, gorgeous strawberry-blonde woman who turns heads as she strides down the hall with those dangerous curves."

"Says the gorgeous, petite woman with perfect skin who could star in ads for luxury Korean skincare."

"Touché," Anna laughs, then she grows serious again. "For what it's worth, I think what you're doing with the orc integration program is important. It must be hard being the first. I want to help however I can."

"Oh, thanks, Anna, for saying that."

The faculty lounge door bangs open and closes again as more teachers arrive.

"Of course. We're friends, aren't we? Besides, I majored in Victorian literature so I know all about repression and how damaging it can be." She winks. "I'm definitely one of those teachers who was hired because I *wanted* to be here for the integration. This moment is going to be written about later in history books, and I'm proud to be part of this. If Professor Irontree needs help with curriculum adaptation, I'm happy to consult."

"Ms. Willis, Ms. Kim," Principal VanWagoner greets as he opens the door for us. "We're about to begin our final meeting before break."

"Ready," I say breezily, as I go past him with my best professional smile.

CHAPTER 6
Ellie

WINTER BREAK HAS OFFICIALLY STARTED, and the holidays are around the corner.

Whoo hoo. My two weeks of staycation have arrived.

The moment I get home I drop my purse and the laptop bag on my desk in my home office downstairs. "Hi you guys," I yell out.

There are muffled shouts of reply.

I race upstairs to my bedroom so I can strip out of my uncomfortable work clothes. Off go the slacks, the blazer and the low heels. My outfit was both professional and sexy at the same time, but the shapewear tank top feels great to peel off. On go the comfy, lounge-around-the-house matching outfit and the fuzzy slippers.

I let out a sigh of happiness.

My hair goes up in a ponytail, and I pause to look at myself in the floor-length mirror. Marcus's terrible words flash in my brain, causing me to turn, assessing what Anna described as my "dangerous curves." And I remember the hungry look on Garlen's features and his tented crotch. I give myself a big smile and leave the bedroom.

Then I make my way downstairs and head toward the sound

of voices in the front room. I find my mom and Zoe sitting on either side of the coffee table engrossed in a very messy project.

"Hey you two. What are you doing out here with all that yarn?" I question, frowning at the mess they've scattered on the table.

Zoe giggles. "Hi Mom. Grandma is teaching me how to make a cat hat."

I put my hands on my hips. "Did you say Cat in the Hat? Are you two writing a new children's book?"

"Nope. She said *cat hat*," my mother confirms, pushing her purple-framed reading glasses higher on her nose. "We're making Christmas presents for my precious kitty."

They both point up at Scarlett, Mom's beloved senior cat who patiently lounges on the nearby cat tree with a bright blue hat perched on her head, tied under her chin, her ears poking out the two holes on the top.

"Oh, she's adorable." I step forward to pet the cat on her fluffy tail, which I know she loves. Scarlett, Mom's twelve-year-old white cat, purrs gently and closes her eyes again. She's such a patient kitty. A saint among cats.

"I bought that hat she's wearing right now from Etsy," my mom explains. "But now we're each making Scarlett new holiday hats by following these steps we found on a YouTube video."

Zoe holds up two crochet needles and a ball of green yarn. "Look, Mom, I'm learning to crow-crow-shay." She smiles wide with one front tooth missing.

"I'm sure it's going to be great," I answer with enthusiasm, then lean down to whisper, "Thanks, Mom."

"You're welcome, honey."

I leave the living room and head into the kitchen to fix dinner for all of us. I smile at the clean counters, ready for me to mess up. Mom always does all the cleaning, but I'm the one who does all the grocery shopping and meal-making. Mainly because these are the chores I enjoy. And the fact that I arrive to a clean kitchen and never have to do the dishes makes it much more enjoyable and less like drudgery.

I start opening drawers and immediately think of Garlen Irontree, that mysterious orc who is supposedly in chains. And I remember the scene that played out on my front yard this morning.

I shake my head, my cheeks hot again as I remember how it all started when I ran out there to yell at Marcus. Really, what was I thinking?

I pull out a cutting board and a knife, then start washing and peeling two large russet potatoes.

Any talk between Marcus and I will now go through law enforcement or lawyers. I should not have to deal with him anymore. That's what the restraining order was for. Again, it was silly of me to go out there. I appreciate that the orcs were there for me. Yes, I have a lot left to say to Marcus to find closure, but I'm going to instead write it all down, because that's more productive. My words mean nothing to him.

The entire day at work, whenever there was the tiniest pause for reflection, I thought of Garlen.

Shouldn't I be happy that Garlen was dragged away in chains, considering he was shouting that I was his bride? Shouldn't I be terrified that there's a group of orcs living next door who have Garlen caged in their basement?

And yet my mind is full of images of Garlen's perfect, muscular chest.

Because of my past wherein I married a narcissist who initially love-bombed me and the subsequent fall out, normally I guard my tender heart with barbed wire, booby traps and a moat filled with genetically modified killer alligators.

But apparently I'm letting in a crack of light.

I preheat the air fryer and roughly cut the two potatoes into French fry shapes, then put them all into a bowl and toss them with olive oil and ranch seasoning. The fries all get dumped into the air fryer and I set the timer for twenty minutes.

Then I wash my hands, heat up a pan and take out a different cutting board so I can chop two chicken breasts.

The last day of the semester was chaos, as usual.

I smiled at all my students in my classes…and never once let on to anyone that my ex-husband, who has a restraining order, showed up on my front lawn in the morning and was removed by a team of mysterious orcs, led by Garlen Irontree, the new Ancient Orc History professor starting at Black Oak in two weeks. Oh, and he said I was his "bride" and warned me away or he'd impregnate me with his orc son.

I shift on my feet because every time I think of that part, heat spreads down my lower stomach and between my thighs.

My orc savior was dragged away in chains by his companions because he wants *me* as his bride?

It still hurts my head.

He barely saw me and was able to decide right then that I was the woman he wanted to have children with? Despite my crazy ex and the fact that I have a six-year-old daughter, he wants *me*?

I pause.

Wait, does he know I have a daughter? I think so…he must've seen Mom and Zoe standing next to me while he was being dragged away. Or he didn't see them because he was being dragged away? And if he did see them both did he know that girl was my daughter? Well, he should because everyone says she's my mini-me. Zoe and I both have long, wavy, strawberry-blonde hair, which works out great because I know exactly how to take care of it and style it pretty.

Which makes me remember… Within the orc species there are only males. There are no female orcs. This is why Garlen said I would give him an orc son. When women decide to marry an orc, they have to make peace with the idea of never having daughters and only giving birth to orc sons. It wouldn't be a child who was half orc and half human, but a child who was entirely orc and looks mainly like other males from the father's family line.

And why am I even thinking this way?

Maybe because I remain an eternal optimist who dreams of meeting the right guy and getting married forever. Despite my nasty divorce and the subsequent restraining order, which I consider but a road bump to my eventual happiness.

I pull out the ingredients for the chicken nuggets and then start cutting two boneless chicken breasts into chunks.

It's good to be home, dressed in my favorite comfy clothes, looking forward to two weeks off with my family. I haven't even started Christmas shopping, so there's a lot to do. Luckily Mom put up all the decorations, except for the tree, which we always wait to decorate on Christmas Eve. It's just going to be the three of us this year for the holiday because my aunt, uncle and cousins are on a European Christmas market river cruise.

I'm not even going to open my work laptop or check my emails during this time off. Nope, not happening. It's time for a real break because there's a lot on my mind.

For instance—is Garlen still in a cage? Did they at least take his chains off? Is he really as dangerous as they say?

Has he eaten dinner?

I heat oil in a pan as I arrange two nearby plates, one with a tempura mix and another with panko crumbs. My fingers get messy as I move the seasoned chicken pieces from the wet tempura batter, roll them into the panko and then place them into the sizzling oil.

I have so many questions about what happened this morning.

The chicken pops, and I use a large spoon to move the golden nuggets around and cook them in batches. All the while I continue to think through the Garlen mess.

I have no idea though how this is all going to work out. I wish I could talk to Garlen. I do have contact information, but can he be accessed if he's in chains?

Well, I've got two weeks to figure something out. He doesn't have a teaching credential, or even an emergency credential for substitute teaching, so that means he can never be alone with the students. I'd planned on being his co-teacher.

The timer dings on the air fryer and now both the fries and the chicken nuggets are done. "Dinner is almost ready," I shout.

"Okay, we'll get the table set," my mom shouts back.

I plate the food on all three of our dishes. Zoe likes the nuggets that are heavily breaded and cut into the smallest pieces, and she needs two types of dipping sauce and only a few fries. Mom likes equal amounts chicken and fries. And I love fries the most.

We all make it to the table at about the same time, with plates, drinks, napkins and utensils. I love eating home-cooked meals most nights at the kitchen table with them. Listening to Zoe chat away about anything she wants to discuss. We tell jokes and laugh together.

"So..." my mom says, cutting her chicken nugget in half, "are we going to talk about what happened this morning?"

"I think we should," I agree.

Zoe looks up from her ketchup-dipping operation. "You mean when the big green guys took away Daddy?"

I sigh, putting down my fork. Shoot, I really thought she hadn't seen that part. "Yes, sweetie. Those were orcs. They helped us by taking Daddy to the police because he wasn't supposed to be here."

"Why was he here?"

I shrug. "I don't really know. It's too bad he didn't just follow the rules and call my lawyer. I could've found out what he wanted."

"One of those orcs is going to be your teacher at school," Mom suddenly interjects.

"*My* teacher? The big one with the tallest horns?" Zoe asks, her blue eyes wide with interest rather than fear. "He looked angry."

"That was Professor Irontree," I explain carefully. "He's going to teach Ancient Orc History to the teenagers at Black Oak next semester. And he is not going to be your teacher. He's only teaching the seniors and not little kids like you."

Laurie dabs her mouth with a napkin. "And we're going to stay far away from him and his house until spring, just like his companions warned." Her tone makes it clear this isn't a suggestion.

"But why, Grandma?" Zoe asks. "He had a cute dog."

"Because orcs can be dangerous in winter. You heard what that other orc said. Garlen Irontree needs to be kept away from people until spring."

"He seemed nice enough before he started roaring," I mutter.

Mom gives me a sharp look. "Ellie, I saw the way you were looking at him. And I heard exactly what he said to you. I have absolutely nothing against orcs. You know I'm happy that you hired an orc for the school and I'd love to get to know our new neighbors at some point. But we need to respect their cultural differences and keep our distance. If his own kind says he's dangerous right now, we should listen."

"I guess you're right," I concede, though I'm not entirely convinced. Because, really, I need to talk to my neighbor soon about what we're going to do about that teaching assignment. I meet Zoe's gaze. "No visiting the orcs next door, or that cute corgi, until spring."

"Promise?" Mom presses.

"Promise," Zoe and I say in unison, although I cross my fingers under the table.

And I glance out the dark window. Not only do I need to talk to him, but I must see Garlen's situation with my own eyes.

Can I sneak over there and look through the windows without being caught?

CHAPTER 7
Garlen

THIS HOUSE that rises above this basement is brand new.

An older, smaller house was demolished and a new two-story house three times the size of the original was built in its place. But they did leave the large basement almost entirely untouched. The realtor who sold this place to us claimed it was purposely left this way so we could turn it into anything we wanted. A blank slate.

And because we're orcs, we turned it into a dank pit to cage one of us.

Meanwhile, I pace the confines of my temporary prison, figuring out how many steps are between the cot, the composting toilet and the large jug of water that's always available.

All I can think of is Ellie and the fact that I might have finally found my mate. There are plenty of obstacles in the way, and yet I remain optimistic that I might be able to come through with this amazing female at my side, swollen with my orc son.

Or I might find myself banished by my elders to live out the rest of my life in the remotest orc commune, without this job at a human school or even my job at the orc university.

And without my female.

What I do in these next few months will determine the entire trajectory of the rest of my life.

No pressure.

The cot is much too small, with my large feet hanging off the end. I managed to sleep here last night, with my chained hands and feet, but it was made for a human and the largest cot that could be purchased but is still too short. There is also a space heater and a heated blanket. I am as comfortable as could be expected in these conditions. Loki remains close, keeping me company. He insists on sleeping with me on the cot, and his bed, food and water bowls were moved down here too.

"Thank you for staying," I whisper to Loki. He barks in response and snuggles closer.

I have to admit that the best course of action would be for me to leave and live out the winter in the commune. Nowadays orcs do this to remain sane until they can return and properly "court" their future bride. But in this instance, I'd rather remain here, chained. I would be calm in the commune because I haven't touched Ellie. We haven't mated. All that happened so far is that her pheromones entered my lungs and lit up my body. For the first time in my life I had an erection, my shaft thickening. In fact, right now as I think of her, I shift on my feet as my cock again grows hard.

It has a mind of its own.

It wants Ellie.

But I'm staying in this cage until March twentieth, the exact date when winter ends. The very next day, March twenty-first, I will be free and unchained.

When I slept on the cot, my mind was filled with sexual images of my future bride. I became obsessed with the curve of her wide hips, the heft of her breasts through the fabric of her shirt. The shine of her long golden-red hair that blew in the wind.

I am a virgin. All orcs are virgins until they claim their female. Yesterday was the first time my shaft had ever hardened in my entire life.

Because I know she's so close, I remain on edge, ready at a moment's notice to grab her and take her away. I dreamt of taking her into the woods, where I would find a cave and tend to my female there, creating bedding with our clothes and any plant material available. I'd then light a warm fire, hunt for dinner and feed her. Then I'd strip her bare and kiss and lick every part of her luscious body until she was begging for more. Then I'd move between her thighs and sink into her wet heat.

Last night, in the dark, for the first time in my life, I touched myself. In the past there were no rushing emotions of heat and desire because I'd never met my mate.

But those urges have been unlocked.

I was surprised at the thickness and texture of my shaft in this state. The slit at the crown was leaking, ready to plant my seed in my female and grow our orc son. I grunted at the thought, urges I couldn't control rushing through me. Soon, my hand was wrapped around...

The door to the basement creaks open.

My uncle Dane appears to bring me breakfast. He returned yesterday afternoon, after dropping Marcus Adams with the police to find me, his favorite nephew, in the throes of a winter mating urge. He inhales the scent of all my releases in the middle of the night and grimaces.

"My blankets need washing and I need to take a shower," I growl.

He rolls his eyes. "Eat first. I'll tell the others and we'll get ready to move you upstairs to get clean."

Thirty minutes later, Dane enters the cage again and unlocks the chain from the wall. They remove my leg chains but keep my wrists chained.

"Is this really necessary?"

"Yes, it is," Dane growls.

All four of them circle me as I stomp up two sets of stairs to reach my bathroom, which is attached to the bedroom I'm no longer allowed to use.

"I will need this shower once a day," I inform them.

"For the entire winter?"

"Yes."

Once inside the bathroom, I kick off my boots, unbuckle my belt and stand in the shower. The door is open and they are all nearby, giving me no privacy. I brace one hand against the tile and grab onto my throbbing cock. "I have to do it again," I growl.

"Oh hell. This is disgusting," Keric snarls.

The door slams closed and I'm left in the bathroom, alone, so I can do my business.

Masturbation won't be as good as sinking into her wet heat. Nothing could be as good as Ellie's pussy. But it must be done because I can barely walk straight with this erection in my way.

I widen my stance and imagine what it would be like if Ellie were mine. What if she was in the shower with me, naked? I groan at this thought and pull on my cock. It's painfully hard and deep green. I will be large for this female; much larger than any human she has mated in the past. I will have to work hard to make sure she is wet and ready for me.

I touch my hand along my thick length, imagining slowly sliding into her wet heat. Will she be able to take me, or will I cause her pain?

"Mine," I growl.

I want to push apart her thick thighs and explore her channel with my fingers, tongue and cock. I continue to touch myself, stroking my shaft. I want her pussy on my dick.

Seed leaks out of the slit at the crown of my green shaft, making my cock slick. I wrap my rough fingers tight and lean forward. The water and the seed give me good purchase and I start in on it with fast, mean strokes. I've learned that this is the way I like to touch myself, that causes the release. Last night, was the first release of my life and all I could think was that I wished I was inside her and this wasn't being wasted in my bedding.

I'm panting, my chest heaving. The chains clink a steady beat as I move back and forth. My balls fill with seed and grow tight. All I can imagine is my female, her hands on me. Touching her sweet body. Sucking on her nipples while I sink in and out.

"Ellie." I throw my head back and groan out her name as my cum jets all over my hands and the tile wall of the shower. It keeps going on and on, the pleasure almost makes me pass out and I have to brace my hand on the wall. I wish I was planting my seed in my female, covering her with my scent.

I slump against the wall, panting and amazed at how that felt. And yet it's not good enough, because it wasn't her. My erection is soft in my hands, for the moment. The only true relief I'll get is with Ellie.

One hour later I'm back in my cage, restless, because the release from earlier is doing nothing to tame my need for this female. I'm obsessed. I've only spoken to her through the video for the job interview and then for minutes in the snow yesterday.

Her scent…her scent and the sight of her beauty filled me with inexplicable need. That small amount of time was enough for my body to understand she was mine.

I realize I was already intrigued by her presence at the interview. I kept looking at her and enjoying the sound of her voice. I felt optimistic, learning that we would teach together and I'd have the opportunity to get to know that female better. And then I accidentally moved next door to her. It really was pure accident.

"Surprise," Jonus announces. "We're bringing all your teaching equipment."

I blink out of my reverie and watch as they all stomp downstairs. I remain chained as my cousins come and go in my cage. Loki follows them back and forth, excited by all the movement. Finally, they are all finished and all four of them crowd into the basement and linger inside or just outside of the bars of my cage.

The teaching station they've assembled is in the corner of my cage, in front of the toilet. It includes equipment I've never seen. Books from my personal library line the shelves they've bolted to the wall, filled with ancient orc texts, human-authored histories, and my own published works. Cables snake across the concrete floor, secured with industrial tape.

"I don't need all of this technology. I only asked for my laptop," I protest.

"You've got everything you could possibly need," Jonus swears, his voice filled with excitement. "There's a desk, ergonomic chair, high-end computer with dual monitors, professional lighting. And this camera that will make you look less terrifying to the human teenagers."

"You're welcome," Aldar grouses, leaning against the bars. "This setup cost more than my first motorcycle."

"The semester doesn't start for two weeks. You didn't need to get all this right now."

Keric drops a heavy box of notes beside the desk. "Consider it our investment in orc academia. The first orc professor at Black Oak Academy needs to look professional, even if he's secretly chained in a basement."

My wrist rattles against the restraints, the special alloy in the orc chains connecting me to the cell bars. They've given me just enough chain to reach the desk but not enough to reach the door. The humiliation burns, but I swallow it down. This is necessary. For Ellie's safety. For my sanity. Actually for the general safety of every human in the neighborhood.

"One more thing," Jonus says, holding up a shiny smartphone. "As promised. Professional communication only."

I reach for it, but Dane, my uncle, intercepts it first. He taps the screen. "Parental controls activated. Monitoring software installed. You'll be able to text, call, and video chat with the school administration. No social media, no unnecessary websites."

"I'm not a human teenager."

"No, you're worse," Aldar comments. "You're a wild orc in the dark of winter who's found his bride. We've all seen what happens to Irontrees in winter. The stories our grandfathers told…"

I bare my tusks at him, proving his point. The chains rattle as I force myself to calm down. "Fine. Give me the damn phone."

Dane hands the phone over and I clutch it like a lifeline. My connection to the outside world. To Ellie.

Jonus clears his throat. "We've set up security cameras. Motion sensors. The works. If anyone approaches the house—"

A sharp beeping interrupts him.

Keric pulls out his own phone, eyes widening. "Speaking of which. Motion is detected on the west side of the property." He glances at a tablet, showing multiple camera views. "It's her. Your department head."

"Ellie?" I lurch forward, straining against the chains. "What is she doing?"

The image on the tablet shows Ellie Willis, bundled in a heavy coat, sneaking along the side of the mansion. She's alone, moving cautiously through the falling snow, peering at windows. I stare at her for far too long, watching her every movement, hungry for any glimpse I can get of the female who is my future.

"Looking for you, apparently," Aldar says dryly. "Didn't take your warnings seriously."

A primal urge surges through me. I want to break free and find her, claim her. My muscles tense, ready to snap the chains. I take a deep breath, forcing the ancient Irontree beast back down. Modern orcs do not kidnap. And I cannot break these particular chains; I've already tried.

For the last ten years, I've been working to prove that orcs and humans can safely coexist, live and work together, with none of the violence of the past. I refuse to be the orc who gains world-wide notoriety as the one who reverted to primitive instincts and kidnapped a coworker and violently took her without her consent.

My body is at war with my mind. My mind refuses to so much as touch my female without her consent. I will only sink inside of her heat and release my seed with her explicit consent and knowledge of what she is getting for life if she chooses to mate with an orc.

A large percentage of orcs want to simply live in their communes their whole lives and either remain alone or happen upon a willing female. They don't want to ever have to live with humans who scream in fright or think the worst of them. They only want females who will be willing to live with them on the orc communes. This isn't unreasonable considering that nowadays many females consider orcs highly compatible, and they will literally ask to be let into communes for planned speed dating rituals in order to see if any of the orcs will want them. And they literally leave crying if they aren't chosen.

But many of us want to live amongst the humans as equal citizens. And my career cannot flourish within the confines of the commune. I will not ruin any possibility of teaching at the academy, or a future relationship with Ellie in the spring by publicly reverting to the type of wild beast they fear. "Don't let her see me like this."

Aldar already heads for the stairs. "Jonus and I will intercept her before she gets too close."

"Treat my bride gently," I order.

"I'll do the talking," Jonus agrees.

"All of us know how to handle humans," Keric grumbles as he follows along.

My uncle stays behind with me. We watch together on the tablet as my three cousins exit through the front door and approach Ellie outside, before she can reach our porch. Even through the grainy security footage, I can see her embarrassment at being caught. I can't hear what they're saying. She hugs herself in the cold, nodding at whatever they're telling her. Eventually, she backs away, turns, and trudges through the snow toward her home.

I sink into the desk chair, relief and disappointment warring within me. She didn't see me like this, but on the other hand I didn't see her either.

The door to the basement opens and all three of them return.

"What did you tell her?"

"The truth," Aldar shrugs. "I reminded her that you're dangerous right now and you need to be kept separate until spring. That she should keep her distance. For her own safety."

"She wanted to see me?"

"She said she wanted to make sure you were all right," Jonus answers, "and I assured her that you were comfortable in your cage."

I let out a disgruntled snort.

"She asked if you were still planning on teaching when winter break ends, and I said you were and that you were ready to teach your classes online if needed. She seemed happy to hear that. And I told her that she could reach you by cell phone and that you know we are monitoring the situation. If anything devolves into unprofessional communication from you we can immediately cut you off."

I nod slowly, staring at the phone in my hand. "She'll text soon. About the teaching arrangement?"

"She didn't say."

"That female will eventually text you," Keric comments. "She didn't run away when you roared that she was your bride. And she came to check on you."

Aldar nods in agreement. "And when she does text, you will keep it professional. This is a rule that must be followed for your safety as well as hers."

My jaw clenches.

"We'll be monitoring every word," he reminds me.

A growl rumbles in my chest. "I know. All of you have said that ten times. There's no need to remind me again." Loki lets out a bark of agreement. I pet him and settle into my cot, focused on the screen in my hand.

Fifteen minutes later, I'm alone and the phone buzzes in my hand, startling me. An unknown number, but I know immediately who it is.

> Good evening, Professor Irontree. This is Ellie Willis from Black Oak Academy. We met this morning. Your cousins said that I can text you about the teaching arrangement?

My lips twitch. She sounds so formal and professional, despite the fact that I devolved into a monster at the sight of her and had to be chained and dragged away. She is also brave, not running away or hiding from me. Instead she continues to try and see me.

Before I can respond, she sends a second text.

> I understand from your...cousins that you'll be teaching remotely when the semester begins. This sounds like an excellent solution. I hadn't yet told anyone at Black Oak of our meeting this morning hoping that we could find a solution over break, and it looks like you found one.

I touch the screen and answer carefully, aware that every word will be scrutinized by those four idiots upstairs. My large fingers are accustomed to using the small human-sized phone.

> Thank you for keeping this confidential. Yes, I'll need to teach remotely for the time being. I appreciate your understanding and flexibility.

Send. Wait. The response comes quickly.

> I'm glad to hear that. Next week, after the holiday, would be a good time for us to talk about the tech you'll need and the curriculum.

My green thumbs hover over the screen. My need to see her and physically touch her is great, but I must remain in control. I respond.

> This sounds good.

> I hope you're…comfortable in your current situation.

I sense the real question beneath her polite inquiry. Is she genuinely concerned about me? It is amazing that she didn't run away or call the police. Most other females would have behaved that way, truly terrified at the sight of an Irontree orc who morphed into a true beast, ready to mate. But my female stood her ground and in fact is worried about me. The thought sends warmth through my chest. But I must always remember that humans are different from orcs. They can pleasure mate. I have no idea if Ellie's arousal for me means she wants something permanent.

> As comfortable as one can be under the circumstances. Thank you for asking. Looking forward to texting you again after the holiday. Thank you again for your understanding about the remote teaching arrangement.

> Of course. Have a good evening, Professor Irontree.

And that's it. The conversation ends. I place the phone on the desk, my mind racing. She's concerned about me. Ellie didn't report the incident to the school. She's willing to work with me despite everything.

Yes, she came to the mansion looking for me, but that could have been strictly professional. She hadn't told anyone at Black Oak how I'd lost my mind that morning and this could blow back on her. But there is one thing that I think none of my cousins know, because they weren't close enough to her. Just before I went wild, I inhaled her compatible pheromones but I also inhaled another tell-tale scent...her arousal. I know that Ellie wants me as much as I want her.

Well, I want her for forever. Because she's human she might only want me as a one-night stand. This has happened to many orcs in the past, falling for a human female who doesn't want them for anything more than a few nights of pleasure. Will I be the same?

Hours later the others have returned upstairs.

I pick up a book on ancient Rome, trying not to think about the security footage of Ellie sneaking around the house, looking for me. Trying my best to refrain from masturbating yet again. At this rate I'll end up with raw skin. The problem is that it never fully satisfies me. I know that only my female can bank this need into something normal and not over the top.

My cousins check on me periodically. Aldar brings dinner, Jonus collects my dishes afterward. Keric stops by to report that all is quiet next door.

It's past midnight when I hear the soft padding of paws on the basement stairs. I put my book down and watch as Loki reappears, having apparently finished spending time with the others. My corgi's stub tail wags frantically as he squeezes through the bars of my cell.

"Come here, traitor," I mutter affectionately, letting him jump into my lap. "Enjoying your new freedom while I'm locked up?"

Loki licks my face, seemingly oblivious to my predicament. I scratch behind his ears, remembering how eagerly he had jumped into Ellie's arms yesterday morning.

An idea forms. It's dangerous, foolish, but irresistible.

I glance at the security camera they've now installed in the corner, knowing my cousins could be watching. But it's late, and most likely they've all gone to bed, trusting the chains to keep me secure. The monitoring software on my phone would catch any unauthorized texts or calls, but there are older methods of communication.

Moving quietly, I find a notepad and pen amongst my supplies. I must tell Ellie the truth about my intentions. And then allow her the room to take me or leave me. It is only right. I hesitate, then begin to write.

When I finish, I fold the paper carefully, considering how to attach it to Loki. There's no collar because we removed it when we moved in, planning to get him a new one, including a tag with updated information. With nothing else available, I tear a strip from the bottom of my shirt, threading it through Loki's front legs and around his chest, creating a makeshift harness. I tuck the folded letter securely into it. I'll make sure to tell them he needs a real harness.

"Ready for a mission?" I whisper, scratching under Loki's chin. "Find Ellie."

The dog's ears perk up. Does he really understand, or am I projecting? He must. This dog was literally bred to send messages. We've gone hunting together and he's done this before, sending messages to other groups of orcs. Either way, I need to get him out of the cell and to the back door.

I stretch my arm through the bars, reaching as far as the chain will allow, and point to the stairs. "Go, outside Loki. Find Ellie."

The corgi tilts his head, seemingly confused by my command.

I sigh, closing my eyes, focusing on Ellie's scent still lingering in my memory. When I open them again, I point more emphatically. "Find Ellie. Find her."

Something in my tone must communicate my urgency. Loki barks once, soft but determined, then darts through the bars and up the stairs.

I wait, listening. The house is silent. Is Loki going to actually try to leave our home through the pet door I know is in the side door? Has he made it outside? Will he really know to go to Ellie's house? Will she even be awake to receive him?

CHAPTER 8
Ellie

I CANNOT BELIEVE I snuck next door while Mom and Zoe went to pick up take-out food. I was in a rush to get there and back because I didn't have much free time. They would expect me to appear in the kitchen to help unpack the Chinese food they'd picked up.

No way can my mom, or even Zoe, learn that I went to check on Garlen. Yesterday I promised my mom I wouldn't do this, but I can't seem to help this insistent need to know what truly happened to him after his companions dragged him away. How can I be expected to not go over there at all and say and do nothing? That's crazy talk. I must know at least the basics before I can be expected to settle down and relax.

Within my small window of opportunity, I boldly stride over to my neighbor's mansion to knock on the massive front door. And maybe I was trying to look through a few windows... They met up with me before I could get that far. I stood there, taking deep breaths of cold air because I've never in my life had orc neighbors and didn't know how any of this worked.

I'd watched this McMansion being built. Do all the orcs own a piece of this property, or did they pool their money together to purchase it? Is Garlen the owner and the rest of them guests?

Three orcs tower over me, and yes, they are a bit frightening. Lots of black horns, green muscles and deep frowns. The one who spoke to me yesterday introduces himself as Jonus and introduces me to the others. Not that I can remember which name goes to which orc, but it's a start. I learn that Garlen lives with his three cousins and his uncle Dane, who is still in the basement with him.

"You must never make any contact with Garlen except through the cell phone, which we will monitor. This will keep you safe, as well as him," an orc named Aldar says. This one isn't as tall as Garlen, but he does have longer hair and a scar on his cheek which will be helpful in identifying and differentiating him from the others. "All five of us are Irontrees, from the Irontree tribe in northern Maine. We will make sure that no Irontree harms a human, and in fact it is important to not only Garlen but also the rest of us that this teaching assignment continues without interruption."

After our brief talk I returned home and immediately fired off texts to Garlen. I'd had a brief talk with his cousins, but I'd learned a lot, especially the correct phone number to use to personally reach him. Yes, it's being monitored so I have to watch what I say, but I was happy to hear his response, no matter how formal. At least now I know he's okay.

Mom and Zoe returned home with my favorite Chinese take-out. I was giddy about my contact with the new neighbors and those texts but had to pretend I'd never walked over there and didn't meet those other orcs. That was a bummer because I would've loved to chat about it over dinner. But instead we ate and watched a Christmas movie together, which was also lovely. I snuggled with Zoe on the couch and daydreamed that Garlen was here with us. How would that work, having an orc husband, who was also the stepfather of my human daughter? Would he accept Zoe as his own and treat her well?

Because an orc husband who didn't want human children from a previous relationship would be a deal breaker. My daughter has had enough angst in her life, and if I'm going to ever remarry, it would have to be with a man who could open his heart to her and treat her as one of his own.

Remarry? Jeez, I've got it bad.

Finally, after dessert and one more Christmas special, all of us end up in our respective bedrooms with the doors closed by 10 o'clock. Zoe might be awake for a bit longer because she likes to lay in bed and play on her kid tablet. I know this because I often find her asleep with it on her chest, or fallen between her and her favorite stuffed animal, Flora.

Mom has the primary bedroom, with the attached bath. Zoe and I have bedrooms next to each other and we share a bathroom.

But I do know this is the quiet time of the evening, with a good amount of alone time for myself.

I'm having a hard time falling asleep so I spend time reading a new romance from my favorite author, but even this can't wholly capture my attention. Eventually, after midnight, I go downstairs to the kitchen for a late-night snack.

And that's when I hear a scratching and whining at the side door to the kitchen.

"Loki?" I whisper. He's at the glass door that leads into the side yard. And if I think about it, that door does have a nice little pathway for a small corgi to navigate. I open the door and kneel, petting the excited dog and notice a paper attached to his makeshift harness. A huge smile spreads across my face. "Oh my gosh, this is why you're here? Are you delivering this to me?" I slip the folded paper from the dog and open it and see it's a letter from…Garlen?

I cannot believe I am receiving a handwritten letter from a caged orc via his darling corgi. If I told this to anyone, they wouldn't believe me and insist I was making it up.

I pet Loki's precious head again. "Thank you for bringing this to me. I've never owned a dog in my life, but if I were to ever have one, I suspect it would be one just like you."

The dog lets out a tiny bark and scampers off into the night and is gone.

I open the letter and start reading.

Dear Ellie,

If you're reading this, then Loki has successfully delivered my letter. I know how strange this must seem, secret letters delivered by my dog, but I needed to explain myself without my cousins monitoring every word on that phone. They believe that I would try to talk you into coming over and letting me loose, but that won't happen, ever.

First, I want to apologize for my behavior when we met. What you witnessed was something most humans never see—a wild orc's first reaction to discovering his mate. Yes, mate. In that moment when I caught your scent, every cell in my body recognized you as the one meant to be my bride.

This doesn't excuse my behavior. During winter, especially for orcs from certain bloodlines like mine, our primal instincts become nearly impossible to control. In ancient times, this resulted in orcs kidnapping human females in the dark of winter, which was a primitive practice we've worked for generations to overcome.

The chains and confinement are necessary. My cousins aren't cruel, they're protecting the both of us. I would never forgive myself if I harmed or frightened you any further than I already have.

The smart thing to do would be for all of us to return to the commune until possibly the middle of spring. But this position is important, and I want to fulfill my obligation.

I know this is an impossible situation. I'm your employee, hired sight unseen, and now I've complicated our situation by screaming for you in the snow. And yes, even while I'm chained, I think of you day and night and my body wants you as much as it did the moment I scented you.

I must tell you the truth, so you understand why you must stay away. If you were to come close again, I would throw you down and fuck you hard, not caring for consent. My body and mind want desperately to fill you with my seed and see you swollen with my orc son. What was said to you before about you needing to stay away from me until spring is true.

We have distance right now and your scent is not within my lungs, but I remain on edge just knowing you are near. Do not be scared. My cousins will keep me chained and you and your mother and your daughter will remain safe.

Your safety is my number one priority. Which is why we must only communicate through letters and text.

> The professional text messages will continue, but if you would like to respond to me privately, Loki can continue to be our messenger.
>
> If the receipt of this letter makes you uncomfortable because you have no interest in mating with me, simply ignore this letter and I'll understand. We can maintain a strictly professional relationship via text messages until spring arrives, when I can meet you again in person and behave in a reasonable manner.
>
> Sincerely,
> Garlen Irontree

Strangely, the first thing I think of is how much I love his handwriting. How is an orc, with those large, rough hands, able to write so nicely? Now I wish I could watch him write. I'm loving the idea of this strong, smart orc, possibly wearing glasses and a blazer... No, there wouldn't be a blazer because they all basically walk around shirtless?

Ugh. My mind is naughty. This guy is my coworker. I can't think of him this way.

And yet how can I not? Yesterday, he said he would impregnate me. He boldly said that in front of everyone on my front lawn, while my ex was being dragged away. And he just told me again that his end game is to fuck me hard.

I smile and pull out my notebook and stay up way too late writing a return letter.

Finally, I fall asleep, wondering how I'm going to find Loki again to send my letter in return.

CHAPTER 9
Garlen

THE SUN RISES behind the frosted basement window, leaving streaks of spooky shadows across the cement floor of my pit. Spending the entire winter here confined within this cage is the biggest test of strength and will power I will have ever endured.

My mind wants to meet this female, speak to her, help her to understand that I want her for life and that I will treat her better than any other male she could ever meet.

My body is constantly enflamed with need and wants Ellie underneath me, no matter what I have to do to get her there.

I'm already awake because I barely slept all night, masturbating again with warring thoughts and feelings causing chaos in my system.

Images replayed in my head of what it must've looked like when Loki reached Ellie's side door. Did she enjoy my letter attached to my corgi? I am now consumed with the anxiety of waiting. Loki returned last night without the letter, or a response, slipping past my sleeping cousins to curl up at the foot of my too-small cot.

Did she read the letter I sent? Was she horrified by my

confession? Or did the letter simply fall into the snow, never reaching her at all?

Keric shows up early for my morning shower. I strip my bedding and carry it with me. It's strange how quickly I've grown accustomed to the heft and weight of the chains. He lets me out and follows me as I walk, still chained. I pause to shove all the fabric in the wash, because again my release is everywhere. Then he follows me upstairs to my bathroom where I then strip off my clothes, shower and shout out another release that sprays the tile. This calms me down. Not satisfied, but able to carry on with my day.

This will be my daily routine for the next two months.

I change into clean pants, and Keric returns to guide me back down to the cage for lock up.

Minutes later my other cousin arrives. Aldar is the best cook amongst us and therefore does most of our meal planning and cooking. "Good morning," he grumbles, stomping down the basement stairs with a tray of food. "I could hear you brooding from two floors up."

I grunt in response and sit upright on the cot, careful not to disturb Loki. "Is that coffee I smell?"

"And meat sticks, seared just the way you like them." He unlocks the door to the cage and steps inside to deliver my food. He also carries extra food to fill up Loki's empty bowl. "You look terrible, despite your shower. Didn't sleep?"

"Would you, locked in a basement cage?"

"It's better than being isolated in a cave with a screaming, kidnapped human female and the entire country literally up in arms and chasing after you."

A low growl rumbles in my chest. I remain seated on the cot and place the food tray on my lap and start eating.

Aldar drags a chair closer to the cot and sits, watching me eat. "Dane has been looking into Marcus Adams. There's something off about that human. The Crimson Tusk connections are possibly true."

I set down my meat stick. "I need to see everything Dane found. Every detail."

"This is just about protecting your boss at the academy, right? And nothing to do with her being your mate?"

"What does it matter?"

"It matters if it makes you do something stupid. Like break those chains and go hunting criminal humans."

"I'm not stupid. There is no way I'd break free and go vigilante alone against Crimson Tusk in the streets of a human city."

"Good." Aldar stands, stretching. "Because one, you'd get arrested. Two, you'd jeopardize your job. And three, you'd scare your future bride. Human women don't find bloodthirsty orcs appealing. He'll be here soon. Dane is checking on the property next door, making sure all three females are safe."

An hour later Keric has already checked on all my restraints again and I'm left alone with Loki and my erotic thoughts of my bride, all of which are dangerous. I take down another book, trying to get lost in the words. The small dog yawns, stretching and turning in a circle on the cot.

"You returned without my letter," I murmur, scratching his ears. "I hope you delivered it properly."

Loki thumps his stubby tail, offering zero insights into the secret world of messenger corgis.

Before I start to entertain ideas of trying to dig my way out of this cell, Dane arrives with a thick folder. "Marcus Adams," he says, sliding it through the bars. "Everything I could find."

I grin and stand up from my cot, stepping forward to take what he is offering. It is good to see my towering uncle. I need something to keep my mind off my Ellie Willis obsession. Dane is twenty-six years older than me, unmated, and a respected member of our commune. I suspect he will soon be voted into a position of authority within my species as one of the elders for our region. I am lucky that he is with us on this mission.

His presence in the basement instantly brings a dose of reality to my addled and irrational state of mind.

I flip through the pages and find arrest records for Marcus Adams. Rehab stays. Missed child support payments. Sealed juvenile records that Jonus somehow unsealed with his tech skills. And worst of all, there are phone records showing calls to known Crimson Tusk members.

I look up at Dane. "He's more than just an ex with addiction issues. This human is indeed connected to Crimson Tusk."

My uncle nods grimly. "This confirms our suspicions about why your start date at the academy was delayed until winter."

"Crimson Tusk made that happen because they knew an Irontree would be more vulnerable to winter urges." I clench my fist, crumpling the edge of a document. "They wanted me to fail."

"The timing is too perfect to be coincidence," Dane agrees. "First, they block your fall semester start through administrative delays, pushing your arrival to winter. Then Marcus shows up the very day you move in, right when you're most likely to lose control."

"And it worked," I growl, rattling my chains. "They couldn't have known that I would react that way to Ellie, but they hoped that at some point one of us here would meet our mate and embarrass ourselves in front of the humans. And I immediately fell right into their trap, on day one. They must be thrilled that I want to mate with Ellie Willis. If they learn I'm chained in a basement, they'll use it as propaganda against orc integration everywhere." I begin pacing the cell again, dragging the heavy chains in my wake. "Have I ruined everything?"

"You're confined, but you will still teach. That's what they truly fear. They want to block the actual teaching, but we've already found a work-around."

"Black Oak Academy is the first school in the country to hire an orc professor. Crimson Tusk doesn't want orc knowledge shared with humans."

"Tusk believes orc wisdom should remain exclusively with orcs," Dane confirms. "Their manifesto calls us the superior species. The idea of an orc teaching human children contradicts everything they stand for."

"Marcus isn't smart enough for this ideological warfare. This unworthy male wouldn't care about orcs versus humans. Why is he involved with them?" I glance at a particular document, showing his impressive debt load. "He's desperate for money, and the Tusk is using him to get to Ellie?"

"I agree. And they'll likely try to use her to sabotage you and the school," Dane says quietly. "They know where she lives."

The ancient winter rage bubbles up, demanding I break free and hunt down every threat to my mate. I force it down, breathing deeply.

"We will protect those three females next door," my uncle vows. "While you are here, unable to protect them yourself, I will be your surrogate. I vow that I will protect them as if they were my own responsibility."

"Thank you. This is bigger than just me now." I stare at the documents. "If I fail, if Black Oak's integration experiment fails, other schools won't risk hiring orcs. Everything we've worked for, everything our species has worked toward…"

"The Irontrees have always been soldiers," Dane reminds me. "For centuries, our ancestors fought to protect orc communes from invading human mobs with pitchforks and torches. And we would battle other invading orcs. In modern times, many of us still feel that ancient call to battle, to protect. The human government requires us to stand down, to integrate peacefully in order to maintain our citizenship status. But that warrior instinct doesn't simply vanish. We all want to fight for what is right and protect not only our species but any being we see being treated unjustly. It's in our blood."

I nod, understanding. My cousins and I have become, in essence, orc vigilantes. We help both humans and orcs while maintaining careful boundaries with law enforcement. It's why we have tight connections with the human authorities, why they can access information about dangerous individuals like Marcus. "We need more security. Cameras on her house, her office at Black Oak. I suspect the Tusk already has infiltrators on the school board."

"Already done," Dane responds. "We are watching the perimeter since yesterday."

"Why didn't you tell me?"

"You didn't need to know."

He's right, but I still resent being kept in the dark. "Show me the feeds. I need to see she's safe."

My uncle merely shrugs in agreement.

The rest of the day passes slowly.

Dane told me every aspect of the impressive security they've set up next door at Ellie's home and at the school. I obsessively review every page of Marcus's file, making notes on possible Crimson Tusk motives, mapping out connections. Mid-afternoon, Dane returns with the promised tablet and books. I spend hours watching the security feeds showing Ellie's house, her classroom at Black Oak, the parking lots. Nothing unusual. Nothing threatening. Just the comforting rhythm of her daily life while on vacation, captured in grainy surveillance footage.

Night falls, casting the basement into shadows.

Keric brings dinner, checks my chains yet again, opens the safe to get some money and leaves without much conversation. Loki returns from an upstairs outing, curling beside me on the cot as I read.

Just after midnight, I sit up suddenly. The house is quiet as an orc tomb and it's now the same time Loki returned last night without the letter. Could Ellie have written back? Would she have read my letter and responded?

I nudge Loki awake. "Time for another mission," I whisper. "Find Ellie. Same as last night. And see if she wants to send a letter back."

The corgi's ears perk up, more alert now because he's done this once before and understands the directive. I create another makeshift harness from the same strip of cloth, but this time there's no letter, only the harness itself, ready to receive one if Ellie has written back.

I stretch my arm through the bars, reaching as far as the chain will allow, and point to the stairs, just like I did yesterday. "Go, Loki. Find Ellie."

The corgi barks softly in understanding, then slips through the bars and up the stairs. I listen intently, hearing the soft click of the pet door as he exits the house.

Now comes the waiting.

I pace the confines of my cage, checking the security feeds on the tablet, watching for a small shape crossing the snow between our houses. A tiny shape moves purposefully toward Ellie's home. I hold my breath, watching as Loki reaches the side door of the house. The door opens almost immediately, as if she's been waiting.

I can't see clearly from this angle, but the small figure disappears inside. Minutes pass. I continue pacing, checking the time every few seconds. What if she decides not to write back? What if my letter offended her?

The tablet chirps with movement at her door again. Loki exits, something clearly attached to his harness now. My heart pounds as I watch his return journey across the snow. I sit on the cot, trying to appear calm despite the anticipation coursing through my veins.

Minutes later, I hear the soft click of dog nails on the basement stairs. Loki appears, triumphant, with an envelope secured to his makeshift harness.

"Great work, Loki."

My hands tremble as I open the envelope, careful not to tear the paper inside. Ellie's lovely scent wafts from the pages, making my body heat with desire. I close my eyes, breathing it in, before forcing myself to focus on her words.

Dear Garlen,

A secret corgi courier service wasn't on my winter break bingo card, but here we are.

Thank you for your honesty about the incident on my front lawn. I appreciate your explanation about what happened when we met. I was more surprised than frightened and certainly not scared.

And thank you for telling me the repercussions that could happen if you weren't restrained. Remaining chained until spring sounded extreme, but I suppose it really is necessary. Are you comfortable? Do they treat you well? I worry about that.

Here I am, writing back, so that means I'm open to us having more between us than simply a coworker relationship.

I hope you understand that humans usually date first and then decide slowly if they want to be serious with a partner. I have questions I need answered first before I would consider us as...well what are we? Do orcs date? Can we date if we're working together?

I guess what I'm saying is that I am open to the idea of pursuing something with you.

But I have questions about what it means to be

your "bride." I've read books about orc-human relationships. If I'm truly your mate, how does that work out? For me? For my daughter? I'm a package deal. My six-year-old daughter, Zoe, comes first in all my decisions.

Please know that if you don't feel comfortable with the idea of adding a human daughter to our "relationship" then we can't start anything. And that's okay, not everyone can make that kind of commitment. But I need to know up front, for the both of us.

And this is very important news that I'm hoping you can tell your cousins too—your citizen's arrest of my ex, Marcus Adams, was helpful, but I believe he's involved with dangerous people now. I'm worried he, or his new friends, might cause trouble for you and I'd feel terrible about that. I just want you to be on the lookout.

Thank you again for helping me when we met. And despite what happened, I'm still happy that we DID meet.

If you'd like to write back, I'll be watching for Loki again tomorrow night.

P.S. Your handwriting is surprisingly elegant for someone with such large hands! I imagine you hunched over a tiny human-sized desk, carefully writing with a pen that looks like a toothpick in your grip. Lol - Ellie

. . .

I read the letter again, then a third time, my chest tight with emotions I can't fully identify. Ellie wasn't afraid. She's worried about my comfort. My female is willing to continue our correspondence. And she notices my handwriting.

Loki whines softly, sensing my agitation. I stroke his fur absently, my mind racing.

My jaw clenches as I imagine how this unworthy human must have mistreated my female and her offspring. He is now involved in Crimson Tusk and I believe trying to use Ellie as a means to get inside access to the Academy.

I should be at her side, helping to protect her and her daughter, not locked in this basement.

The good news is that Ellie doesn't sound repulsed by the idea of being my mate. She has reasonable questions, but she's curious, not horrified.

I carefully fold her letter and hide it beneath my mattress, away from the security cameras' view. Then I find the paper and pen Keric brought earlier, sitting at the small desk they've provided.

My cell phone vibrates. I receive a text from Ellie.

> Good news. I have everything set up for remote lessons. The principal and school board were surprisingly accommodating when I explained you'd had a "family emergency" that required remote work for a while. They're excited to have an orc professor, especially one with your credentials, and are willing to be flexible.

I smile, pleased to see her following the deception of professional talk via text and personal exchange through our letters. My female is sneaky. This is the perfect way to throw my cousins upstairs off the scent, while we write real words to each other through pen and ink.

I send back an equally professional and dispassionate text in return. Then I sit at the small desk, trying to recreate the image of myself she imagined and begin writing a long letter to my female.

Dear Ellie,

Loki enjoys helping us out. He is of a messenger breed and therefore thrilled to be doing exactly what he was bred to do.

Yes, I will remain confined until spring. It's not as bad as it sounds. My cousins have made the basement comfortable, with books, a laptop, and everything I need for teaching. The orc-weight chains are frustrating but necessary. I would never want to harm you, which is why I accept this confinement without fighting it (much).

You ask what it means to be my mate. How would a relationship work out between a human and an orc?

Unfortunately, orcs who find a possible mate in the dark of winter can't date like a human. If we'd met at any other time of the year I could have behaved in a civilized manner and I would've met you and then asked you on a human-style date and we could have taken this relationship slowly. By the time winter arrived hopefully I would have already charmed you into becoming my mate and then there would be no winter frenzy because we would be mated.

But instead, we met in the dark of winter, the worst possible time.

It's important that you know what you're getting yourself into if you decide to take me on.

First, after we have sex and exchange scents and solidify our relationship, I would be bound to you for life. There will never be another for me. I would be physically unable to have sex with another female while you are my bride.

Second, there is no divorce amongst orcs. Marriage is considered a flimsy construct amongst humans because it isn't a true bond as with orcs. I will never want another. I will age with you, protect you, care for you and our orc sons. This protection will of course include Zoe. I would never expect you to abandon or sideline your daughter. If anything, I would hope to be another source of support and love in her life, should you ever allow me that privilege.

But this does not mean that you cannot ever leave me. You always have the choice to leave, or to never start a relationship with me. Your consent, your choice, is so important to me that I remain chained next door to make sure that I never harm you in any way.

Humans can choose freely, and I would never presume to claim you without your explicit consent.

Many orcs live their entire lives having found their mate but never being chosen in return. They stay on the commune in order to remain separate from their female who did not choose them. There are many orcs in my commune that are raising their orc sons alone. It's painful, but we manage.

What troubles me most about your letter is the mention of Marcus. Orc instincts to protect our mates are overwhelming, especially in winter. My cousins have installed security around your house and at Black Oak. If you notice anything suspicious, please text me immediately. I will alert my cousins, who can respond faster than human law enforcement.

I come from a long line of warrior orcs. The Irontrees have traditionally been protectors and soldiers, fighting to defend our species from threats. In modern times, many of us still feel that call to protect, though we must do so within the boundaries of human law. My cousins have found ways to use those instincts constructively, working alongside law enforcement when possible. We have connections that allow us to investigate someone like Marcus. And why we are inclined to provide citizen's arrests when warranted.

We believe your ex-husband might be involved with a criminal organization called the Crimson Tusk, a gang of rogue orcs who abandoned the communes for illegal enterprises. They're dangerous and have been expanding their operations in Northern California.

Be on the lookout and text me if you see anything unusual. Meanwhile, know that you are safe because you have five orcs living next door and all of us are making sure you, your mother and Zoe are perfectly safe during this human holiday season.

Your P.S. made me laugh. It's true that human pens are absurdly small in my hands. I have custom stationery made with larger dimensions. The irony of being a teacher with oversized hands isn't lost on me. I've been to a few human conferences, and they watch in fascination as I delicately handle their business cards without crushing them.

Loki will be ready for another mission tomorrow night.

Garlen

I fold the letter carefully, creating a small, neat envelope from another sheet of paper. Writing my feelings out has calmed me somewhat, though the thought of threats to Ellie and the school where she works still makes my blood boil.

My letter is ready, but I can't send it yet. I fashion another simple harness for Loki. "Tomorrow night," I whisper to him, "you'll return to Ellie. Understand?"

The corgi tilts his head, then licks my hand.

I choose to interpret this as agreement.

Ellie's letter is stashed securely with the other one, beneath a loose floor tile I discovered, which is a better hiding place than underneath the mattress. For the first time since my confinement began, I feel something beyond frustration and primitive need.

I feel hope.

CHAPTER 10
Ellie

THREE DAYS HAVE PASSED since I began exchanging love letters with my orc boyfriend.

A snort-laugh escapes my lips.

Okay, so he isn't technically my boyfriend, and those letters can't really be classified as "love letters" since neither of us have declared any love for the other. Garlen is simply the new teacher hired for Black Oak Academy who happens to live next door and is the same orc that called me his "bride" the moment he met me, and who now communicates via letters delivered by his adorable corgi.

Totally normal situation.

I have to admit I've decided he's my secret boyfriend, even though he said that orcs don't date.

And I like toying with the idea in my head that he's not only my boyfriend but a possible future husband. Yes, it's kinda crazy to be thinking this way, considering we haven't spent any real time together, but...I really like that wild orc next door.

I had no idea that I would like exchanging letters so much. I've never sent handwritten letters to anyone before. I've written messages in cards before to family, but that's about it. Garlen's handwriting is nicer than mine. When the letter arrives it even smells like him, that same scent I remember from when I stood near him that first day—a woodsy mix of leather and leaves.

It could be said that I need to take things slowly considering my ex is most likely still in jail in Truckee and hasn't left yet. This does not bode well. And Garlen remains caged.

But an orc who would never cheat on me and would remain with me forever and treat my daughter as his own sounds like my idea of heaven.

I glance over at Zoe, sitting at the kitchen table, finishing cereal while watching a show on her tablet.

I still have no idea if he'd get along well with Zoe, and if Zoe even wants an orc stepfather. Does my mom want an orc as her son-in-law? Would Garlen fit in well with my little family and would I fit in well with his family?

What if we start to work together and discover that we hate each other?

There are still so many unknowns. But I'm moving along with the fact that my attraction for this guy I only saw once in real life is off the charts. That's got to mean something. I've had to walk around and continue with life as if I don't want to sneak next door and unchain that orc and let him fuck me hard, despite the chance that it could turn ugly and I might end up with him in a cave in the mountains.

I suppose this is because he goes on and on about consent. Despite everything, I can't help this deep feeling of trust for him and the other Irontrees living next door.

And so far, our letter exchanges have been a success. He hints at his attraction for me, but not in a yucky way. I feel I've really gotten to know him. He's told me all about growing up in his commune with his parents, who are still together. His parents, Lori and Thorin Irontree, happily live on the commune where Garlen was born and raised in northern Maine. His uncle, Dane Irontree, and Thorin are brothers and best friends. It sounds like Dane was sent with this group as the adult in the room to make sure nothing went wrong. Which Garlen admits is ironic considering in his own words "everything went wrong."

Last week I had no idea I'd meet my co-teacher and he would be such a force in my life. This orc fills most of my waking thoughts. I literally lay in bed at night, getting all hot and bothered, thinking of him. Images run through my mind of that muscular chest and those thick thighs and his strong arms. And I caught the hint of that huge package between his legs.

I'm in a great mood today, in the kitchen, again wearing super-comfy clothes, rolling out gingerbread cookie dough. Mom is upstairs wrapping presents, with strict instructions for all of us to not come up or open the door until she texts the all-clear.

My favorite Christmas music plays in the background, and I loudly sing along to my favorite parts. This one was my dad's favorite song too.

Sadness hits me hard. This is only our second Christmas without dad, and I still miss him terribly. Mom is sad too but tries her best to carry on.

I take a deep breath and refocus on the job on the marble counter in front of me.

Cookies need to be made for the people I want to say "thank you" to for their niceness, or even to people I want to become closer to by giving them something I made by hand. And the only thing I know how to make well by hand is cookies, so I dig in.

I'm going to make a special dog cookie for Loki (in the shape of a dog bone), and snowman-shaped cookies for Garlen and his family members.

"Mom, can I decorate the doggy one?" Zoe asks, not looking up from her tablet.

"Absolutely. But first, it's got to get made and baked. Get ready, you're going to help me press all of these into the dough and cut the shapes in just a few moments."

"Okay," she answers absently.

The dog-shaped cookie cutter slips in my hand, falling to the floor with a clatter. I bend to pick it up, and when I straighten, I see Loki sitting patiently by the back door, a letter attached to his harness.

I bite my lip and look around. Why is this corgi so early today? I wasn't expecting him until past midnight. I glance over at Zoe, who seems unaware. For once, her addiction to her screen is coming in handy. "Zoe, honey, can you please go upstairs and go into my room and grab me that box that's on my bed?"

"But my show…"

"You can take your tablet with you. Hurry, I need it right now to help with the baking."

She sighs dramatically but slides off the chair, taking her tablet with her. As soon as she's gone, I rush to let Loki inside.

"Hello," I whisper as the corgi excitedly enters, his nails clicking on the tile. "Sssh. Sit. Sit." I crouch to untie the letter. "You're early today, aren't you?" I comment. Then I quickly hide Garlen's newest letter in my apron pocket and give Loki a small piece of leftover ham from my breakfast. "Our little secret," I tell him, scratching behind his ears. "Wait here." My pre-written letter from last night hides inside a cookbook on the shelf. I take it out and attach it to his harness. I give a few pets of his soft fur. "Is Garlen doing okay?" I ask the dog, as if he could answer. "He's not sending you early because he's sick, right?

Loki's fluffy rear end shakes enthusiastically. I choose to take this as a good sign. Maybe the answer is as simple as Garlen wanting to send two letters a day, instead of one. Which is fine with me.

"Stay safe," I whisper, letting him out the back door. I watch until Loki's small form disappears between the houses.

"Mom," Zoe grumbles from behind me. "What box were you talking about? There wasn't a box on your bed."

I turn towards her. "Oh, sorry, honey. Ooops, here it is. My bad."

I return to my baking, eager to read Garlen's letter but knowing I need to wait until I have privacy.

An hour later the front door opens and closes, and Mom appears, carrying the mail.

"Anything interesting?" I ask, trying to sound casual despite that letter I still haven't had a chance to read.

A whole batch of cookies burnt because I wasn't paying attention and now I have to mix a whole other batch of dough. And I'm not sure if I even have enough ingredients anymore.

"Bills, catalogs, and…oh, look at this, I bet it's an invitation." Mom holds up a red envelope, waves it in the air and immediately tears it open. "I'd heard that the Petersons always have an annual Christmas open house. To be truthful I was hurt that we didn't get an invitation when it seemed everyone else had. Yep, we're invited. Look, it's postmarked a week ago." She snorts. "It would've gotten here much sooner if they'd just walked over and put it in our mailbox. But we can still make it, right? It's scheduled for the day before Christmas Eve, tomorrow night. The whole neighborhood is invited."

"Yeah, I can make it. We don't exactly have anything else going on."

"I was just talking to Dane about this yesterday," Mom says, her voice too casual.

"Dane? As in Dane Irontree? Garlen's uncle? You know him?"

She nods, busying herself with sorting the mail. "We ran into each other at the mailboxes again. He was asking me for advice on how to find the best large size clothes for orcs. I told him I'd do some research."

I let out a snort. "Since when did you develop an interest in menswear?"

"I've always been interested in menswear," she says defensively. "Anyway, he mentioned the Petersons had invited them too."

"All the Irontrees are going to the neighborhood Christmas party?"

"Apparently just Dane and Jonus are going so that Keric and Aldar can stay behind and watch Garlen."

Something in her tone makes me pause. "Mom, have you been talking to Dane about Garlen?"

"Well, a little." She sets down the mail and leans against the counter. "Actually, quite a bit. I've been talking to Dane about this, and I spoke to my lawyer…"

I look over my shoulder. "You have a lawyer?"

"Yes, of course." She picks up her tablet, taps on it and walks over to show me the screen. "This is what I've learned about whether Marcus will stay in jail or not. Dane told me that—"

"Dane? Again?"

"Yes. Can I finish?"

My lips twitch. "Sorry for interrupting, go ahead."

"After Dane dropped Marcus off at the police station he was immediately arrested for violating the restraining order. He's been in jail, waiting to see what the judge decides his bail will be and if he can make that bail."

"I'd assumed he was going to be in jail for a while considering he doesn't have anyone he can call who will pay that bail, whatever it is."

"Yes, I agree. His family has cut him off and last I'd heard he'd lost all his old friends too. He doesn't have anyone we know of who can pay that bail and there's still the FBI matter that's up in the air. But Dane thinks there's the possibility that he's been hired by an orc criminal organization called Crimson Tusk to cause trouble for Black Oak Academy. He thinks he's here to cause trouble for Garlen's teaching assignment through his co-teacher."

"Crimson Tusk?" I ask, pretending like I've never heard this before, although I'd already heard this theory from Garlen. I'm relieved that she knows, so now we can talk about it. "Will they think he's worth paying the bail for?" I question.

"I don't—" And then her phone vibrates. She grabs for the additional screen. "Darn it, Marcus was let out on bail earlier this morning."

My eyebrow crooks. "Is that a text from Dane?"

She grins. "Yes. He's my new connection."

I push my hair back from my face and let out a breath. Even the Christmas music can't brighten my spirits. "Marcus is out on bail and roaming the streets again? Well, great, I was just starting to feel comfortable in this new house and neighborhood and I'm back to not feeling safe."

"I feel very safe."

"I don't," I whisper, making sure Zoe can't hear us. "We don't know why Marcus is here or what he wants. Him arriving here doesn't make sense. And if he's here because he's getting paid by some orc gang, that's even scarier."

She points next door. "I feel safe because Garlen Irontree thinks you're his mate. I don't know if that's true or not or if the two of you are ever going to eventually get together. And yes, it's very weird that an orc that's chained and caged is in the basement next door, because if he got free he'd come over here and kidnap you. But on the other hand, that orc would give his life for you."

My mouth drops open. "You only like him because you think he'd take a bullet for me?"

"Yeah, what's wrong with that? I'm your mother. I want you safe. I want Zoe safe too. Marcus made bail and what if he tries to come back here and this time tries to hurt you," she chokes up. "What if he goes beyond shouts and does something else to you and I'm not here or can't protect you from him…those orcs next door would be here in a moment."

"You know what's weird about all of this is that Marcus always hated orcs."

"He did?"

"Yeah, that's why I can't understand him working together with this orc gang. He'd rant about how none of them should be allowed to work with humans. He was really pissed when that new law passed, making the orcs citizens."

"Hmm. I didn't know that. Another piece of the puzzle."

"I've moved across the state to another town and started a new job, and my ex has managed to find me and he's here again. Normally I'd be freaking out about this but you're right, I'm strangely calm. It must be because…"

"Because we already saw those orcs take care of him in a minute and pin him to the ground and ship him off to the police station. And they are looking out for us, right now."

"How do you know that?"

She shrugs. "Dane told me."

"Let me guess," I chuckle. "While you were at the mailbox?"

"Yes…" She lifts her phone. "And he texts me about it sometimes too."

I stare at her for a long moment, not sure how to process this new information. My mother, who's always been cautious around strangers, is suddenly exchanging texts with an orc we barely know? And apparently discussing our safety with him? Not that I can talk…I'm also quickly growing close and exchanging messages with my own Irontree. "Well. I guess I should be grateful we have neighbors looking out for us."

"You should. In fact…I was thinking we could bake some cookies for them. As a thank you."

I glance down at the cookie shapes already arranged on the baking sheet. "Great minds think alike."

I'm ready to start another batch of cookies when I realize I'm running out of ingredients. "Oh, darn it, I need to run to the store." I lift my chin and shout to be heard above the TV. "Zoe, you want to go to the grocery store with me?"

"No," a tiny voice replies from the other room.

"Mom, can you please stay to watch Zoe and get these out of the oven when the timer dings and then put this other tray in for another twelve minutes? I'll be right back. I just need more sugar and some frosting."

"Sure." Mom picks up the oven mitts. "You go ahead."

I grab my coat and keys, stepping out into the freezing cold December air. The sun is already setting, casting long shadows across our snowy front yard. This is still all so weird to me, living with actual snow. When I moved here, I had to quiz my coworkers, who were very helpful with tips on what to wear and how to take care of my driveway and car in weather this cold.

Although since those orcs moved in next door, they've been taking care of me. I haven't had to lift a finger and all my snow removal gadgets remain idle. There isn't a bit of snow on my car, the driveway or my sidewalk.

Nice.

As I approach my car, something catches my eye. White paper flutters under the windshield wiper. Probably an advertisement. But as I get closer, a chill runs down my spine. I recognize that handwriting.

I pull the paper free and unfold it.

Merry Christmas, I'll be seeing you soon –
Marcus

Anger flashes through me hard as I refold the note and slip it into my pocket and look around.

Dammit, dammit, dammit. I slide into my car, lock the doors, and sit for a moment, trying to calm my racing heart. I don't want to scare Zoe with my feels, so I can't rush back into the house and let her see me upset. But I need to let someone know this happened.

The note looks innocuous, simply a happy holiday wish, but in reality, it's a threat. And now that I know Marcus is being used by this gang in order to get to Garlen and Black Oak, through me, I'm worried. What would they be willing to do?

I bite at my lip and realize there's a way I can alert everyone at once, including the police, from where I'm sitting, in my car. I take out my phone and snap a picture of the note, then send it to my mom with a quick text:

> Found this on my car. Don't tell Zoe.

She instantly replies:

> Sending to Dane now. Just a sec…

I sit for a moment, the weight of the situation pressing down on me. I'm responsible for Zoe's safety. For my mom's safety. Heat burns behind my eyes. I married this guy once upon a time. I was the one who brought him into our lives. I'm the one who made him Zoe's father.

After the holidays I'm definitely going to need to get a hold of my therapist again and restart our sessions.

My phone dings.

I read Mom's response.

> Dane is sending your info to the police. He said for you to go ahead and go shopping and he and his family will keep you safe. Love you.

I put the phone down and blow out a breath. Well, okay, that sounds good. I look around, not seeing a single thing in the neighborhood out of the ordinary that could signal a threat. Goddammit, I'm not going to let Marcus ruin our Christmas. I'm not going to let him change the way I live my life. If I want to go to the store, I'm going to the damn store.

I start the engine, pull out of the driveway and turn the Christmas music up louder.

At the store, I move through the aisles, looking over my

shoulder. Every tall, skinny man makes my heart skip a beat. And then, when I stop in the frozen foods section, because of course I'm finding more things I need to buy beside sugar and frosting, I see an orc I recognize.

I give Dane a small hand wave.

He lifts his chin and stomps away.

Hmm.

I keep shopping and when I reach the sugar and flour aisle, I see another orc. Is that Keric? I smile at him.

He also gives me a chin lift and walks away.

I finish shopping and don't see either of them again, but they've made my day. I drive back feeling safe and secure.

Later that night, Mom and Zoe go next door to deliver our gift box of homemade Christmas cookies, and a little separate bag that holds the special cookie for Loki.

Meanwhile, I finally have a chance to read Garlen's most recent letter, which was written either last night or early this morning, before I found the message from Marcus. Garlen must be upset, not being able to reach out to me personally.

Dear Ellie,

You asked about my cousins...Aldar is the second son of our healer and unable to train as a healer, still trying to find his place amongst our species. Jonus is an orphan. His mother left him soon after he was born and his father died from a disease soon after. Keric was sent to us as a child from a remote commune in Siberia and little is known about his past, but I think he knows more than he's letting on. I'm the son of the best hunter in our commune, who wanted to become a teacher. We're all misfits, including my uncle Dane, and this is probably why we get along so well.

You also asked about orc holiday traditions. We celebrate the winter solstice rather than Christmas, though many orcs who live among humans have adopted both. On the longest night of the year, we light bonfires and tell stories of our ancestors, honoring those who came before us. Each family carves a token from wood or stone to represent the year's major events, which is then added to the family collection.

One more thing about Zoe. If I were lucky enough to have you accept me as your mate, I would consider Zoe my daughter in every way that matters. Her happiness and well-being would be as important to me as our future sons'.

P.S. I've learned my uncle and cousin are attending a neighborhood gathering soon with you, Laurie and Zoe. I wish I could join you and walk proudly beside the sexiest and most fantasti-cally beautiful female I've ever seen.

Garlen

I fold the letter carefully, holding it to my chest for a moment. He thinks I'm sexy and beautiful.

And his words about Zoe bring unexpected tears to my eyes. In all my thoughts about dating attempts since the divorce, I was never certain any man would be able to treat my daughter as his own. But I feel there is a distinct possibility with Garlen.

Letters like this are exactly why I consider Garlen my new boyfriend.

I take out a fresh sheet of paper and write my response, pouring out my fears about Marcus, my gratitude for his family's protection, and admit more about my growing feelings for him despite the impossibility of our situation.

Dear Garlen,

I was finally able to read your letter, after I went out to the car and found that note from Marcus. It must've been hard for you to hear from Dane that I got that message from Marcus on my car. Please know I sent it to my mother, who I knew would send it to Dane.

I'm wondering if your relatives are softening yet about communicating? Maybe they might let you start calling me, with no one listening in? I don't know about you, but I'd love to be able to talk to you late at night, each night. Or call you whenever I needed.

Please tell me when I'm being too much. I'd hate to accidentally do anything that could cause your winter frenzy to start again. Sometimes, I can't help but think like a human and wish for things I *can't have.*

And yes, I wish you were going with me to that neighborhood party too. I would love it if we could stop by your house and pick all of you up on our way over and we could all show up together, one big happy group.

Wouldn't that be lovely?

Hope all is well and that you are comfortable.

Counting down the days until the first day of spring.

Ellie

When I'm finished, I fold the letter carefully and make my way downstairs. At midnight, right on schedule, Loki arrives. I give the happy dog all the pets and another treat. Then I secure my letter to his harness and let him go on his merry way.

Before bed, I step onto the front porch to pick up a package that was delivered earlier in the evening. I breathe in the cold night air, trying to clear my head. That's when I see two dark figures standing across the street, partially hidden by a redwood tree. Watching our house.

I step back inside, locking the door behind me. What the heck? With trembling fingers, I take out my phone again, but this time I text Garlen's number, which is essentially the same as putting my message on blast.

> Message for all: I think I saw an orc and Marcus standing together in the park across the street. I'm unsure because it was dark, but I am certain I was being watched. Did anyone else see this too? Am I right or overreacting?

Almost immediately, my phone starts buzzing with replies:

From Garlen:

> Stay inside. Lock all doors.

From Aldar:

> We saw it too. It was Marcus and an orc we are trying to identify. Don't worry.

From Keric:

> I'm following as they leave.

From Jonus:

> Got the north side covered. Rest easy. All is quiet again.

And finally, from Dane:

> Laurie has been informed. We're handling it.

I sit on the edge of my bed, clutching my phone, a strange mixture of fear and security washing over me.

Eventually, I fall asleep, wishing Garlen was in bed with me.

CHAPTER 11
Ellie

"MOM, I don't like what you're wearing," Zoe declares. Her nose wrinkles as she studies my outfit.

I sputter with disbelief and look down at my black shirt and dark jeans, which I thought looked great until just a few moments ago. "What's wrong with this?"

"We're going to a Christmas party," she wails, with all the authority her six years can muster. "You've got to wear something sparkly with Christmas colors. That's boring."

"Boring? Girl, the Petersons' neighborhood party isn't exactly a red-carpet event. I want to be comfortable."

"You need an outfit like mine," she shouts and then points at herself with pride.

Zoe wears a red velvet dress with white tights and looks like a Christmas card come to life. This is because we went shopping today for that exact outfit, then I spent the last forty minutes bathing her, getting her perfectly dressed and then brushing and braiding her long strawberry-blonde hair, tying back the front with matching holiday bows. Her shiny ballet flats click on the hardwood floor.

"Well, not all of us can look as cute as Zoe Willis."

"It's true, I'm the cutest." She laughs and runs off down the hallway, chasing after a beleaguered Scarlett.

"Don't get those clothes dirty before we get there," I yell after her. "I will lose my mind if you mess up your hair."

"Okay, okay, Mom."

And then she's down the stairs and gone.

I shake my head and chuckle. Zoe has been bouncing off the walls with excitement. This is the first real social event all three of us have attended together since moving to Truckee. It makes me happy that my baby girl feels safe enough to go to this party without worries. She hasn't even asked about her dad since she learned that he was taken away by the orcs and given to the police for showing up at our house when he wasn't supposed to. And I do my best to not talk about it again in front of her either, helping to retain this mood of holiday vacay happiness.

I catch a glimpse of myself in the hallway mirror and secretly agree with Zoe's assessment. The hair and makeup look good, but the shirt is way too oversized and not the best to show off my curves. Why did I also choose my baggiest jeans for this party? And I'm wearing my oldest pair of black flats. I'll look frumpy next to her, not matching my own daughter's level of Christmas cheer.

What if I end up in pictures of the party that are sent to Garlen?

I rush back into my bedroom and enter the closet, looking for something special to wear. This is hard to find, considering most of my clothes are either teacher appropriate workwear, or loungewear. Not much in between.

I haven't bought anything that was purely for looking good and didn't have to do double duty as something I could also wear to work since…since that green dress I bought years ago for an anniversary date with Marcus that never happened. Soon afterwards, I gained about fifteen pounds and it was pushed to the back of the closet. It was hella expensive and I kept saying I'd lose weight and wear it again.

Until now.

I pull it out from the back of my closet and smile.

The dress is a size eighteen and I've dropped fifteen pounds in the last six months, mainly because of stress. Maybe it will fit again? No harm in trying. And I still have the shapewear I'd originally bought to wear it with. I strip out of my jeans and sweater, wiggle into the shapewear that helps disguise that roll in my back and the rubbing between my thighs. I slide the green wrap dress over my head and adjust it correctly.

Then I walk over to the full-length mirror in my room and assess the situation. And smile. Well, damn, I look pretty good if I must say so myself.

I turn around from all angles and feel pleased with what I see. It fits perfectly, in fact better than the last time I wore it. It's a little bit looser, in all the right places. I have a pear shape, which means my best outfits emphasize my waist and torso. My legs are okay, but my torso is my best feature. My waist is my smallest part of my body and my breasts aren't too bad—not too big or too small and still reasonably perky despite having had a baby. This dress is at least three years old but it's a classic look. And even though my legs are too pale right now, no worries, I can wear tall boots because it's a midi dress that borders on maxi.

It feels good to remind myself that I look good now, exactly as I am. My hair is thick, long and shiny and a natural color that is hard to get, even from a colorist. My eyes are green and I love the freckles on my face and body. My ankles are still reasonably small. And I've got straight teeth, without the need of braces. How lucky am I?

This strong body birthed a baby. It takes me for long walks in the neighborhood. And this body is the one I will have for the rest of my life and I love it just the way it is.

And Garlen likes it too.

I take a minute to fluff up my hair, apply more makeup, put

on a bracelet and lastly, I slip on my nicest pair of tall brown boots, the ones with a bit of heel.

Then I spray on some perfume.

And I'm ready.

Mom emerges from her bedroom and the two of us meet in the hallway.

I raise an eyebrow.

She looks stunning in a long, champagne-colored silk skirt and a darker cashmere sweater. Kitten-heeled brown boots peek out from under the hem of the skirt. Her blond hair is blown out and silky. A leather purse is over one shoulder and gold jewelry shines at her ears and on her wrist. My mom always looks amazing, but even for her, this is kicking it up a notch.

"New skirt?" I ask innocently as I help her pin a Christmas brooch on her sweater.

"I haven't worn this jewelry since your dad was still with us..." Our gazes meet and we exchange sad smiles then give each other an impromptu hug.

"I miss him too," I whisper.

My mother lets go first and backs away. She smooths an invisible wrinkle. "This is just something I picked up on the Nordstrom Black Friday sale," she says, answering my original question.

"Huh. Anyone in particular you're hoping to impress?"

"Don't be ridiculous," she responds, but the flush on her cheeks tells a different story. "And what about you? Ellie Willis, you look amazing. I've never seen that dress before. That's been hiding in your closet this whole time and you've never worn it?"

"I haven't had reason."

She loops her arm through mine and guides me down the stairs with her. "All eyes are going to be on the three of us tonight."

"Do you think we're overdressed?"

"Honey, there's no such thing."

And suddenly I'm surprised too at how much I'm looking

forward to this event, which is great considering I was sad to be going without Garlen.

Zoe meets us downstairs and the three of us gather in the foyer, in front of the coat closet. "Can Loki come to the party?" my little girl suddenly asks, while pulling on her coat.

"Loki, the dog from next door?" Mom questions with a look of pure amazement. "Are you kidding? No, he can't go with us. He needs to stay home with his family."

"But Dane is going, and he's Loki's family."

I exchange glances with my mother. How does Zoe know this? "That's true," I answer, "but Loki's a dog, and the party is for people. They don't allow people to bring their own pets."

Zoe sighs dramatically. "Fine. But if I ever have my own Christmas party, I'm going to let everyone bring their pets."

"Sounds like a great idea." I put on my grey wool coat.

My mom slips on a long, black coat and opens the front door. "The Willis girls are ready. Let's go forth and show them what we've got."

CHAPTER 12
Ellie

WE LAUGH AND STEP OUTSIDE, ready to take on the world.

Luckily, it's a short walk, over cleared sidewalks, to the Petersons' house.

Our heels click on the cement. I take a deep breath and smile. The air smells of fresh pine and smokey fireplaces. Our neighborhood is picture-perfect, with snow dusting the trees and holiday lights twinkling from every house.

I've learned that this was a planned community designed and built over fifty years ago. There is a central park right across the street from our house, and the houses are in a square around it. A few cul-de-sacs branch off from the park. This is a small, close-knit community, without an official homeowners association, but we do have an informal Facebook group for homeowners.

I glance ahead as we get close to Garlen's home. Warmth sweeps across my stomach as I think of Garlen Irontree. Is he watching from somewhere inside? Can he see us walk past through the security cameras I know they've installed? I find myself hoping that he can somehow see me in this dress, that he knows we're thinking of him. Would he like how I'm dressed? And how would Garlen dress for an evening like this?

Do orcs enjoy human parties?

"The sidewalks are always perfectly clear nowadays," Mom notes as we make our way. "Not a speck of snow."

I nod. "Our orc neighbors have been a huge help."

"Very," she agrees with a big smile. "And they loved those Christmas cookies we delivered."

"Keric said I can help shovel snow tomorrow," Zoe announces as she stops to check on a small pinecone. "I'll have my own little shovel."

I glance down at her, then step forward and bend down, shifting her jacket and redoing a button in front so it fits better. "When were you talking to Keric?"

"He was in our driveway this morning. I went out and we talked. He's a nice orc."

"Oh."

We start walking again. Zoe and my mom start a lengthy conversation about which house on the street is decorated the best for Christmas. We did our best to put up our own lights out front and all the décor the day after Thanksgiving and were pleased with the results, but our house is still a wimpy display compared to everyone else.

The orc McMansion has no lights or Christmas decorations.

We pass directly in front of Garlen's house, and I swear I can feel eyes on us. Not in a creepy way, but in a protective way. I stop and look straight into a dark overhang because I feel ninety-nine percent certain this spot contains a security cam, possibly monitored by Garlen.

I blink because I think I hear something... "Did you hear that?"

"Hear what?" my mom turns back to ask.

"I thought I heard a..." I shake my head. "Guess I'm just imagining things. Never mind. It's probably the music from the party."

The Petersons' home is two doors down from Garlen's house. It's an impressive, white, two-story colonial with every inch decorated for the holiday season. Wreaths on every window, a life-sized Santa and sleigh on the roof, and so many lights I'm surprised they haven't caused a neighborhood blackout. I've driven past here many times, and I can tell they've put up a bunch of new lights, I assume just for this party.

"Oh wow," Zoe whispers, eyes wide. "Look Mom, it's Santa and the reindeer."

I take her hand. "I love it too."

We step up onto the porch and can easily hear the hum of conversation and Christmas music inside. I press the doorbell.

The door opens with a rush. "Welcome," a loud voice greets. A middle-aged blonde woman with a gaudy Christmas sweater and plaid skirt gives us a brilliant smile. "You must be the Willises. We're so glad you could make it. I love getting to know all the new neighbors. Please call me Emily. My husband Robert is on the back patio. Come inside."

We step into the entryway, a winter wonderland with garlands and twinkling lights draped across every surface. The house is packed with neighbors mingling, drinks in hand and platters of food on every table.

And I already see Dane and Jonus, two huge orcs standing near the fireplace, each holding a glass of something amber. They don't look out of place at all amongst this large crowd, despite being the only orcs in the room. Both wear nice shirts that are actually buttoned closed and tucked into their black pants. Jonus is surrounded by a small group of humans, all laughing at something he's saying.

"You know the Irontrees?" Emily Peterson asks, following my gaze.

"They're our next-door neighbors," I explain.

"Oh, that's right. You're the ones who live beside the orc mansion," she exclaims, a bit too loudly. A few heads turn our way. "How fascinating. The house on the other side of the orcs is empty right now because the Millertons are in Florida for the holiday season. Are they…good neighbors?"

There's something in her tone I don't like. "The best," I answer firmly. "All of the Irontrees have been incredibly helpful and kind."

"Of course, of course. I met Dane and he's such a gentleman. The other one, Jonus, is quite charming, isn't he? Hard to believe they're the same species as that Crimson Tusk gang you hear about on the news."

Before I can answer, the doorbell rings again and Emily waves us on, busy answering the door for the next wave of guests.

Mom has already drifted toward the refreshment table, where, coincidentally, Dane is now standing.

Zoe tugs at my hand. "Can I go play with those kids?" she asks, pointing to a group of children gathered around a Christmas tree in the adjacent room.

I notice a few teenagers are there too, starting activities with the children. "Sure. Don't get in trouble and…"

"Mom, I won't mess up my hair."

I laugh as she bounces away.

Then I turn and start making my way through the crowd, accepting a glass of wine from a passing tray. Several neighbors introduce themselves, asking the usual questions about where we moved from and how we like Truckee so far. It's nice getting to know the people who live in the houses I pass by daily.

Eventually, I find myself gravitating toward Jonus, curious about what's made him the center of attention. As I approach, I catch the tail end of his story.

"…and that's when we realized the entire commune had been preparing for the wrong celebration date. Two hundred orcs standing in rows, wondering why the sun hadn't aligned with the sacred stones."

The group erupts in laughter, and I find myself smiling too. Jonus notices me hovering and waves me over.

"Ellie. Come join us. I was just explaining orc winter celebrations to our neighbors."

"Which apparently involve a lot of calendar miscalculations," I quip, earning another round of laughter.

"Only that one time," Jonus grins, exposing his white tusks. "I was telling them about Black Oak Academy as well. Several humans here have been curious about the new school."

"Oh, you work at Black Oak?" a woman eagerly questions.

"Yes, I do."

"I'm so happy that a new school has opened. This town is growing so much these last few years, and all the other schools are at maximum capacity, having to bring in rows of portables as classrooms. My friend's daughter is starting at Black Oak after break. What exactly do you teach?"

"We're a K-12 school and I'm the head of the social studies department."

"And is it true you've hired an orc professor?" a balding man in a red sweater interrupts.

I make sure to smile wide. "Yes, that's what's exciting about Black Oak Academy and why I'm happy to work there. We are the first school in the country to integrate orc teachers, and eventually orc students, into a human private school setting. We've been lucky to hire Professor Garlen Irontree to teach with us. He starts after winter break. He's going to teach our seniors Ancient Orc History. We're extremely fortunate to have him."

"I'm just not sure if mixing species in education is appropriate," the man mutters, just loudly enough to be heard.

The group falls silent.

Before I can respond, Jonus speaks up. "Garlen Irontree is my cousin and Dane's nephew. His research in orc history has been praised by scholars of all species. Good teaching doesn't recognize biological boundaries, does it?" His words are light, but there's a hardness to his tone.

The man mumbles something noncommittal and moves away.

"Sorry about that," a woman with silver hair proclaims. "I think it's wonderful that you're bringing our two species together in this way. It's long overdue."

"Thank you. No worries. We're the first in the country to do this and all eyes are on us. I know some people are uncomfortable with this, but I believe it's going to be a great way for all of us to live together in peace and understanding. I've even been contacted by news organizations who want to come and interview Professor Irontree and me and the students. It's going to be interesting."

The conversation eventually shifts to safer topics, but I find myself distracted, scanning the room. Is my family okay? Mom and Dane are still by the refreshments table, deep in conversation. They look surprisingly comfortable together. Mom laughs at something he says, touching his arm briefly.

I walk over to check on Zoe and find that she's playing with the other kids. The teenagers are helping them to decorate paper ornaments. She looks up, catches my eye, and waves excitedly.

Well, Mom and Zoe are happy, so I force myself to let go of any lingering shyness and mingle more amongst these strangers. I could return to the people I know, but that won't get me new contacts. I'm not only the head of a department, but I'm also a parent who is on the school board. I need to spread the good news that Black Oak is open and ready for enrollment.

As I grab another glass of wine and move onto the back patio which has heaters and more Christmas decorations, I see more groups of partygoers. And I overhear snippets of a conversation about "strange cars" in the neighborhood and "suspicious characters." I move closer and find a group of men discussing home security systems.

"...been seeing a black SUV driving slow past my house. Called the police, but by the time they show up, it's gone."

"My security camera caught someone crossing my front yard last week," another adds. "Tall guy, couldn't see his face. Nothing stolen but still gives you the creeps."

I drift closer as I sip on my wine, wondering if this is related to Marcus or something else entirely.

"The police said there's been an uptick in activity from that orc gang—what's it called? Crimson something?"

"Crimson Tusk," I supply, joining their circle. "My ex-husband may be involved with them."

All eyes turn to me, and I immediately regret how open I was about my situation. I'm normally a very transparent person who has trouble telling even lies of omission. It's a part of my personality that often gets me in trouble, especially after a glass or two of wine. But to my surprise, instead of awkward silence, I'm met with concern.

"You've had trouble with that gang?" asks a gray-haired man with dark skin and kind brown eyes. "I'm Raymond Morris, by the way. Retired sheriff's deputy."

"Hi, nice to meet you. I'm Ellie Willis. I moved into the neighborhood six months ago with my mother and my six-year-old daughter. I teach at the new Black Oak Academy. A few days ago, my ex followed me here and violated a restraining order. The Irontrees helped handle the situation, but he's out on bail now. And I know he's involved in something he shouldn't. He's being investigated by the FBI and they told me they thought Marcus might have ties to Crimson Tusk. I don't know if that's true or not, but it's a good idea to keep your eyes open for that."

Raymond nods thoughtfully. "We've been thinking of organizing a neighborhood watch. Sounds like we should fast-track that."

"I've got cameras I can share footage from," another man offers.

"And I can coordinate with other neighborhoods," adds a third.

I feel a warm rush of gratitude. These people barely know me, yet they're ready to help protect my family. "Thank you," I say sincerely. "It means a lot. After the divorce, I moved my daughter all the way from Southern to Northern California to start a new job here in Truckee. I thought I was free and clear. But now he's followed us, and I can't help but feel bad that I've brought my problems into your neighborhood."

"This is your neighborhood too and we help our own. You said that you are under the Irontrees' protection?" The man glances across the room at Dane. "I will keep in contact with them, and we can all work together on this. Go ahead and enjoy your evening. We will take care of this."

And then the neighborhood watch group walks away and I'm immediately included in a new conversation with a group of parents interested in possibly having their children attend Black Oak.

As the evening progresses, I find myself enjoying the party. The Chardonnay is so good I end up having one more glass of wine above my limit. This causes me to giggle and talk too much, but I'm having fun and I don't have to drive, so what the heck. Two different women stop me to tell me how much they love my dress and ask where I got it, which makes my day.

The house is warm and filled with holiday cheer, the food is delicious, and despite the occasional awkward moment, most of the neighbors seem genuinely welcoming. I'm having a great time talking and laughing with my neighbors, and I believe quite a few of them are now convinced that Black Oak would be a great place to send their kids. Perfect.

Still, I can't help wishing Garlen was here, his warm body next to mine, his arm around my waist. I'm all hot and tingly and loving the idea of stumbling back home and having someone there with me to strip me bare for some sweaty sex.

Naughty, naughty thoughts surface of what it would be like to have his face between my thighs. Those tusks nicking my soft skin and that tongue getting me off. Damn, that's hot.

"Would you like another glass of Chardonnay?" someone asks.

My eyes widen as images of myself throwing up in a toilet emerge. Instead I offer my empty wine glass and force myself to slowly respond in complete sentences. "Um, no thanks. Could I instead have a glass of water, please?"

An hour and a half later I'm mostly sober and it's time to leave. Zoe is reluctant, having made several new friends. Mom, too, seems in no hurry, lingering to say a lengthy goodbye to Dane.

"Did you have a good time?" I ask Zoe as we walk home amongst groups of other neighbors who are also walking to their own homes. The night sky is clear and star-filled above us. Most importantly, Zoe still has both holiday bows securely clipped in her hair.

"Yes. Dane told funny stories," she answers. "He showed us how to make shadow animals with our hands."

I raise an eyebrow. "Dane Irontree? He went into the other room and hung out with the kids?"

"Uh-huh. Grandma was there too. Dane knows all about Santa's elves."

I glance back at Mom, who's walking a few paces behind us, occasionally looking over her shoulder at the Petersons' house. I slow down so I can get close. "Dane seems nice," I comment casually.

"Oh, he is," she replies, too quickly. "Did you know he taught botany at the orc university for twenty years?"

"No, I didn't."

"And he grows the most extraordinary orchids. He's invited me to see his greenhouse after the new year."

I hide a smile. "How nice."

As we approach our house, I notice a small package wrapped in simple brown paper, with a familiar paw print in the snow beside it.

"What's that?" Zoe asks, rushing forward.

"Probably just something a neighbor dropped off," I say, taking it from her hands and quickly putting it in my pocket.

I open the front door and quickly start giving Zoe directions, trying to distract her from the package I want for myself.

Later that night, after Zoe is tucked in bed, I retrieve the package from my pocket and unwrap it carefully. Inside is a beautiful, roughhewn, wooden carving of a fox and her kit, with a note:

> *Please accept this gift as a token of what you and your daughter mean to me.*
> *Sincerely, Garlen*

I press the carving to my chest, warmth spreading through me despite the cold outside. Then I place it on my nightstand.

I take off my dress slowly, wishing Garlen was here with me. What if I were to go into the closet, take off this dress and the shapewear and step back out in a skimpy nightgown? How would he react?

One day, I will find out.

CHAPTER 13
Garlen

Orcs are stronger and have better hearing and vision than humans. This is why I can easily hear the stomp of the other orcs in the domicile. Deep voices and grunts sometimes drift into my space. The clash of their powerful bodies during practice sessions are somehow comforting.

The mansion feels emptier with Jonus and Dane gone.

I sit alone in my basement cage, staring at the security tablet propped on my makeshift desk, hoping to catch a glimpse of my bride.

I'm on edge because my cousin and uncle left for the neighborhood Christmas party, dressed in their best human-style clothes. Both wore button-down shirts that were actually buttoned and tucked into their normal black pants with the black belt and silver buckles that bear the Irontree crest.

They looked almost human-normal, if you ignored the horns, green skin, and tusks.

Meanwhile, I sit in my cage, wearing only my black pants, in a state of barely contained rage, considering the two of them are there with Ellie, and I am not. I should be with my female right now, my hand on the small of her back, greeting other humans and letting them know that this gorgeous creature is mine.

My fists clench.

Mine.

"Stay calm," Aldar warns before heading upstairs. "Jonus and Dane are at the party, you are down here, and Keric and I will be monitoring the feeds. All of us have a role this evening and yours is to remain calm so the rest of us can do our work and make sure that neither Marcus or Crimson Tusk can infiltrate. I need to be upstairs and not having to rush down here and deal with you. If you start getting worked up, we'll cut the connection."

I grunt in response while petting Loki. Being treated like a rabid animal is humiliating. At least they're letting me watch.

The tablet chimes with a motion alert. My fingers tighten around the edges as I pull the screen off the desk and onto my lap. The front camera shows movement at Ellie's house. Her front door opens, and three figures emerge. Zoe is first, jumping down the front step in a dark coat and red dress. Laurie is next, elegant in another long coat and hints of something silky and cream-colored.

And then…Ellie.

My breath catches in my throat. She wears another coat, which is unbuttoned, allowing me to see how her clothing molds to her curves. I can see the sweep of a glittering, deep green dress, flowing around her legs. Her hair falls in loose waves past her shoulders, catching the light from the porch lamps. This isn't the professional department head I glimpsed during our video interview, or even the surprised woman in proper teacher clothing from our first real meeting on her front yard.

This is Ellie transformed, radiant. And sexy as hell.

Something primal stirs deep within me.

I zoom the camera in, needing to see more of her. I haven't gotten this good of a glimpse of my female since that first day we met. The dress emphasizes her waist, then flares slightly over her wide hips. Her breasts are large and tempting. She looks down, adjusting something on Zoe's coat, and the fabric pulls across her chest. Then she turns in such a way that I am presented with her backside. This helps me to imagine what she'd look like, bent over, her ass exposed for me as I take her from behind. I swallow hard, my mouth suddenly dry. My shaft is hard and leaking, ready to plant my seed in my bride. My mind fills with dirty, filthy images of her bent forward, naked, so wet that her juices run down her thighs. I want that golden hair wrapped around my green hand.

Ellie buttons the front of her coat. Then the three of them walk down the driveway and head in the direction of the Petersons' house. This means they'll pass directly in front of our mansion.

I switch cameras to track their progress. "Control," I mutter. "Maintain control."

But the sight of Ellie in that green dress has awakened something ancient in my blood. My skin feels too hot, my clothes too restrictive. My shaft obscenely tents my crotch. Every day since we met, I need to release as I shower. Late each night, before I fall asleep, I think of her again as I masturbate while lying in my cot. And this only takes the edge away, leaving a deep feeling of discontent. I want my seed inside of my female, not wasted, sprayed on my stomach or dripping on the tile wall of the shower.

I stand and pace the confines of my cage, dragging the chain behind me, my eyes never leaving the tablet in my hand.

Loki runs around in circles and whimpers with distress.

Now they're on the sidewalk in front of our property. Ellie glances up at the house, as if searching for something. Does she know I'm watching? Can she feel my eyes on her? I lean closer to the screen, tracing the outline of her face with my finger.

Suddenly, as if responding to my touch, she stops. She looks directly at one of our security cameras, and for a surreal moment, it feels as if she's looking straight into my eyes.

Something inside me snaps.

Explosive need builds in my chest, rising through my throat. "Ellie!" I roar.

Loki races up the stairs, barking.

The chains burn against my wrists as I pull against them with all my strength. One of the anchoring bolts cracks free from the concrete. I lunge forward, reaching for the bars, needing to break free, to go to her.

"Mine." The word erupts from somewhere deep and ancient, a place I've never accessed before. My tusks have fully extended, sharp and white against my lips. "My bride."

The basement door crashes open. Aldar and Keric thunder down the stairs, eyes wide with alarm.

"Garlen, stop," Aldar shouts.

His voice sounds distant, unimportant.

All that matters is reaching Ellie. I need to feel her in my arms, to mark her as mine, to carry her somewhere safe where no one else can touch her. My rational side has disappeared, replaced by something wild and possessive.

I strain against the chains until blood seeps from beneath the metal cuffs. One more bolt pulls loose from the wall.

The cage door bangs open. Keric tackles me from the side, driving me to the ground. "He's breaking through the restraints."

Aldar joins the struggle, pinning my shoulders while Keric works to secure the chains again. I thrash beneath them, my strength magnified by winter's rage. I knock them both aside and stand again, heading for escape.

I'm knocked against the bars, next to the exit. My freedom is so close. These two need to learn their lesson, they cannot keep me caged. Another growl rumbles in my chest. I grab a hand and yank it at an awkward angle to pull it free. A voice screams in pain.

"Get the sedative," Aldar yells.

"Got it. I just need to…"

"No," I snarl, fighting harder, one step away from getting these two off my back. "She's mine. My bride."

"Your *bride* is going to a party, you idiot." Keric grunts, as my elbow connects with his ribs. "You cannot kidnap her while she's on a mission to convince other humans that hiring you for their school was a good idea."

I throw him off, sending him crashing into the bars. Aldar tries to hold me down alone, but I'm too strong. I rise to my feet, dragging him with me, the chains hanging broken from one wrist.

"Ellie!" I roar again, the sound echoing through the entire mansion.

Keric returns with a syringe. I see it coming but can't dodge with Aldar still clinging to me. The needle plunges into my thigh, and almost immediately, my limbs grow heavy. The rage dims, replaced by a cold numbness that spreads fast through my entire body.

"Sorry, cousin," Aldar grits as I slump to the floor. "It's for your own good."

An hour later, I come back to myself, groggy and aching.

Loki is on my chest, licking my face.

I'm back on my cot, with new, heavier chains binding me to the wall. The remains of the broken restraints lie in a pile in the corner of the cage.

Shame fills my heart and mind. I again lost control completely and became exactly the primitive beast humans believe all orcs to be. What if I had actually escaped? If Ellie had seen me like that...

I flex my fingers, feeling the deep soreness in my muscles from straining against the chains. Dried blood crusts the skin around my wrists. I reverted to the type of savage orc humans have nightmares about.

"You're awake. We didn't give you that much sedative. Just

enough to knock you down for a bit so your bride could pass and create enough distance between the two of you. And when she walks back to her house, you are not allowed to watch with the tablet."

I look up to see Aldar sitting outside the cage.

"Sorry," I grumble, my voice hoarse. "I don't know what happened."

"I do." He slides a water bottle through the bars. "You saw your bride dressed up for that party and lost your mind."

I drink deeply, the cool water soothing my raw throat. "Did anyone hear...?"

"Your mating roar? The house is well-insulated, and the Petersons' place is noisy. I doubt they noticed."

Relief flows through my senses, followed immediately again by the deep shame. I'm supposed to be better than this. I'm the integration pioneer. Instead, I'm chained in a basement, sedated to keep from kidnapping the department head. "I need to do something while they are still at that party. I can't just sit here with these thoughts."

He points. "Your carving tools are in the drawer. Just stay where I can see you."

I nod with agreement. Woodcarving has always calmed me. Back on the commune, I'd spend winter evenings by the fire, shaping figures from blocks of maple and pine. I retrieve my tools from the desk drawer, along with a piece of cherry wood I've been working on for days.

As I carve, working with my hands and focusing on the smooth rhythm of blade against wood, my breathing slows. With each curl of wood that falls to the floor, a little more of the wild rage dissipates. Gradually, a shape emerges. A mother fox and her kit nestle together protectively. The physical act of shaping wood centers me, pushing back both the winter urges and the anxiety about Crimson Tusk. My fingers move with practiced precision, smoothing the curves of the mother fox's body, adding delicate details to the kit's fur.

Yes, I want Ellie as mine, so I can have her underneath me and plant my seed and see her swollen with my orc son. But I also want to start a complete family with her, combining the orcs we will have together and the human child she has already birthed. I fantasize that we are all together, in this house, with my female making homemade food and offering it to me with her hand.

In my letters, I've tried to convey how seriously orcs take their responsibility to all children, not just biological offspring. This carving says what my words cannot, that I would protect them both, always.

The carving is complete. I hold it up to the light, examining my work. The mother fox curves protectively around her young, a perfect symbol of what I hope to convey to Ellie about my intentions for her and Zoe.

I wrap the figure carefully in simple brown paper, then take out my writing materials. I write a short note to accompany the gift. When finished, I fold the letter and tuck it into the package, tying the whole bundle with string.

Using more string, I fashion a simple harness for Loki, who has been dozing near my feet. "Come here, boy," I call softly.

Loki stretches and pads over, letting me attach the package securely to his makeshift harness. "Take this to Ellie's house," I tell him, scratching behind his ears. "Leave it where they'll find it."

The corgi understands his mission. He squeezes through the bars and trots up the stairs, his nails clicking against the wood.

By the time I hear Jonus and Dane return from the party, I've regained most of my composure.

"Oh good, he's conscious," Jonus announces cheerfully as he stomps down the stairs. The button-down shirt is already changed and he's dressed in black pajama pants. "Keric told us what happened while we were gone."

Dane follows behind, his expression unreadable as always. Both seem unharmed, which I take as a good sign. The humans must have been relatively welcoming.

"How was the party?" I question, setting aside my new carving and forcing myself to not immediately ask about Ellie.

"Not that bad," Jonus admits, dragging a chair close to my cage. "Humans make excellent mulled wine. And I enjoyed overhearing all their conversations from around the room without them fully realizing how much better orc hearing is than human hearing."

"And Ellie? Did she enjoy herself?" I question, trying to sound casual.

"She was quite popular," Jonus answers, leaning back in his chair. "That green dress made quite an impression. Other humans kept walking up to her and starting conversations."

I clench my jaw and both fists but say nothing. He's baiting me and I will not fall into the trap.

"She asked about you," Dane offers unexpectedly. "Wanted to know if you were comfortable."

I sit up straight. "What did you tell her?"

"That you were managing as well as could be expected."

"She talked to many different human males," Jonus adds, clearly enjoying my discomfort.

A low growl escapes before I can stop it.

Jonus laughs. "Don't be concerned. I was there, watching her every movement and keeping her safe. I intercepted a few of those males and redirected them elsewhere. I would never do anything to jeopardize my way of getting more of those home-made Christmas cookies."

Dane gives him a warning look.

"What Christmas cookies?" I snarl.

"Laurie and her granddaughter brought them over and they are already gone, eaten by all of us in moments," Dane admits. "There was one special cookie in a dog bone shape for Loki, and it is gone too."

My chains rattle. "How did I not see this? Did you turn off the security feed? And why didn't I get any of this food?"

"Calm down. We couldn't give them to you because they were made by her hand. Laurie made many cookies too, but most of them were made by your possible bride. You know that would be triggering for you. And she did not make them and then give them to any of us as a mating ritual. She is an innocent human who does not know how they might affect you."

"They did not affect any of us."

"Right, we simply ate."

I sit up, yanking against my chains. "I want these cookies."

Dane sits back and crosses his arms. "Well, when spring arrives you can ask Ellie to bake cookies in your home that you share together, and until then you get nothing."

I let out a roar.

"Stop," Dane growls. "I am changing the subject from cookies. Ellie Willis spent most of her time discussing the Black Oak Academy with the other humans. Defending your position there. Several neighbors expressed reservations about orc integration."

"Of course they did," I mutter, sitting back. "Humans fear what they don't understand."

"But many were supportive," Jonus says, his tone turning serious. "Especially after Ellie explained how they were lucky to have such a distinguished orc teacher on staff."

"She defended me?" The thought warms my chest.

"Several times," Dane confirms. "She's committed to the school's mission."

"And possibly committed to you as more than a coworker," Jonus comments, "although this is not confirmed yet."

I choose to ignore this part because I know already that my female wants me at the very least as a pleasure mate and hopefully more.

Jonus looks over at Dane. "I noticed you spent quite a bit of time with Laurie Willis."

My uncle's normally impassive face shows a hint of discomfort. "We have common interests."

"What common interests do you have with that older grandmother?" Jonus presses.

"She isn't old," Dane growls. "Only an orc as young and stupid as you would think a woman as beautiful as Laurie is *old*. I get along with that female because we are the same age and she's easy to talk to."

"And she doesn't look too bad for a grandmother."

A growl rumbles in my uncle's chest.

"Wait," I lean forward. "You're interested in Laurie Willis as a mate? Is that even possible at your age?"

"I'm not dead," Dane growls. "I can form a mating connection with a female."

I look him up and down. "Your shaft thickens for her?"

"Yes," Dane coughs. "I feel physical changes when she is near."

"You've never felt this before?"

"Never. Finally, at fifty-six years old I am around a female that enflames my body and finally feeling the need to mate."

"But this female cannot become pregnant. I can scent that she is incompatible for breeding," Jonus says. "How is this possible? I thought orcs mated in order to breed."

"No, the winter mating frenzy happens to younger orcs who inhale the pheromones of a breeding compatible female who is their future mate. When you reach my age, a change occurs that calms your blood and you're able to find matches with females of similar age who can't become pregnant. I can appreciate a female without succumbing to winter madness. Age has its advantages."

"Without the need for chains and sedatives," Jonus remarks.

Dane raises a hand. "Enough about the Willis females. There is more information to report. Several neighbors reported suspicious vehicles in the area. Black SUVs with tinted windows."

"Crimson Tusk?"

Dane nods. "Raymond Morris, a retired sheriff's deputy who lives across the park, is organizing a neighborhood watch. Ellie spoke to him about her concerns. She gave them Marcus's name."

"And she mentioned Marcus's potential ties to Crimson Tusk," Jonus explains. "The neighbors were surprisingly supportive. They're taking it seriously."

"As they should," I growl. "If Crimson Tusk is targeting Ellie because of me—"

"Keric and Aldar are setting up additional cameras around the Willis property tonight and also in the park across the street."

I nod, grateful. "What about the school? If they're opposed to integration it might be a target. Do we have enough cameras there yet?"

"We're aware. Precautions are being taken."

The knowledge that Ellie is being drawn into danger because of what I represent settles like a stone in my stomach. Yet I can't withdraw from the position at Black Oak, letting the integration experiment fail. And we can't let Crimson Tusk win. This is unacceptable. Not just for me, but for all orcs hoping to share their knowledge with the wider world.

And I suspect Ellie wouldn't want me to quit either.

CHAPTER 14
Ellie

THE BACK DOOR rattles with a familiar scratching.

I bite my lip with excitement and wipe my hands on a nearby cloth. Can it be Loki? I glance at the kitchen clock. It's super early on the morning of Christmas Eve. We'd originally sent our letters to each other at midnight, but lately this has morphed into whenever Garlen wants, which is fine with me.

Mom's already up too, flour dusting her hands as she rolls out sugar cookie dough on a nearby counter. I've upgraded to coconut macaroons and snickerdoodles. Waking up ridiculously early is normal for her, but only on special occasions like this will I be found happily baking before the crack of dawn. I like to sway to Christmas jazz music while I sip huge cups of coffee. The smell of cinnamon and vanilla fills the kitchen.

It's a fun morning, bringing memories of us doing this together, with Dad strolling through the kitchen, looking to sneak a cookie or two. All the Christmas shopping and wrapping of gifts is done. We've already purchased the food to make a yummy dinner tonight and an excellent Christmas morning breakfast. We have already decided to give those orcs next door yet another batch of cookies because they seemed to like the others so much.

"Your friend is here," Mom comments without looking up.

My brow furrows as I move over to open the door. Hold on, does Mom know that Loki arrives for me to bring letters from Garlen? Or does she think this dog wants to see me because of how we instantly bonded on that first day?

"Oh, look it's Loki," I say with a hint of surprise in my voice, trying to play this off.

Loki sits on the mat, snow dusting his black and white fur, a folded paper secured to his harness but no package this time. He wears a red and black checkered sweater and little red snow boots.

This dog is so cute I can't handle the cute. Every single time he arrives at the side door like this, he's adorable. This time I pause to take a picture of him with my phone. "Morning, handsome," I whisper, crouching to untie the letter. The corgi licks my face enthusiastically before I can dodge the wet tongue. "It's good to see you again," I chuckle. "Yes, yes, I missed you too."

The paper smells faintly of leather and winter air.

Loki scurries off, following the path between our two houses. I should be much more covert about this and wait to read this letter later, but I can't help myself. The last time I tried that, I had to wait hours to have a chance, and I can't wait that long. I stand, already unfolding it, eager to read Garlen's words.

Ellie,

I've finally learned you baked cookies for me with your own hand! None of these cookies reached me. They were all eaten by my greedy uncle and cousins. Loki got his cookie, of course, but I got none of what you made. Yes, I sound like a petulant child, complaining about my lack of treats, but receiving handmade food from a mate's hand is erotic to orcs.

I can only hope you will gift me a new batch in the spring.

Tomorrow we choose to celebrate the winter solstice in alignment with the human's winter holiday. While you celebrate Christmas Eve with your mother and daughter, we'll be lighting a bonfire as orcs do on the commune grounds. We'll tell stories of our ancestors and carve tokens to mark the year's significant events.

My cousins will build their own fire in our backyard tonight. I'll watch from the window...

A throat clears behind me.

Oh hell. I spin around, letter still in hand.

Mom stands with her hands on her hips. "I saw the dog deliver that to you. That's a letter from Garlen, isn't it? He sent that package for you last night too and he's also been delivering letters through his dog? How long has this been going on?"

My mouth opens but no words come out.

"We need to talk about this. Now."

Zoe's footsteps creak overhead, letting me know my little girl is stirring. I follow Mom to the living room, sinking onto the couch beside her. The fake, pre-lit, Christmas tree is set up, without ornaments yet, but the lights twinkle cheerfully, at odds with the serious atmosphere.

I fold the letter and shove it in my pocket. "Mom, I can explain—"

"Ellie, don't bother with any lies," my mom grumbles, "I know that you must care about that orc and are growing close with him. Believe me, I understand how that could happen. I'm not upset at all that you're obviously having ideas of taking Garlen's offer of becoming his wife."

"Oh good," I exhale, "because it's true. I'm getting to know him through his letters and I think…I think there's something there," I admit.

"That's fine. But like I said before and like all his cousins and Dane have said, you need to wait until spring."

"I am. I haven't seen Garlen in person since they dragged him away in the snow. Both Garlen and I are following all the rules."

Her brow furrows. "No, you're not, Ellie. You're riling him up through your love letters because neither of you can be trusted to follow the rules that protect us all."

I can't help but pout at this description, no matter how accurate.

"Ellie, I'm only saying this because I think you're forgetting those rules about staying away. The chains and that cage are all there for a reason. You forget that you could be ruining everything for them."

"What?"

"You and I are keeping quiet about what happened out front on that first day that we met them. Anyone else would've screamed, freaking out over how they performed that citizen's arrest and then how Garlen, the biggest orc of them all, lost his mind at your scent and lunged for you. Garlen Irontree had to be knocked to the ground by three other orcs who could barely contain him. They had to chain and drag him to a cage that they'd preplanned and already built in their basement. Luckily for them, all three of us are sympathetic toward orc integration. Most people would've gone to the media and the police with that story. We remained calm and told no one. No one in this neighborhood knows that Garlen is in that cage. Luckily for us a lot of our closest neighbors were at work or gone for a holiday vacation already and didn't see it happen. Marcus doesn't even know that part either, where Garlen declared you his bride. He only knows he was arrested by the orcs. The cops around here already love that group of orcs and view them as law-abiding, meaning the police don't know that he's caged. Why would you ruin everything for the Irontrees by doing something that would cause Garlen to lose his mind again in the dark of winter? He could break loose and do something worse that we're not able to hide. And then he'd lose his job at Black Oak. The other orcs would have to banish him to his commune. Your school would probably be dragged for creating this risky situation in the community. And all the other orc teachers would be blacklisted too. The idea of orc teachers and students in human schools would be set back decades. And Garlen and the others next door could lose their ability to live amongst humans and be sent back to live on their commune for the rest of their lives, or maybe even sent to orc prison."

"Are there orc prisons?"

"Are you listening to me? This is important."

"I'm listening."

She moves closer to me. "This might sound like I'm changing the subject but…you know I moved here to be with you and Zoe because family is important."

"I know. You always say that and…"

She raises her voice. "No, really, family is important."

My eyes widen.

"Ellie, my parents have both passed away. My husband died much too early. I've moved away from my friends to be here with you two. Of course, friends are important too but…"

I take her hand in mine and give it a squeeze. "We love you too, Mom. Zoe and I both consider you not only our mom and grandmother but also our best friend. You know I love that we are all living together like this. It was the best idea we had, buying this house and moving in together. We all need each other."

She wipes at her eyes. "Thank you, that's so sweet. I'm just bringing all of this up because I want you to know I'm saying this about Garlen not to be mean but because I care. I feel like I did a terrible job with my advice concerning your first husband and maybe I was one of the reasons why you thought he was a great guy."

"Mom, he was a narcissist who love-bombed me and tricked us all into thinking he was something he wasn't, and that was *before* we dealt with the addiction disease, the lies and the criminality."

"I really thought he was a great guy. I told you to marry him."

"I thought he was a great guy too. When he proposed I said yes. Dad thought he was wonderful too."

"I'm hoping that this time around, I'm someone who can give you better advice. And all I'm saying is, be careful because what Garlen does here reflects on his entire species and can affect the rest of his life. They have a plan in place so that at the end you two can be together if you'd like, or not if that's what you decide too. You just need to follow the plan."

"Of course, I understand."

We're both quiet. This is the place where I should probably vow that I won't exchange letters anymore, but I can't seem to get the words out.

She glances over at the sparkling Christmas tree lights, then back at me again. "I almost wish your father had never seen the part where Marcus changed into a man who needed a restraining order."

"Yeah, me too."

"I wish he could've happily thought you'd married the right man. A man who would treat you with respect. Instead, his stroke happened right after Marcus had stolen most of the money from your accounts and disappeared." She squeezes my hand. "But I do wish he was still around to see how we've all ended up. I would want him to see how strong and brave you are. You carried on, got a new and better job, and Zoe is doing great."

My eyes heat up at my mother's kind words. "And I believe that Dad would be happy to see you doing well too."

She exhales. "I still miss him so much."

I rub at my eyes. "The holidays make it harder."

She nods in agreement.

I lean back into the couch. "Mom."

"Yes?"

"I want you to know that if you decide to start dating again that's perfectly fine with me. And I don't consider it any kind of thing that tarnishes what you had with Dad. You still have a long life ahead of you and I want you to be happy. You and I both can, of course, be happy without a man in our lives, but if the opportunity for a great guy presents itself, then I say we both take the opportunity."

She lets out a snort-laugh. "I love you, Ellie."

"Love you too, Mom."

CHAPTER 15

Ellie

"MOM, can I put the Santa hat on top of the tree?" Zoe asks, bouncing on her toes.

"No, baby girl. That's Grandma's job. She likes to do the Minnie Mouse hat topper. But you can hang these." I hand her a box of delicate glass icicles.

"Careful with those," Mom warns. "They were my mother's."

I turn up the music and grab my daughter's hands and pull Zoe into my arms for a quick dance, then let her go so we can continue decorating. She laughs with delight and starts trying to put the ornaments on the tree.

It's so strange, celebrating Christmas with only the three of us, but we're doing our best to make it fun.

Dad is gone. I'm no longer married. And yet we still decorate the tree in the main room on Christmas Eve day, as we've always done, since I was little.

When I was a kid and even into my teens, the holidays seemed large and rowdy, overflowing with family. But most of those older grandparents and other relatives have sadly passed away too. Cousins have moved. My aunt and uncle on my mom's side, who we would usually spend Christmas with, are on that river cruise in Germany. And we've even moved to a new town, very far away from our old network of friends.

It's just the three of us here, alone, for this first holiday in Truckee.

It's been a good day. We're all dressed in comfy loungewear, one step above actual pajamas. A playlist of "Oldies Christmas Songs" blares in the background as we work in a comfortable rhythm, pulling out ornaments from boxes and deciding where they go.

Zoe chatters about Santa's route. Mom sips on a glass of wine and hums along to her favorite songs. I try not to obsess about Garlen being chained and living alone, watching the solstice fire from his basement window.

Marcus keeps entering my mind too.

Ugh.

I've come to the inescapable conclusion that he's here most likely to work together with that orc supremacist gang called Crimson Tusk, to ruin the hiring of the first orc teacher at an orc school, to prove it can't be done. I wasn't sure before, but now I'm certain. And beyond that, who knows what other nefarious reasons he has for lingering in our vicinity. Certainly not to see Zoe, as he first claimed.

I take a deep breath and hang more ornaments. A deep conversation with my mom and Irontrees about Marcus can wait until after Christmas. Instead, I need to concentrate on making this holiday special for my baby girl.

I follow behind Zoe, quietly fixing her work, spacing ornaments better, or making sure they are hung sturdier on each limb of our seven-foot Christmas tree.

"Does Garlen celebrate Christmas?" Zoe asks suddenly.

I freeze, about to put up a precious ornament that holds a small picture of Zoe with Santa, taken three years ago at the shopping mall. "Well," I answer, "I don't think so. Orcs have their own winter celebration. They call it the winter solstice."

"What's that?"

"The solstice is the longest night of the year. The orcs light big bonfires to celebrate and tell stories and—"

"How do you know all this about orc customs?" Mom interrupts, her tone suspiciously casual.

"Um, I've been researching, so I know more for Black Oak's curriculum and because I'm going to eventually have not only more orc coworkers but maybe orc students too."

Mom gives me a knowing look.

"I want to see a real orc bonfire," Zoe declares. "Can we go next door and watch?"

"Not this year, baby. We haven't been invited and maybe it's only for their family."

"Maybe next year?"

I swallow hard. "Maybe."

We continue decorating, the conversation shifting to safer topics: what cookies to leave for Santa, whether reindeer really like carrots, how many marshmallows constitute the perfect hot chocolate ratio.

Finally, the tree is done, the ornament boxes put away and I'm exhausted. I fall onto the couch to rest. Zoe sits at my feet, experimenting with accessorizing her dolls with different decorations.

It's been a busy day. We baked, did last-minute shopping together and hand delivered more Christmas cookies to neighbors, including our orcs next door. I know the cookies won't make it downstairs to Garlen, but that's okay. I'll bake him a new batch in the spring. I love the idea that he will love what I make.

In fact, my mind is glued onto the fact that he said handmade food from a mate is erotic to orcs. I've literally taken that letter out and reread that part three different times.

Erotic?

Meanwhile, my ex was never big on my baking or cooking. He preferred to eat out.

It never ceases to amaze me how little we had in common. How did I not see this before we married? I suppose I was so thrilled Marcus Adams, one of the best looking and most popular guys on campus, wanted *me*. He wooed me in such a grand way, with all the fancy dates and the eventual proposal in front of my family on bended knee. I had to say yes, right? Of course he was the right man.

And now, the "right man" for me might be someone who at first glance would appear all wrong. Someone who must be chained next door so that he doesn't hurt me in his haste to impregnate me.

Yes, this sounds bad to most women, but it's making me hot and bothered. I've always wanted more kids. I'd love the opportunity to give Zoe some brothers. I'm an only child and I've always secretly wanted siblings. I'd like to give Zoe some siblings.

I close my eyes for a moment and twirl my hair.

Maybe I like the idea of having an orc son. I've challenged Garlen, letting him know that Zoe and I are a packaged deal and if he's going to take me on, he has to love my daughter as his own. Conversely, I will be impregnated with an orc son, never daughters, and am I okay with that?

Does Zoe want an orc brother?

Will my mother accept orc grandsons?

It's a lot for all of us to think about.

Just as my eyes start to drift closed for a well-deserved nap, the doorbell chimes.

Darn it. "Who is that?" I yawn, looking over at my mom reclining in her favorite chair. "We're not expecting anyone, are we?"

"No. I don't know who that could be."

"I'll get it," Zoe shouts. She races to the door before I can stop her. I groan and push myself off the couch. "Zoe," I shout, "we don't know who's at the door. Let me..." But by the time I get there she's already turning the handle.

The door swings open and Jonus and Dane stand on our porch with wide smiles.

I blink with surprise.

Both orcs wear unbuttoned flannel shirts. Dane holds a potted plant. Loki sits between them, his tiny tail wagging furiously.

"Merry Christmas Eve," Jonus booms. "We are here to thank you for the cookies and because we wanted to perform a quick visit with our favorite neighbors on this human holiday eve."

My eyebrow lifts because I can't help but think they have an ulterior motive. Why would these two want to visit us for a holiday they don't even celebrate?

"You mentioned enjoying Christmas poinsettia," Dane says to my mother, offering her the plant.

Mom steps forward, her face lit up with joy. "Oh, Dane, that's so thoughtful. Please, come in. We're happy you two are here to visit. I just made fresh cookies."

"Cookies?"

They rush forward, stomping into the entryway, bringing cold air and the scent of pine. I move back to make room for them. Loki immediately races inside too and ignores me, zooming straight for Zoe, who drops to her knees to hug him.

"Traitor," I whisper in jest to the little dog as I close the front door.

"Would you like some hot chocolate to go with the cookies?" Mom asks Dane, already heading to the kitchen "Or coffee?"

"Hot chocolate," he replies, following her.

I'm left with Jonus, Zoe, and an overexcited corgi in the living room. Not that I'm bothered. These two are Garlen's relatives and I feel like we're becoming close. How can it be bad for me to take the time to get to know his family better? What if one day he asked me to marry him? These orcs would be my actual family.

I glance towards the kitchen because I'm starting to wonder if Dane is going to be my mother's new husband.

Jonus and I settle on opposite couches around the coffee table, with the blinking tree behind us.

Zoe lands on the carpet with Loki.

Before I can even start a conversation, my inquisitive daughter asks the first of what turns into a whole series of intrusive questions. "Jonus, why are orc horns different sizes?"

Jonus leans forward, his forearms on his knees. "Every orc is unique. Like human fingerprints, but much more obvious. Garlen has the tallest horns in our group and mine happen to be the shortest horns, but mine are also sharper than anyone else."

"Do baby orcs have horns?"

"Yes, they have horns," Jonus chuckles, "but they are very small and soft. They stay small like that and don't grow in until orcs are teenagers. Very awkward phase."

"Why is your skin green?"

I look down at her with surprise.

"Evolution," Jonus patiently answers. "Our ancestors lived in cold northern forests for thousands of years. Green skin provided camouflage for hunting."

"Why are your teeth so big?"

"Those are called tusks and we need them to help shred our meat when we eat, and also to battle other orcs for dominance."

"Oh…do orcs have mommies?"

The question makes Jonus pause. I lean forward, curious to hear his answer.

"Orcs are all male," he replies. "We form families with human women who become mothers to our orc sons."

Zoe tilts her head. "There aren't any girl orcs?"

"No."

"How do orcs get wives then?"

"Most adult orcs hope to eventually meet a human female who will want to marry them."

"Oh, like how Garlen wants to marry Mommy?"

I sit up straight. "Zoe, why do you think that?"

"What? I heard him shouting that you were his bride. Doesn't that mean that after he feels all better and can come back to work, he wants to marry you?"

Jonus hides a smile. "Well, for right now, your mother and Garlen are only coworkers."

"Mom is going to be his boss," my little girl says with obvious pride.

I take a sip of coffee, trying to hide my smile.

Mom and Dane reappear with a plate of cookies and hot chocolate for everyone.

"Can Loki do tricks?" Zoe asks, moving on to a different subject.

This launches Dane into an unexpected explanation. "Loki is a special breed of orc corgi. These corgis are traditional orc hunting dogs," he begins, settling into Dad's old armchair. "Originally bred for silent tracking and message delivery."

My eyes widen. *Message delivery?*

"Their short legs are perfect for moving under forest brush," Dane continues, oblivious to my reaction. "They have exceptional memory for routes and locations."

"So they're like living GPS systems?" I ask carefully.

"Better. They can deliver messages between homes within communes or between hunting parties without training. Just show them a route once."

Mom and I exchange quick glances. She hides her expression behind her mug.

"That's fascinating," Mom says innocently. "So they just... know where to go?"

"They memorize routes after one trip. On the commune, we had one corgi who could navigate between seven different homesites and buildings," Jonus adds. "Carried medical supplies during a harsh winter when the paths were blocked."

"Not only are these orc corgis cute, but they're loyal."

"Once they bond with a family, it's for life."

Just like the orcs themselves, I think but don't say. "Am I right that Loki is Garlen's dog?"

"Yes," Jonus answers quickly. "Loki was given to him as a gift from a grateful student and arrived as a puppy. Loki is three years old."

The conversation settles into a comfortable rhythm. We talk about dogs in general, cookies are passed around, Zoe shows off her Christmas crafts, Loki performs a few basic tricks for treats. It feels so…normal. Like orcs belong here in our living room on Christmas Eve. But someone important is missing.

"Since we're all being honest here…" I begin, setting down my cup. "Tell me, how is Garlen really doing?"

The room goes silent. Even Loki stops begging for cookies.

"You can't ask about him…" Jonus frowns.

"Why can't I ask? He can't hear us. I just need to know. And I also don't think it's right for us to pretend as if he doesn't exist."

The orcs exchange uncomfortable glances.

"Come on. I'm also his boss. I have a right to know if he's okay."

More silence.

Dane exhales. "We had to sedate him."

I sit up straight, anger flashing through my veins, ready to respond.

"What does sedate mean?" Zoe questions.

I bite my lip. "It means he got so upset the only way they had to calm him down was to give him medicine so he could sleep it off and feel better."

"Oh."

"Is he still asleep right now?" I grit. "Does he need to be given this sleep medicine often, as in every day?"

"No, no, of course not. The administration of the medicine so he could sleep happened last night and it's the only time we've had to give it to him. When he saw you walking to the party in that green dress he got very…upset," Jonus admits quietly. "Aldar and Keric were barely able to keep him contained long enough to give him the medicine so he could sleep in peace."

"Oh." Heat floods my face, half with embarrassment and half

secretly thrilled to know he reacted so violently to the sight of me all dressed up. He saw me in that dress and lost control so completely they had to drug him. The thought should terrify me. Instead, it sends an inappropriate flutter through my stomach.

"The intense feelings Garlen has sometimes aren't lessening yet, as we'd hoped," Dane adds.

"But he refuses to give up the teaching position," Jonus says. "Do you think he should stay?"

I purse my lips. "I believe he should stay and start the semester with us. If he leaves, everyone who thinks orcs can't integrate or that they will devolve into ancient ways, will be proven right. If he leaves, they win."

"Mommy?"

I look down. "Hmm, yes, what, baby?"

"Is Garlen going to be my new daddy?"

Zoe's question explodes into the room like a ticking bomb. I'm mid-sip, hot chocolate suspended between cup and lips. Mom's eyes go wide. The orcs look at each other in panic. Loki even looks surprised.

Before anyone can form a response, the dog suddenly barks and races to the window.

We all turn to look.

"What's wrong, Loki?" Zoe questions, following behind.

Dane moves to the window. His expression grows hard, but his voice remains light. "Looks like someone's lost."

Jonus joins him and speaks in code again, for Zoe's benefit. "Probably looking for the right address for a Christmas party."

They exchange a quick, meaningful glance that makes my stomach drop. I walk over and look out the window with them. All I catch is the distant view of a retreating black SUV.

"Well, we should head back," Dane tells my mother. "Christmas Eve, lots to do. Right, Jonus?"

"Are you going back to light fires and celebrate Winter sol... sol...siz?" Zoe asks.

"Yes, that too."

"Thank you for the cookies."

They're already gathering their dog, moving with subtle urgency.

"But you just got here…" Mom protests.

"Christmas Eve," Dane repeats. He touches her arm briefly. "Keep your doors locked tonight. Just a normal precaution."

"Is everything all right…" I start.

"Everything's fine," Dane assures me.

At the door, Zoe tugs on Dane's sleeve. "Will Garlen be okay?"

He pauses. "Always, little Zoe. Orcs take care of each other, and we also take extra care of the humans we care about most."

The door shuts behind them and they're gone.

CHAPTER 16
Garlen

MY FIRST WINTER solstice outside of the commune, technically what humans might consider Christmas Day, is spent, per usual, in chains.

Black, heavy chains clink against my wrists for the seventh day in a row. One week of this and I hate it, and I've got two more months to go until the start of spring can set me free. Every single day I look down at them and I'm angered. I should be remaining calm, viewing them as a necessary evil, and most days I accomplish this optimistic objective, and at other times, like today, I'm purely irritated.

Yes, my body remains enflamed, in a constant state of ready-to-mate, and my mind fixates on Ellie, but does this require chains? Couldn't I feel this way in my own bedroom?

And then I flex my arm, testing the chain, and noting a crack in the cement.

Yes, I need to remain here.

In one week's time I will begin co-teaching with my bride as we teach a large unit on ancient orc history together, from the perspective of both human and orc. For the first time in history, humans will be taught orc history by an actual orc. Usually, our history is only learned by humans through what their history books in school, written by humans, teach them with what I consider purposely vague details. As a history teacher I will not bring in anything beyond the standards that the school requires, but I will for the first time provide a few primary source artifacts that have never been seen. I plan to focus on teaching the students orc culture and how we got to where we are now with orcs as citizens.

I glance at the bars again because I sometimes wonder if it will be able to fully withstand an Irontree in the dark of winter. The cage was partially tested two nights ago, when I lost my mind and saw Ellie decked out and sexy in her green dress. The bars are made of the same steel as my chains, handcrafted by our best blacksmith, made strong enough to withstand an orc in the dark of winter. It's already been tested and stood strong, although I have noticed those cracks in the cement, but I haven't mentioned this to the others.

What would happen if I were thrown into a full-blown violent rage?

There's no way that could happen. I'm only allowed a covert visual of Ellie when she accepts a delivery from Loki. I have her letters, and I've noticed that the scent that lingers on the paper has a calming effect.

I roll to my side on the cot. My feet continue to hang off the edge, and the metal creaks under my weight. I suppose I could complain about needing a new bed, but I already feel bad that my relatives do so much as it is to keep me fed, bathed and restrained, not to mention the composting toilet in the corner.

Because my orc skin runs hot, this basement is always comfortably warm, but the chains around my ankles and wrists remain cold against my skin. A constant reminder of what I am —a wild orc in the dark of winter.

The latest letter from Ellie remains tucked underneath my pillow. The others remain hidden under the floor, but I always keep the most recent under my head at night so I can inhale her scent. I've kept and read all her letters so many times the paper is starting to wear thin along the folds. Her flowery scent lingers on the paper, faint but present.

This whole last week, sending secret letters back and forth with Ellie has kept me from exploding into another winter mating frenzy. I haven't told any of my family about this because I know they wouldn't understand.

I continue to masturbate to the thought of her at night and again during my morning shower. In the dark of night, under the covers, I take out my throbbing cock and jet my come into my hand and on my stomach, shouting out her name. Each time I wish she was here, so she could watch, because this is for her.

I inhale Ellie's scent, which brings calm and peace.

Today is the start of the humans' biggest holiday.

In the commune where I grew up, the winter solstice was our most sacred time. My thoughts drift to my childhood in northern Maine, to the Great Lodge with its timber ceiling and massive stone hearth. Every orc in the settlement would gather there as the winter reached its peak. The oldest members would lead the fire ceremony, tossing fragrant branches onto the flames while acting out ancient stories of our ancestors. The scent of pine sap and woodsmoke would fill the air, along with the rich aroma of roasting meat.

The Irontree commune in northern Maine brewed some of the finest ale on the east coast. We drank it from tankards passed down through generations, often getting louder and more raucous as the night progressed. Young orcs would receive their first taste at sixteen, usually resulting in them passing out under tables while the adults laughed.

The elders would tell tales of the greatest warriors of our people and how they protected and preserved our way of life. As a child, I would sit mesmerized, imagining myself as one of those great orcs. I never imagined my path would lead me to becoming a teacher at the orc university and then a teacher at a human school.

And I most certainly did not envision myself chained in a

basement to protect the human female whose pheromones enflamed my body.

The door at the top of the stairs opens. Aldar and Jonus talk as they descend. "Merry Christmas," Jonus calls out, his deep voice carrying across the basement.

Aldar carries a large wooden tray with covered dishes that release steam into the cool air. "Yes, we're here to celebrate Christmas like a human, but we've also brought you a proper solstice meal," he adds, placing the tray beside my cot. "The meat sticks are burned exactly as you like."

Uncle Dane follows them down. "Happy solstice, nephew," he booms. "Better late than never. I trust you are well?"

"As well as can be expected." I eye the food with interest. My stomach growls loudly, earning chuckles from my cousins.

"We found a cask of orc ale on our doorstep this morning," Jonus offers, a hint of amusement in his voice.

I straighten immediately. "From whom?"

"Crimson Tusk," Dane confirms, shaking his head with a mixture of disbelief and begrudging respect. "We left out a basket of our special venison jerky on the curb for the actual date of Winter Solstice and they reciprocated on the date we are celebrating. Ancient traditions persist, even between enemies."

"The Winter Solstice Truce," I murmur. Every orc child learns about this custom. Warring tribes or even family units set aside their differences in honor of the solstice. "They actually honored it?"

"Seems so," Aldar says. "We've tested the ale already, of course. No poison, just damn good ale."

"Alaskan brew," Jonus adds with appreciation. "Those extreme northern communes make it with glacier water. You can taste the difference."

"You brought some for me, right?" I eye them hopefully.

Dane laughs and produces a large tankard he'd managed to keep hidden. "Of course. We're not monsters."

I take it eagerly. My first sip confirms Jonus's assessment. It's excellent ale, with complex notes of pine, berries, and something distinctly mineral that speaks of glacial origins. The liquid warms me from the inside out, a pleasant fire spreading through my veins. "Damn good," I agree, taking another longer pull. "Their brewmaster knows his craft."

"Don't drink it all at once," Dane cautions. "That's Alaskan strength. It's twice as potent as our Maine brew."

"I'm chained in a basement with nothing else to do," I point out, enjoying another deep swig. "Besides, my tolerance is legendary."

Jonus snorts. "That's not how I remember the solstice gathering three years ago. Didn't you climb a tree and declare yourself 'King of the Forest' before falling asleep on a branch?"

"That never happened," I say with as much dignity as I can muster, though my ears heat with the memory. "And if it did, I blame that experimental juniper batch that Thorne was so proud of."

My cousins laugh, and I find myself smiling despite my confinement. The ale loosens something tight in my chest. For a moment, it almost feels like a normal family solstice celebration. But then I look down at my chained arms and legs, and my family sitting outside of my cage. "Give me another tankard," I grouse.

Dane takes my empty tankard and pulls out a huge flask, he uses it to refill my tankard and hands it back to me. "You might be interested to know that I dropped by to check on the Willis women again, purely for security purposes," he admits, pouring himself another measure from his flask. "I shared some of this with your department head too."

I nearly choke on my ale. "You gave Ellie orc ale? Uncle, that stuff is twice as strong as human whiskey."

"I gave them all the proper warnings, to treat it not like their human beer."

All of us grimace at the thought of that water-like substance the humans call their ale.

"I once had beer with a human male who I knew was sharing it with me as a bonding exercise," Aldar says. "It was like drinking flavored water."

"Did you finish it or spit it out?" Jonus questions.

"I managed to finish it but made excuses when they offered more."

"I am thankful for that orc brewery that recently opened nearby."

"Brewery?" I question. "Where?"

"It's just outside of town. We'll take you there in the spring."

I look over at my uncle. "And when you returned alone this evening, did Laurie Willis happen to offer you coffee and cookies during your security check?"

"She did," Dane responds. "She's a kind woman. Very... hospitable."

Jonus snorts. "He came back smelling like her perfume and whistling. And slightly drunk."

"As I said before, older males can form a connection with a beautiful human without winter's rage," Dane says with dignity. "It's perfectly natural."

"Heh," I rumble, feeling jealous at my own uncle's easy ability to start a relationship with the mother. "And how is Ellie this evening?" My heart rate increases just saying her name. The chains clink as I shift position, trying to appear casual.

"She seemed well. Excited about Christmas morning with her daughter. And quite giggly after half a cup of our ale."

I groan, imagining Ellie tipsy on potent orc ale. "You're a terrible influence."

"She asked about you when both Jonus and I were there," Dane mentions casually. "Wanted to know if you were comfortable, if you needed anything. She's always worried about your state of being."

My chest tightens at this information. My female was thinking of me? "What did you tell her?"

"What I always say…that you were as comfortable as a chained orc could be," Jonus says with a shrug.

I glare at my cousin, who only grins wider.

"About that car we spotted yesterday," I say as I chug the last of my tankard, changing the subject. "Any news?"

Dane's expression darkens, though the ale keeps some of the sparkle in his eyes. "It circled the block three times. Crimson Tusk. We've increased patrols around both properties."

"They're getting bolder," Jonus adds. "We found footprints in the snow behind Ellie's house."

My muscles tense, chains jangling as I stand abruptly. "What? When?"

"Late last night," Aldar says. "Don't worry, we've stationed Keric around her property. That's why he's not with us right now. He will do the first watch, and we will take the others. No one will get close. They only do this to show us what they are capable of, and yet they are holding back. They wouldn't harm Ellie because it wouldn't help their stance and their image with the media. They are only doing this to rattle us and therefore we need to take it in stride. And the Solstice Truce holds until tomorrow."

I pace the length of my chains, frustration burning through me. I should be the one protecting her. Instead, I'm the one being protected from myself. "We should move them in here with us," I growl. "The security is better."

"And have you tear through reinforced steel to get to her?" Aldar raises an eyebrow. "No, you will remain exactly as you are."

He's right, but I hate it. I rake my fingers through my hair, fighting for calm.

"Eat your meal and drink your ale," Dane says. "We'll continue monitoring the situation. I'll return later with any updates."

• • •

They leave me with my solstice feast, my tankard of excellent Alaskan orc ale, and my churning thoughts. The food is delicious, and the ale helps quiet my mind. After two more large swigs, a pleasant warmth spreads through me, dulling the edges of my worry.

Hours pass. I read one of the new books my cousins brought, the words swimming slightly as the ale takes full effect. Then I hear the familiar scratch of paws at the door at the top of the stairs. My heart rate increases.

Loki.

The door opens slightly, and my corgi bounds down the stairs, tongue lolling and his fluffy bottom wagging furiously. He wears the special harness I designed, and attached is an envelope.

I drop to my knees as he reaches me, removing the letter before rewarding him with affectionate ear scratches and treats I've been saving. "Good job, Loki, you are the best messenger. Legendary."

He lets out a deep bark in agreement, circling twice before settling at my feet.

I hold the envelope to my nose, inhaling deeply. Ellie's scent —vanilla and cinnamon. And something else...the unmistakable trace of orc ale. My body responds instantly, heat flooding my veins. My tusks lengthen slightly, pressing up from my lower lip. I struggle for control before carefully opening the envelope.

Inside is a sheet of pale blue paper covered in Ellie's neat handwriting, though I notice it's slightly less precise than usual. The letters are looser, more flowing. I position myself to hide from the security cameras in the corners of the room. These words are for me alone.

Dear Garlen,

Merry Christmas Eve! And Happy Winter Solstice!

Tomorrow morning is Christmas, and I want you to know I'll be thinking about you and wishing we were together. I know all the very valid reasons that you must remained chained and isolated from me for so long, but it doesn't make it any easier. I am beginning to believe that when we met that day on my lawn, you weren't the only one who was instantly smitten. Maybe I scented something too? Because I tell you, I've been hot and bothered since that very first day!

Earlier today Dane and Jonus came by and we visited, then they left because you know, Crimson Tusk was watching us again. Why do they do that? I lead a boring life. What else are they seeing today that they didn't see yesterday? I can only assume they literally want to frighten me. Intimidate me?

Not happening!

Next week you and I are going to figure out our lessons and then we are going to kick ass, teaching those students orc history from primary sources. The first time this has happened in our country, or even in the world.

I want you to know I'm proud to be helping you with this—to be the one who supports you being able to bring your truth to the wider world. I think you and your brothers are pretty wonderful.

Did you know Dane returned about two hours ago, bringing six bottles of orc ale as a gift? I tried some of it and it tastes good. I had no idea I liked orc ale so much.

I hope this is okay to say, but I wish you were here in bed with me tonight. Christmas Eve with my family was wonderful, but now that everyone has gone to bed, I wish you were here with me. I want to touch you all over and know what it's like to kiss you. We've grown so close now and haven't even shared a kiss. How does kissing work when you have those big tusks? Would I be able to touch your horns?

Warm (and slightly tipsily), Ellie

I read the letter twice, and heat spreads through me at the thought of my face between her spread thighs and my bride's hands clutching my horns as she shouts out her release. The ale has loosened her inhibitions, it seems. I take another long swig from my tankard, enjoying the thought of kissing my bride.

In her letter, I find two slightly crumbled gingerbread cookies wrapped in a paper napkin. I bring one to my nose, inhaling the spicy-sweet scent before taking a careful bite. The taste explodes on my tongue—cinnamon, ginger, molasses. I close my eyes, savoring it.

Something made by her hands, for me.

CHAPTER 17

Ellie

ONE WEEK LATER…

The first day back after a school break is always the hardest.

I'm a couple pounds heavier because I ate my way through cookies, candy and big holiday meals. Those were fun times—the baking, movie-watching, resting and gift-giving and receiving. Lots of time spent with Zoe and Mom, making memories. And also, lots of romantic letters exchanged between me and Garlen.

But I'm glad that most of the treats are out of the house now and that amazing orc ale is all gone. I'm ready for all of us to return to our normal eating patterns.

"Ellie. You're going to be late for work," Mom calls from downstairs.

"Just a second," I yell back, wrestling with my new black blazer.

Zoe and I are notorious for having trouble waking up early, which I think is universal, well except for my mom, the nutty morning person. I was able to wake up early for Christmas baking and cooking, and that was about it. The rest of the vacation was spent sleeping in as much as I'd ever wanted.

Having to return to a 6 am alarm each weekday morning

sucks. My mother's morning perkiness caused conflict when I was growing up, but now I love this part of her personality. She makes sure no one oversleeps and that we all get our butts out the door in time.

It's funny how you gain a different perspective as you grow older.

Zoe appears in my doorway, fully dressed and ready to catch her bus. "Mom, is Garlen teaching today?"

"Yep. Today is the first day he's going to try teaching from the basement next door. He's going to talk to the students using his computer."

"Are you nervous?"

I blink down at her, surprised my little girl is asking such a deep question. "Yes," I answer. "A little bit, sweetie. But the good kind of nervous."

"Like that same kind of nervous when we're excited for Christmas morning?"

I pull her close and give her a kiss on top of her head. "Yes, baby girl. Exactly like that."

We all say our goodbyes and I get outside and start my short drive to work. I wave good morning at Aldar and Keric, who are out too, shoveling snow after last night's snowstorm.

Despite the fact that I have to return to this brutal morning schedule and dress in uncomfortable, professional clothes again, I'm happy to return to work. I missed my students. For reals. I've always been the type who gets close with the students and parents. And per usual, I really enjoy all my classes this year but this time there's something different. Something memorable. A heady feeling of excitement permeates amongst the staff, students and parents. We know we're all taking part in something special and important—the first orc integration in education in history. Principal VanWagoner even had nice staff shirts made with the school colors, the mascot and small embroidery declaring the establishment year of Black Oak Academy. All of us who are here to open the school, from the admin and teachers to the office staff and custodians, can forever keep this as a memento.

The students and parents know I'm ground zero in this integration. This is the tester class that will get the first orc teacher. Next year hopefully we'll be able to bring in more orc staff and students.

But this all depends on how Garlen and I perform.

No pressure.

Yes, two years ago I won Teacher of the Year for the entire state. And I'm almost done with my administrative credential. But this is a big job for anyone.

And today is the day, the first day Garlen and I will teach together. It's strange to think of how, if we'd met on the front lawn two weeks ago and there had been no mating spark between us, nothing beyond simple coworker camaraderie, my winter break would've been very different.

It's good that I know my orc co-teacher now and orcs in general. Prior to meeting Garlen and his relatives, I'd only seen orcs on TV and in books and movies. I was born and raised in a sunny, warm area. North American orcs are warm-blooded and prefer cold, mountainous, forested climates. This is another reason why Black Oak was founded in Truckee, so that the climate would be pleasant for orcs.

Knowing Garlen ahead of time makes me much more comfortable and will make our teaching better for the students. His family still thinks that the two of us only communicate via text. Mom knows what we were up to with the letter writing, but I'm impressed that as far as I can tell she's been keeping our secret from Dane, which I appreciate.

I truly believe that the exchange of letters these last two weeks helped instead of hindered. How could I not use that time to get to know him better? I've definitely learned that Garlen isn't simply someone I'm attracted to, he's someone I want as a…future husband?

Father of my future orc sons?

It's amazing how in the space of two weeks so much has changed in my life. And in Mom's and Zoe's lives too. Mom and Dane are obviously falling hard for each other. And Zoe seems to have thoughts of Garlen as her future stepfather and is happy about this? I haven't specifically talked to her about this yet because I've been biding my time, waiting until I know this is really happening between us. But at some point, I'm going to have to sit my baby girl down and have a long talk with her about our future.

Strangely, this last week I ended up texting Garlen more often than using the letter exchange. Letter writing was too slow for us figuring out our lesson plans together. We needed to work hard on the preplanning of a month-long unit and leave nothing to chance. I discovered I really enjoy working with him in this way. We'd been getting to know each other the week prior, through our sexy, emotional, romantic letter writing. But now I've seen another professional side of Garlen and I like him even more. Yes, I was part of the team that hired him because I thought he was a good choice. I must admit that because I knew he didn't have an actual teaching credential, I assumed he'd need a lot more help. This isn't true at all.

Garlen basically has all the California grade level standards for K-12 memorized, which is great considering our school's curriculum is highly aligned with those common core standards. I was hired because the school board wanted teachers picked not only from private schools but from those who had worked in public education too.

I'd sent him possible lesson plan ideas we could do together so we'd be aligned to the standards and create brand new teaching that I hoped would impress anyone who wanted to learn later what we were doing here. He's a perfect partner in this. Going back and forth with Garlen via text about lesson planning makes him sexier. He's not only the right man for my body but for my mind too. I've already been in a marriage where we really had nothing in common, and I know what a disaster that can create.

I snag my favorite parking spot at the school, turn off the car and take a deep breath.

An hour later, it's all about to start. Excitement tingles in my stomach. Principal VanWagoner is in my room, as are two members of the school board and a few parents. They are all squeezed into the back of the classroom on extra chairs. The first bell rings and the seniors begin to enter and settle in their seats. It's a packed crowd.

The students are buzzing with excitement.

"Is he really going to have horns?" one student whispers.

"My dad says orcs are super smart," another adds.

My phone buzzes and I check to see a message from Garlen. *Are we ready?*

Ready! All the students are entering and the big wigs are seated in the back. I'll make the connection in about ten minutes.

Sounds good.

I love it that this man is completely on the ball and ready to go. In fact, prompting me. A smile widens across my face. All the audio/visual equipment and internet connections are set up and prechecked. This should be a go.

"This is it, Ms. Willis," Principal VanWagoner says, adjusting his tie. "History in the making."

"No pressure at all," I mutter under my breath.

Shelly Xiong, one of the board members, laughs. "We have complete confidence in you both."

"The technology better cooperate today," I say, fiddling again with the screen connection.

The bell rings and I step in front of the class. "Okay, settle down. Class has started. You're about to make history today," I tell them. They quiet down and I smile and welcome the students back from break and start my lesson. After a bit of background knowledge and an introduction, I tap on the keyboard and make the connection with Garlen and there he is, live, on a big screen. We made sure to change his background to book-cases, so no one knows he's chained, in a cage.

The students and our guests all clap loudly.

Garlen looks surprised and pleased at their warm welcome and obvious happiness to see him there, even if it's through a screen.

And all I can think is that his features look handsome to me… those shiny black horns and his full lips. I even like the gleam of his tusks. His dark eyes and those long eyelashes are dazzling.

First, I introduce Garlen, letting everyone know that Professor Irontree is teaching remotely for the next two months. I don't explain why, just say it as a statement, and they all accept it easily. I do my best to keep everything inside and not show any feelings toward Garlen, besides professional connection. I must look like someone who knows her co-teacher only because, yes, we worked on the lesson plan together during break via email and messages, and now we're starting today. No one can know what he said or did on my front lawn, where he declared that I was his bride. No one can know about the fact that he's been caged and chained for the last two weeks next door, or that we have been exchanging love letters.

Sometimes I have doubts about this situation. I haven't said this to anyone yet, but I have secret worries. Late at night, twirling my hair, I wonder: Am I hiding knowledge about some-thing that could be dangerous to the community? Something that could be dangerous to the students or to the school?

But I've thought about it long and hard, and I don't think of Garlen as dangerous to anybody. To be truthful—and this is hard to say—but the only person he's dangerous toward is *me*. I am the one he reacts to. I'm the one he wants to kidnap. His cousins and uncle are keeping him caged because it is so important to them that modern orcs don't behave in the ways of old, and that modern orcs are seen as a species that can work together with humans.

Humans and orcs were always apart for so long, our two

species at cross purposes and distrustful of each other. There was hatred, mobs with pitchforks, and bad behavior on both sides toward the other, but in the last century as humans gained a technological and warfare advantage, the worst behavior came from my fellow humans.

But things are changing between us, and orcs are citizens now. There are reparations. There's been an orc sheriff, and an orc firefighter, an orc senator, orc representatives. And here, at Black Oak Academy, is going to be the first orc teacher. But Garlen doesn't have his credential, or is not even allowed a waiver, because orcs aren't allowed yet in human colleges, and therefore he can't get the appropriate teaching credential. I'm the official credentialed teacher in the room, the teacher of record, so I have to be here with him. I really believe it when he says that the reason why he wants to be a teacher so badly is that he wants to be a role model for bringing our two species together.

So I have to help him.

Not telling anyone that Garlen is teaching remotely because he's chained in his basement is a terrible lie of omission. I glance back and feel a bit of nervousness. There's the principal. There are two school board members. I have not said word one to them about what happened over winter break, or my relationship with Garlen. They think he can't start because I made up some story about not being able to get out of his contract yet at the orc college in Maine, then he can be here in person after spring break to finish out the year.

I fall into old teaching patterns. I'm a little bit nervous, but then it goes away. I know the students. I know this lesson. I know what we're going to do. He knows his part, I know my part. It's a good lesson, and even though the world is watching in a way, I can do this.

I glance around at the class. How exciting, too, for the students. All of them are being so good and attentive. I don't have to monitor anyone's behavior. I'd say it's because they're as excited as I am. These teenagers know too that this is a historical moment. Their parents went through the bother of placing them here at this expensive private school so that they could have this type of instruction and be here for this historic moment.

Next year I'm hoping we can start giving out scholarships so that we can open this school to more students from a variety of backgrounds.

I've never seen Garlen teach. I couldn't go and watch him teach a demonstration lesson at the orc university in Maine. I stand to the side and watch as he starts speaking, and very soon I come to realize he's wonderful. I am so impressed.

"Who can tell me what ancient civilizations had in common?" Garlen asks from the screen.

Hands shoot up. "Trade routes." "Writing systems." "Social hierarchies."

"Excellent. Now, here's something that might surprise you about ancient orc settlements..." He launches into his lecture with such natural charisma that I find myself leaning forward, captivated along with the students.

Garlen Irontree stops often to do comprehension checks with them. He engages them. We go back and forth in the lesson. There are parts where he has them break into groups, which I monitor. He adds humor and has them laughing. I'm laughing at some of the things he's saying. I had no idea this orc was so charming, really.

"Professor Irontree, did orcs really build underground cities?" one student asks.

"We did indeed. In fact, my direct ancestors helped design the tunnel systems beneath the Canadian Appalachian Mountains. They were abandoned long ago due to an earthquake. Would you like to know why we originally built them underground?"

The students lean forward eagerly, and I catch myself doing the same thing.

In the back, the principal and the two school board members are laughing too. They don't remain seated the whole time but come forward and wander up and down the aisles, checking on the students' group work and their responses, and then at the end, their exit essays.

The hour and a half goes by swiftly and I'm stunned to look at the clock again and see we're almost over.

"Any final questions before we wrap up?" Garlen asks.

"Will you tell us more stories about how orcs hunting techniques are different from humans next time?" a student calls out.

"Absolutely. I have plenty more where those came from."

I bring us back and let them know what to look forward to in the next class, and the bell is ringing. The students are animated as they leave for their next class. I walk over to the computer, because I feel it would look unnatural for me to not congratulate Garlen or speak to him in some way.

Right then the principal walks up, and the two school board members too, so I'm not alone with him. They wave and make sure all their faces are in the screen, and I'm sort of pushed to the side.

"Outstanding work, Professor Irontree," Principal VanWagoner says.

"When can you join us in person?" asks a board member.

"I can teach in person after spring break. I'm excited to meet everyone face to face."

"This lesson you did today is why we were here. This was the mission statement of the school," Mrs. Xiong adds. "You should be proud to be the first."

"This should be the first of many," Garlen responds graciously.

They continue to gush over him, and I am just really impressed at his composure and how he's able to do this much level-headed, professional communicating considering his state of mind when I'm near. We didn't talk about this, but I feel instinctively like this must be hard for him. He'd told me that there are many hours in the day where he's just sitting there calmly, bored out of his mind, chained in the cage. This must be that Garlen.

He heard my voice when I was teaching and there were times when we had to talk to each other through the screen. And we still have to do this same lesson two more times today. Is he going to be able to carry on with this for the rest of the day?

I feel euphoria at a lesson well done, and I have to keep the faith that we can move on and do this again two more times. We've done this first run-through and worked out the bugs. Next time we can modify the exit question and give more time for the group work. There's just a small break, and then the next class will be here soon.

Finally, the others leave and I think we're alone for a moment. I take the opportunity to talk to him about how I felt it all went. "That was incredible. The students loved you," I whisper to the screen, noting that the next class begins to already trickle in. Darn it.

"Thank you. And I can see why you won Teacher of the Year. You made that seamless."

His voice is warm, and I feel my cheeks heat at his kind words.

"Ready for round two?" he questions.

"Always." I look around. The classroom is already half full and we don't have any privacy.

My phone buzzes. "When does the next class start?" he asks via text.

I look at my watch and then tap a response on my phone. "Five minutes. The students are already arriving."

He nods on the screen but answers via text. "Let's get going."

CHAPTER 18
Garlen

SOMETHING IS WRONG. I don't know exactly what it is, but I feel on edge.

The sensation has been building all afternoon, a restless energy crawling beneath my skin. I've tried to focus on reviewing student responses to the exit essay and fine-tuning the plan for tomorrow's lesson, but after teaching the third class of the day, my concentration keeps dissolving, and I find myself either rereading letters from Ellie or fiddling with curriculum.

Every few minutes, I pace the small confines of my reinforced chamber, the chains around my ankles clanking against the stone floor.

Despite the off and on concentration, I've already spent time grading the exit essay each student was expected to write, letting Ellie and I know if they clearly understood the lesson objective or if we need to reteach. The results were encouraging. Today was a successful teaching experience. Most students grasped the concepts we'd presented, and several asked thoughtful follow-up questions that showed genuine engagement. One student wrote about wanting to learn more about orc building techniques, while another expressed fascination with orc tribal tattoos and healing arts. Reading their human enthusiasm should have filled me with satisfaction and hope for the future of integration.

Instead, all I can think about is the sound of Ellie's voice during the lesson. The way she laughed at my joke about underground orc architecture. The slight breathlessness in her tone when she complimented my teaching during our brief unmuted moment. Each word sent heat racing through my veins, and now, hours later, my body still burns with unfulfilled need.

Tomorrow, we are going to build upon what we taught today, adding a new element. We teach the same lesson three times per day, to three different classes of thirty students each. Ellie told me that three classes is less than the normal course load of four classes that the school gives to teachers, giving us more time to lesson plan, grade and even deal with parents or the media if that becomes necessary.

The reduced schedule was meant to be a kindness, allowing us time to perfect our collaborative teaching method. But sitting here in isolation, replaying every moment of today's success, I find myself craving more. More time hearing her voice. More opportunities to watch her animated expressions through the camera. More chances to witness her brilliant mind at work.

Ellie is an amazing teacher.

I suspected this from her credentials and our text exchanges but seeing her in action today exceeded all my expectations. She commanded the classroom with natural authority while maintaining warmth and approachability. When that one student struggled with a concept, she rephrased it three different ways until understanding dawned in his eyes. When another became too excited and started talking over classmates, she redirected his energy without dampening his enthusiasm.

She's exactly the kind of educator I aspired to be when I first dreamed of teaching. I began at the orc university, wanting to teach the history of our species, so that knowledge was not lost. And now I want to give that knowledge to humans as well.

Watching her work alongside me, seamlessly weaving our

different perspectives into a cohesive lesson, felt like glimpsing our future. Not just as colleagues, but as true partners in every sense.

I'm not physically in the classroom with her, but I can hear everything she says. Her laughter continues to trigger my emotions.

Each time she laughed today, whether at my attempts at humor or in response to student comments, triggered primal and possessive reactions. My enhanced orc hearing means I catch every subtle intonation, every soft breath, every quiet "mmhmm" of encouragement she offers struggling students.

This is torture.

I shift on the narrow cot, trying to find a position that doesn't emphasize the persistent ache in my body. The chains allow me to move freely within the chamber, but they serve as a constant reminder of my confinement. Of the distance between us. Of the fact that I am not at the school, wherein at lunch break I could simply walk across the hall, lock the door behind us and take her in my arms for a deep kiss.

I'm all alone downstairs and I think alone in the entire domicile. Aldar and Keric are at the school, making sure the first day goes well and that the second day is even better. Jonus and Dane are outside, keeping an eye out on the perimeter of both of our properties.

The silence presses against me like a physical weight. For weeks, I've grown accustomed to the constant presence of my family members. Their orc voices drift down from upstairs, their heavy footsteps move on the floorboards above, and their occasional visits to check on my condition. Now, with everyone dispersed on various security duties, the basement feels cavernous and oppressive.

I understand the necessity. Our first day of integrated teaching has drawn attention from media outlets, government officials, and unfortunately, groups like Crimson Tusk who oppose our efforts. My cousins are ensuring no one can disrupt tomorrow's lessons, while Dane coordinates with local law enforcement to maintain a secure perimeter.

But understanding doesn't make the isolation easier to bear.

I glance at the clock, noting that the school should be letting out soon, therefore Ellie and Zoe will return to the house next door. In fifteen minutes, the final bell will ring and students will flood out of Black Oak Academy. Ellie will gather her materials, probably stay to chat with the other teachers or address any parent questions, then make her way to the parking lot. She'll drive home thinking about today's success, maybe mentally preparing for tomorrow's lessons.

Does this mean she will think about me during that drive? Will she replay our brief private moment the way I've been obsessing over it? Will she feel the same electric anticipation for tomorrow that's currently setting my nerves ablaze?

Will she write me a letter?

I lean back against the stone wall, closing my eyes, trying to center myself through meditation techniques Uncle Dane taught me years ago. Breathe in for four counts. Hold for four. Breathe out for six. I try to focus on the sensation of air filling my lungs rather than the phantom taste of my mate's skin.

It's not working.

If anything, the quiet meditation makes me more aware of every sensation. The fabric of my black pants against hypersensitive skin, wafts of cool air raising goosebumps along my arms, the steady throb of arousal that hasn't abated since I first caught Ellie's scent two weeks ago.

And then I look up and see Loki making his way down the stairs again in that adorable lurch, on his short stubby legs. He's a tiny beast but still full of strength and loyalty. I notice there is something attached to his harness. I'm puzzled because Ellie isn't here yet to deliver a letter. Where did he get this?

My confusion sharpens to concern as I take in Loki's appearance. The little corgi is panting heavily, more than usual, and there's something frantic in his movements. His usual confident trot has been replaced by an urgent scramble, his claws clicking rapidly against the stone steps. The small package bouncing against his side looks different from Ellie's usual letter attachments, its rounder, metallic, with an odd shimmer that catches the artificial light.

Did Ellie arrive home early and leave me a gift of some sort? But that doesn't make sense. The timing is all wrong. And why would she use this strange container instead of her usual folded paper secured with ribbon?

Unease prickles along my spine as I watch Loki navigate down the final few steps. Something about this feels wrong, but I can't identify what. I'm picking up scents I don't recognize clinging to his fur. There's the scent of chemicals, metal and something else, something that makes my nostrils flare with instinctive wariness.

I stand and drag the chains with me to the bars of the cage. "What do you have?"

Loki makes his way through the bars and sits at my feet. He's looking up at me with trusting eyes. My dog truly feels he's being a loyal messenger and following the instincts of his breed.

But as I kneel to examine the attachment more closely, a low whine escapes his throat. This is not his usual happy greeting, but a sound of distress. "Easy, Loki," I murmur, reaching down to stroke his head. "What happened? Where did you get this?"

His rear end wags half-heartedly at my touch, but the anxious energy doesn't leave his small frame. If anything, my attention seems to agitate him further.

A soft, circular object is attached to his harness, and I take it out. The device is warm to the touch, with tiny holes perforating its metallic surface. And then I hear it ticking, which grows faster, more urgent, and I have just enough time to register the sophisticated craftsmanship, and the fact that this is no amateur contraption. And before I can toss it aside the object explodes in my hands, covering me with a cloud of scent.

The explosion isn't fire or shrapnel, but something equally

dangerous to an orc. A fine mist erupts from the device, filling the air around me with particles so small they're almost invisible. The cloud expands rapidly, enveloping me completely. I try to keep my eyes and mouth closed and fall back, away from it, but it is too potent and already permeating my entire body.

The scent hits my lungs like a sledgehammer. It's concentrated beyond anything natural, chemically amplified to trigger maximum response. My lungs burn as the foreign particles infiltrate them, and my eyes water from the intensity. But it's not just the potency that devastates me, it's the specific combination of scents that have been weaponized against me.

This is Ellie's amazing scent, with a hint of...terror. Pain. Distress pheromones that speak directly to the most primitive parts of my brain. The scent tells a story that bypasses all rational thought and strikes straight at my core instincts: my mate is in danger. She's hurt, afraid, calling out for me to save her.

The rational part of my mind, the educated, civilized orc who understands chemistry and psychological manipulation, tries to assert itself. This is artificial. This is a trap. Someone has created a chemical cocktail designed to override my self-control and trigger my winter mating frenzy.

But that voice is immediately drowned out by something far older and more powerful.

And my mind fills with every instinct I've been trying to keep down for the last two weeks. The instincts I said I could keep under control until spring arrived, but I am defenseless in the wake of the scent of my bride's distress.

The change begins at my core, a heat that spreads outward like molten lava through my veins. My heartbeat doubles, then triples, pumping superheated blood to every extremity. The careful mental barriers I've constructed over weeks of meditation and self-discipline crumble like sand.

Winter's full power crashes over me with devastating force. Ten thousand years of orc evolution cannot be denied.

My vision sharpens until I can see individual bits of dust floating in the air. My hearing becomes so acute that I can distinguish the different heartbeats of small animals in the walls. My sense of smell maps the entire house, tracking the fading trails of everyone who's been here in the past week.

But overriding everything else is the phantom scent of Ellie's fear, growing stronger instead of weaker, driving me toward madness with each passing second.

I must get to her.

Nothing else matters. Not consequences, not integration efforts, not the careful plans we've made for our future. My mate is in danger, and every second I waste in this cage brings her closer to harm.

"Ellie!" I roar.

The sound that emerges from my throat is barely recognizable as my own voice. It's deeper, carrying vibrations through the stone walls that shake dust from the ceiling. It's the battle cry of an ancient warrior, the territorial claim of a predator, the anguished call of a male who will tear the world apart to reach his female.

Loki barks and runs in circles, as if to tell me to calm down, or alert the others that he needs help to tame this wild orc.

Red haze fills my vision.

The dog runs back and forth between me and the stairs, whimpering and yapping in obvious agitation. Some distant part of me recognizes that he's trying to communicate something important, but that awareness is buried beneath layers of primal fury.

My lungs fill with her scent. My body changes, morphs into the beast that cannot be contained. I throw back my head and let out a thunderous roar. My bones stretch and thicken, adding inches to my height. My arms and legs grow bigger and thicker. My tusks elongate, as do my horns. Muscle mass increases exponentially, my pants strain against the rapid expansion before finally tearing apart. My hands become claws, while my feet develop the broad, powerful proportions needed to carry my increased weight at incredible speeds.

The winter weight chains that have confined me for weeks and were forged specifically to contain an orc, prove inadequate against the full fury of my enhanced state. In moments I burst from the chains that were meant to keep me contained.

The reinforced cage door that has kept me safely contained presents more of a challenge. The first time I throw myself against it, the frame buckles but holds. The metal reinforcements were installed by orcs who understood what they were trying to contain. But I am beyond what they planned for. The second impact shatters the lock mechanism completely, and the door swings open with a tortured shriek of twisted metal.

Freedom.

Now I'm stomping up the stairs and I burst out of the door from the basement. I pause, taking a deep breath, and reorient. I need to get to Ellie. I am out of the cage because she needs me. My bride needs me to get to her right now and then I will take her to a cave in the nearby mountains and keep her there and fill her with my seed. She will bear my orc sons.

The main floor of the house seems impossibly small after weeks in the basement. Furniture that once appeared normal sized now looks like dollhouse miniatures beneath my enhanced bulk. I have to duck to avoid hitting my horns on doorframes, and my footsteps crack the hardwood flooring.

The scent trail is clearer here, more complex. She has never been inside, but she was on the front porch and outside the house. I can smell where Ellie walked two weeks ago during her first visit. But underneath that precious memory lies the artificial chemical signature of the device, still clinging to my nostrils and driving me toward madness.

She's not here. She's never been in real danger in this house.

But the scent tells a different story, and my winter-addled brain cannot distinguish between manipulation and reality.

I must care for her. Ellie is my bride, and I will not allow any harm to come to her.

The protective instinct burns even brighter than the mating drive. Whatever has threatened her will be destroyed. Whatever has caused her pain will face my wrath. I will tear apart anyone who stands between us, then carry her somewhere safe where no harm can ever reach her again.

The mountains call to me, ancient orc strongholds where my ancestors kept their mates during the dangerous months. Caves with fresh water and narrow entrances that can be easily defended. Places where I can keep her warm and safe while filling her belly with my offspring.

But first, I have to reach her.

I lift my chin and take a deep breath. She is not in this domicile. Her scent faintly lingers in the home next door, but I know she is not there either. The distant sound of a school bell rings. My bride is at Black Oak Academy, and she is in trouble.

The front door explodes outward in a shower of wood splinters and twisted hinges. The cold air hits my superheated skin, but instead of discomfort, it brings clarity. My enhanced senses map the neighborhood in detail. I locate every scent trail, every potential threat or obstacle.

Ellie's scent next door is hours old and confirms what my rational mind already knew, that she's not here, has never been in danger here. She's at the school, probably gathering her things after a successful day of teaching, unaware that forces are moving against us. She'll be emerging from the building soon, surrounded by students and parents, vulnerable in ways she doesn't understand.

"Garlen," a deep voice bellows.

The voice belongs to Dane. I register this dimly as I launch myself into a ground-eating run. He's shouting orders from the house next door, probably calling for backup, trying to coordinate some kind of intervention. But he's too far away, and I'm moving too fast.

By the time my uncle reaches the front of the house, I'm already gaining speed. I race through the snow, across streets. Nothing will get in the way of me getting to my bride. Cars skid to a stop and honk and yet I continue forward.

My legs pump with mechanical precision and I take even breaths. Cold air fills my lungs without burning, my heart operates at levels that could kill a normal orc.

More cars screech to a halt as I burst onto the main road, their drivers staring in shock at the massive figure racing through their midst. I leap over the hood of a sedan that can't stop in time, my momentum barely affected by the obstacle. The driver leans on his horn, adding to the growing chaos of alarm spreading through the neighborhood.

But none of it matters. The only thing that exists is the distance between me and Ellie, shrinking with every powerful stride. Another deep voice yells my name, but I ignore it. Nothing will get in my way. I run faster than ever before, pumping my legs and taking even breaths. I can run like this forever; whatever it takes to get to her and keep her safe. I will protect her and get rid of anyone who is in my way.

She must be taken by me to a safe place in the mountains, where I can be alone with her and impregnate my female. No more separation, no more careful control, no more denying what we both want.

This fantasy drives me faster, my legs eating up the distance to the school. Humans shout in distress. I ignore them and keep going. I can see the school in the distance. There are children and adults all over, along with yellow school buses and cars from parents picking up offspring.

The scene ahead would normally fill me with satisfaction. Parents arriving to collect their children after a historic first day, students chattering excitedly about their orc teacher, the successful beginning of the integration program I've worked so hard to achieve.

Instead, all I see are potential threats.

Too many humans with unknown intentions. Too many opportunities for someone to harm my mate while I'm still too far away to protect her. The parking lot swarms with activity. Car doors slam, engines start, voices calling out. Any one of these humans could be an enemy in disguise.

I crash through a snowy hedge separating the residential area from the school grounds, branches tearing at my skin without slowing me down. Security cameras track my movement, but I'm moving too fast for any human response. By the time anyone processes what they're seeing, I'll already have reached Ellie.

Parents notice me now, their cheerful post-school conversations cutting off abruptly as they register the massive orc charging across the snow. Some cry out as they grab their children and run for their cars. Others pull out phones, either to call for help or to record what they're witnessing.

Let them watch. Let them see what happens to anyone who threatens an orc's mate.

Focus. Focus.

And there she is, my bride. I catch sight of her exiting the building alongside another human female. I let out another roar.

She's even more beautiful than my memory suggested, professional and confident in her jacket and skirt. The wide hips and thick thighs are the stuff of erotic dreams. Her hair catches the afternoon sunlight as she walks, and her laugh, that sexy sound that has tormented me all day, carries across the parking lot as she responds to something her companion has said.

The sight of her safe and unharmed should bring relief, but the scents still flooding my system won't allow for rational thought. My bride is here, within reach, but still not in my arms where she belongs.

My roar echoes off the school building, causing windows to rattle and birds to burst from nearby trees in panicked flight.

Ellie lifts her head at the sound and looks right for me. Her eyes widen. "Garlen?" she whimpers.

And then I speed up and rush right for her.

CHAPTER 19
Ellie

A MASSIVE, wild orc charges across the parking lot.

The same male I've exchanged love letters with for the last two weeks and taught classes with earlier today. He's now transformed beyond anything I could have imagined.

How did he escape?

Garlen's pants hang in tatters and barely cling to his expanded frame. Every muscle is defined and bulging, his green skin stretched over a body that's gained at least fifty pounds of pure power. His tusks jut up from his lower lip like ivory daggers, and his horns have curved into wicked points that catch the afternoon sunlight. But his beautiful, dark eyes are still the same and entirely recognizable.

"Ellie, we need to run." Anna's voice cuts through my shock. She grabs my arm, trying to pull me toward the school building.

"It's okay," I hear myself say with a certainty that surprises me. "It's Garlen. I've got this."

"But Ellie…" she cries.

"No, go back. I'm staying. Don't worry, I'm okay. I'll take care of this."

All around us, parents scream and scoop up their children. Car doors slam as people flee the parking lot. In the distance, I hear security alarms and sirens are approaching. But I step forward instead of back, my body moving on pure instinct.

They are all afraid of what he's become, but this is Garlen. My Garlen. He won't hurt me.

He reaches me in three massive strides, and suddenly my orc is towering over me, breathing hard and wild-eyed. Up close, I can see how his pants hang like rags on his transformed body, barely decent. And yes, his crotch is again obscenely tented, just like our first confrontation at the front of my house. Poor guy. This is the second, no, the third time this has happened to him. And this time is obviously the worst. His chest heaves with each breath, and there's something desperate in his expression, like he's fighting a war inside his own mind.

Despite his size, despite the way others are fleeing in terror like it's the apocalypse, I'm not afraid. Instead, my heart races with something else entirely. Concern. Love. The overwhelming need to help him.

"Garlen?" I say his name again, softer this time. "It's me. It's Ellie."

"My bride," he rasps.

My hand reaches up, trembling but determined. He moves close, until there is almost no space between us and he bends down and allows me to touch his face. The moment my palm connects with his heated skin, his body shudders. The wildness in his eyes flickers. "Need…need to make sure you are safe."

"I'm safe," I whisper, my thumb stroking across the stubble on his jaw. "I'm here. You found me. Everything's okay."

Around us, the chaos has settled into an eerie silence. Our audience has quieted down to watch and listen what's happening between us. I'm dimly aware of phones lifted and recording, but all that matters is the way Garlen's body appears to already be softening.

"Ellie," he rumbles, his voice deeper and more guttural than usual. "You…you're safe?"

"Completely safe." My other hand joins the first, framing his face as I watch him fight for control. "You came for me. You always come for me."

"Yes." His eyes close for a moment, and when they open again, there's more of the Garlen I know looking back at me. Still wild, still dangerous, but fighting his way back to the surface. "You always come first."

Watching him struggle, seeing his gentleness despite his transformation, something warm and certain settles in my chest. This overwhelming feeling that's been growing for the last two weeks, this connection that defies logic and reason.

This is love, isn't it? I'm falling in love with this orc.

The realization should terrify me, but instead it feels right. Garlen is my future husband, chains, winter madness and all.

"Ellie. Get away from him."

The shout breaks our bubble of intimacy. I turn to see Dane, Jonus, Aldar, and Keric pound across the parking lot with heavy chains and other orc-like weapons. Their faces are grim with shame and panic.

"We're sorry. This should never have happened," Dane calls out as they approach in a semi-circle. "Step back. We'll contain him immediately."

At the sight of the chains, Garlen's progress toward calm instantly reverses. A low growl rumbles from his chest, and I feel his muscles tense beneath my hands.

"No." The word comes out sharp and clear as I step between them and Garlen. "Absolutely not."

"Ellie, you don't understand—" Aldar starts.

"I understand perfectly." My voice carries across the parking lot, and I know every phone is capturing this moment. "He doesn't need chains. He needs me."

Gasps ripple through the crowd. The significance of my words echoes off the school building, practically going viral in real time. But I don't care. This is my choice, my declaration, my future I'm claiming.

"But we need to…"

"No, you don't need to do anything. I can bring him in."

I slide my arm around Garlen's waist, or as much of it as I can reach around his expanded frame. "Come on," I murmur to him. "Let's go home."

He looks down at me with something like wonder in his eyes. His arms wrap around me, and he pulls me in close. I feel the heat of his body and the ridge of that enormous erection, which sends a rush of heat between my thighs.

He rests his forehead against mine. "My bride," he sighs.

I remain in his arms for a few moments, loving the feel of him surrounding me. His scent, the rub of his tusks against my cheeks. I love it all.

Finally, Garlen exhales and loosens his hold on me and steps back. I take his huge hand and he allows me to slowly lead him away from the school, his family, away from the chains, away from the chaos we've created.

I don't look back or even around. I just keep myself focused on the long walk home. It seems quick to take by car, but the walk from the school back to his house will take about thirty minutes. But this is okay, it will give Garlen plenty of time to calm down.

According to the sounds I hear around me, it also gives the local and national media time to arrive and track our progress.

I'm dressed for the cold, in a long coat, with a scarf. My mittens are in my pocket. And I have on my tall boots that I spent a lot of money on, but they are invaluable right now. They have a bit of a heel and look elegant, but I can also walk miles in them.

It's amazing to me how Garlen seems perfectly comfortable, barefoot, with only shredded pants. Steam rises off his shoulders, so I suppose his internal heat is enough to keep him warm.

The quiet walk through the neighborhoods feels surreal, like something out of a fairy tale. Beauty and the Beast strolling down suburban streets while the world watches. With each block we cover, I notice changes in Garlen. His breathing becomes less labored. His stride is shorter because his legs and feet become slightly smaller. Most noticeably, his tusks begin to retract, and his horns start shrinking back toward their normal size.

By the second block, he's holding up his torn pants with one hand while I hold onto the other.

"My clothes…" he murmurs in an almost normal-sounding voice.

"We'll get you inside soon and you can change," I assure him, fighting back a smile at how odd my day has turned out. Here I am, walking home with an orc who is transforming back from winter madness, and I'm worried about his pants. I take another peek at his crotch. Although, it is important for him to get covered, he's lucky that the shredded fabric covers his erection that has only partially faded.

Neighbors peek from their windows but keep a respectful distance. A few wave hesitantly, and I wave back as if this is the most normal thing in the world. As if I always take afternoon strolls with my half-naked orc boyfriend after he breaks out of a basement cage to rescue me from some imaginary danger.

"Ellie," Garlen says quietly as we finally turn onto our street. "What I did back there… I'm so sorry. I couldn't control—"

"It's okay." I squeeze his hand. "I know you couldn't control what happened to you. You thought I was in danger, and you came for me. Do you know how incredible that is?"

He looks down at me with those spectacular dark eyes, now fully his own again. "You're not afraid of me?"

"Never." The certainty in my voice surprises even me. "Not of you. Not ever. Instead I…I think it's sweet that you would come to protect me like that. But I'm also worried for you, because you didn't seem like yourself at all. Why would you think I was in danger, when I was just at work?" I squeeze his hand again. "We'll get to the bottom of what happened. Together."

We pass the Petersons' house and can clearly see media vans already gathered up ahead. They are at a respectable distance, reporters setting up cameras and adjusting microphones from the park across the street. They all stare at us and alert each other that we're here and start recording, but none of them call out to us.

I pull out my phone and quickly text my mom. *I'm fine and I'm next door with Garlen. Please watch Zoe. Will explain everything later.*

She sends back a thumbs up emoji.

We reach the porch of Garlen's home, and I let go of his hand for a moment. He fumbles with his keys, still holding up his pants. I bite my lip to keep from giggling at how endearingly ridiculous he looks. This powerful, dangerous orc who accidentally terrorized half the town, now struggles with something as basic as opening the front door.

He pauses and looks down at me. "Do you want to go home instead?"

"I'm staying," I tell him as he finally gets the door open. "We'll figure this out together."

"Are you sure?" His voice is uncertain, vulnerable in a way that makes my heart ache. "After what just happened, everyone's going to have opinions about us. About you. You know how I feel, but I only want what's best for you. This is your chance to go back to the way things were. They can put me back in the cage again."

I look back at the cameras flashing, at the reporters who stand in the park and are doing their broadcast with us and the house in their background. The world is about to scrutinize every aspect of our relationship. Then I look up at Garlen. This huge orc is rumpled, embarrassed, still holding up his pants, but looking at me like I'm the most precious thing in his universe.

"Yes, I'm sure I want to stay with you," I say, stepping into his house with him. "I choose *you*, consequences and all."

CHAPTER 20

Garlen

WE ENTER the house and find all three of my cousins and my uncle waiting inside.

None of them look happy.

The front room, which usually feels spacious and welcoming with its warm wood furnishings and stone fireplace, now feels cramped and tense. Dane stands with arms crossed near the mantel. Aldar paces by the large windows that overlook the street. Keric is positioned by the front door, and Jonus sits in a leather armchair.

The contrast between this scene and the raucous audience outside is jarring. Through those same windows, I can see the glow of camera lights and hear the distant murmur of reporters setting up for what will undoubtedly be a long night of coverage. Inside, the house feels like a fortress under siege, heavy curtains drawn against prying eyes.

My cock is still thick but not as hard and throbbing as before. My pants are shredded and hang from my body. I am happy to be within the shelter of my domicile and away from the prying eyes of all those humans. I need food, drink, sleep and sex with my female, in no particular order.

Plus, I suffer from a heavy dose of shame for my behavior in public in front of all those humans. The careful image I've been building for months of the educated orc professor, the bridge between our species, lies in ruins somewhere between the basement cage and the school parking lot.

The students I taught today saw me revert to an Irontree of old, after I'd explicitly told them that modern orcs aren't the same as ancient orcs.

What do the principal and the members of the school board think of me now?

After a day like today, the last thing I want is to be grilled by the other Irontrees. But as I look around the room at their grim faces, I realize this interrogation is unavoidable. They need answers, and frankly, so do I.

Keric points at the front door. "Luckily for you I bought a replacement door as back up when we first arrived and I was able to quickly replace what you destroyed."

I glance back at the entrance, noting the fresh wood and gleaming hinges. The old door had been solid oak, installed when this house was built. The fact that I destroyed it so completely that it needed immediate replacement is another reminder of how far I lost control.

"All those humans are outside now," Aldar growls, gesturing toward the windows where camera flashes continue to strobe through the curtains. "Now the whole world knows that this generation of Irontrees is risky."

Dane nods. "The elders are not pleased. They've called for your immediate removal and return to your commune. I managed to convince them to wait until I could speak with you and get a better look at the situation. But they are waiting impatiently for my reply."

I nod, grateful that my uncle is providing cover.

A growl rumbles in Keric's chest. "The whole point of you taking this human job and us coming here was to prove that orcs could work and live alongside humans with no incident. And here we are."

The accusation in his voice cuts deep because it's justified. We came to Truckee with such hope, such determination to prove that integration could work. Senator Overthrow had personally endorsed this program. Representatives Overland and Goldtree had vouched for the Irontree clan specifically. And I've potentially destroyed all of that in one afternoon of winter madness.

I take a deep breath and glance down at Ellie. My female holds my hand again and appears strangely calm and in fact smiles at the orcs in attendance.

Her composure amazes me. She should be traumatized, angry, demanding explanations. Instead, she stands beside me like we're greeting guests at a dinner party rather than facing the aftermath of a crisis. Her small hand in mine anchors me, reminding me that not everything is lost.

"Hi," she greets my family. "I brought Garlen home."

The simple statement hangs in the air, and I see something shift in my relatives' expressions. She's not presenting herself as a victim or an outsider looking in. She's claiming ownership of the situation, of me, of our relationship.

Jonus grins. "Yes, you did."

His approval is evident, and I remember his words from weeks ago about humans needing to prove themselves worthy of orc protection. Ellie has certainly done that today.

Dane exhales. "Thank you, female, for how you responded to Garlen's winter mating instinct. We appreciate your level-headed response to a wild orc running straight for you. Most females would have screamed and ran."

"And if you'd ran," Aldar explains, "that would've made things worse. It would've ignited his worst instincts. Garlen would've ran after you, kidnapped you off the street in front of everyone and right now we'd instead be part of a search team, trying to find you within his lair in the remotest part of the mountain range."

She squeezes my hand. "I suddenly knew that the right move

wasn't to run from Garlen, but to go toward him. I could see that he needed me."

Her words send a warm pulse through my chest. She saw me, truly saw me, even in my most dangerous state. Not just the beast, but the male beneath who was desperately trying to reach his mate.

"Can we all sit and talk about what happened?" Ellie questions.

We all give nods of acceptance. The other three orcs take seats in the living area. Aldar settles heavily into the sectional sofa. Keric remains perched on the edge of the coffee table like he's ready to spring into action. Dane takes the chair opposite Jonus. Ellie pulls me to sit next to her on the couch. It feels good to have her so close.

The familiar weight of cushions beneath us reminds me of the life I've been missing these last two weeks. Now Ellie is here, her thigh pressed against mine, her scent filling my nostrils with every breath. It's intoxicating and comforting and terrifying all at once.

Dane crosses his arms. "While the two of you were walking back, we returned to the basement to investigate what happened. What could have made you so triggered you were able to break through the chains and the cage? Those are supposed to be unbreakable."

The memory is still fragmented, coming back in flashes. "Yes, I was working, then Loki came downstairs."

"We found the remnants of a scent bomb in the basement." Keric's expression darkens. "Sophisticated work. Military grade chemical amplification. How was it delivered to you without us knowing?"

More bits of my memory return. "There was something unusual attached to Loki's harness. Loki brought the scent bomb. My loyal companion, from a breed of corgis bred for thousands of years to serve orc families, was turned into a weapon against me."

Ellie pulls our joined hands onto her lap. "I don't even know what this bomb is. I've never heard of it before."

"A scent bomb is a chemical device designed to trigger orc mating instincts," Keric explains grimly. "They combined your natural scent with distress pheromones. To Garlen's already winter-frenzied brain, it would have seemed like you were in mortal danger. He instantly thought he needed to get to you, that it was a life-or-death situation."

Ellie's eyes widen as the implications sink in. "So that's why he said he was there to make sure I was safe. He said that to me, but I didn't understand why he'd think I needed saving in the first place, considering I was at work and he'd seen me just an hour before, at the end of our last lesson." She turns to me. "Why would your dog allow those orcs near him and to attach something to him and bring it to you?"

"Because it held your scent," Keric explains. "Loki thought he was doing the right thing."

"But Jonus and Dane were out there too. He could have gone to them…"

I shake my head, better understanding what happened. "Loki could scent the distressed pheromones too. He thought you were in trouble and that I needed to know so I could protect you."

Loki whines at our feet.

"Oh Loki," Ellie exclaims. "Come here, we still love you." She lets go of my hand in order to bend down and scoop Loki up onto her lap. "You were trying to protect me too, which I appreciate. You were tricked too, as much as Garlen was." She kisses the dog's nose, and he seems to settle down.

"It had to have been Crimson Tusk," I say. "Humans don't know how to manufacture a scent bomb. And Loki wouldn't have let a human attach anything to his harness. Crimson Tusk didn't just attack me; they turned my own protective instincts and my dog's loyalty into weapons. They knew exactly how to manipulate both of us."

"Sneaky."

"Yes."

"Which member of Tusk planted this scent bomb on Loki? It had to have been someone high up."

"We're still investigating," Aldar says. "This was a coordinated attack designed to discredit the integration program."

Ellie leans forward. "They wanted Garlen to lose his mind and come rushing at me like that, while school was letting out, to cause a scene?"

"Yes."

"Well, it's a good thing then that I didn't run."

We all nod in agreement.

"The good news is that even though the chains are broken, we have a backup pair," Dane explains. "We have already fixed the cage. If the elders decide to let Garlen stay, we can return to the same situation as before. We know the restraints will hold in normal winter frenzy. He was able to break free because the scent bomb caused a rare condition amongst orcs where we can grow even larger in response to a mate in danger. This almost never happens, but it has been recorded in our histories."

Aldar nods in agreement. "There will not be another scent bomb so that situation will not repeat itself."

"But wait," Ellie interrupts. "Does Garlen really need to remain chained and in that cage if the whole point was to keep him away from me? I'm staying with him, so doesn't that mean since I'll be close he won't need the chains or even the cage anymore?"

The words hit the room like a thunderclap. Everyone freezes, and I feel my heart skip a beat.

"You're staying?" Dane questions.

"You're staying?" My voice cracks. Yes, she'd said that when we entered my domicile, but I thought she meant temporarily, until she'd talked to my relatives and saw me settled and then she'd go back to her own home and I would have to return to the way things were before. Or I'd have to return to the commune. Either is still an option. The hope and terror warring in my chest make it hard to breathe. She wants to stay with me, but the danger…

Keric stands. "You're staying *here*, in this domicile, with Garlen?"

"Yes, yes, I'm staying. I have to, don't you think?"

I frown. I don't want her to stay with me only out of a sense of obligation. "You don't have to do this," I reply. "We can return to you living next door and teaching at the school and I'm co-teaching again remotely." The thought of returning to that isolation, especially now that I've held her, feels like a death sentence. But I won't trap her here out of guilt or misplaced heroism.

She shakes her head. "We cannot go back to that arrangement. It obviously doesn't work. What if they are able to plant another scent bomb? Plus, now we know that you can remain calm with my touch and my scent in your lungs. It makes more sense for me to simply stay close, rather than have you kept in a cage."

"He's sane because you don't present a distressed scent, but like you said, you're calm and in fact slightly submissive." Dane's clinical explanation is hard to hear, but he's not wrong. Ellie's presence soothes the winter madness in ways I hadn't thought possible.

"You can't do this," I growl. "It's not safe." The protectiveness surges through me again, though thankfully without the chemical amplification that drove me to madness earlier. She's too precious to risk, her caring is too important to lose to my lack of control.

Her eyes narrow. "Are you as committed as I am to you being able to finish out this school year in the classroom with me, teaching until the last day of the school year?"

The question cuts straight to the heart of everything I've worked for. This position, this opportunity to prove that orcs and humans can work together, is bigger than just me. It's the foundation for everything that comes after. "Yes, I am."

"Well, I think the only way that's going to happen is if I stay right by your side." She squeezes my hand and looks deep into my eyes. "And I'm not with you only for that reason. I'm here because I want to be with *you*." She looks around at my assembled relatives. "I am staying close with this orc of my own free will and because I care. This is exactly where I want to be, with Garlen."

My eyes grow hot. How am I so lucky to have found the bravest human female and she wants to take me on? Her logic is sound, but the implications terrify me. Living together, sharing space, maintaining my control for two more months while she's within reach…

"What about the police? Is the human law enforcement going to allow us to monitor Garlen in our own way, or will they interfere?"

The question comes from Jonus, ever practical about legal ramifications.

"The police are leaving this alone," Aldar answers.

"Why?"

"Well, the principal didn't press any charges. No parents have called in to file complaints or press charges either. And Ellie is here of her own free will, so…" Keric's explanation brings a measure of relief. At least we won't be dealing with criminal charges on top of everything else.

Ellie lets go of my hand and glances down at her phone. "I do have a text from principal VanWagoner. He wants me to get in touch with him ASAP to let me know if we're still able to teach tomorrow." She throws her head back and laughs.

"What's so funny?"

"After everything that happened I have to admit I was a little worried we were both fired and you were probably going to be arrested and instead nothing much is happening and our principal wants to know if we're still on for tomorrow."

The absurdity of it strikes me too. A chuckle of relief rumbles in my chest. After everything that's happened, the human is focused on logistics rather than liability.

"You're both famous now."

Jonus's observation is accompanied by the distant sound of more vehicles arriving outside. The media circus is only growing, and by tomorrow our faces will be on every news channel in the country.

"I will only agree to this," I say, "if I remain chained. I refuse to touch my female while I'm like this."

All the orcs in the room nod in acceptance.

"It is only right," Dane agrees. "This will go a long way towards the elders allowing you to remain."

Ellie looks hurt, and it tears at my heart to see her expression fall. "But I thought you wouldn't need the chains because…"

"Ellie, it's wonderful that you are choosing to stay with me and support me in this way. But I still need to protect you. I will wait until spring to remain at your side unchained, when I can treat you with respect. You cannot stay with me without restraints. It isn't safe. It's already been established that sometimes I can't stop myself. I won't risk your safety for my comfort." My voice deepens. "Anything that might happen between us must always be because of your genuine consent, given freely. What if I later came back to myself and discovered I'd done something to you without your consent? I'd never forgive myself. I refuse to put the both of us in that situation. I will remain chained."

My bride nods slowly. "I will live here with you until spring break." She looks at the other orcs in the room. "I will stay with Garlen and put up with him being chained. But there is no way I'm living in a cage in the basement."

The finality in her voice makes it clear this isn't a negotiation. Dane and I exchange glances, and I can see him calculating sleeping arrangements and security protocols.

"The good news," Aldar confirms, "is that with you here, it's true that he at least doesn't have to live in the cage. And maybe he won't need the leg chains either."

Keric grumbles but then gives a curt nod of agreement.

"What about Zoe?" I ask.

Ellie flashes a brilliant smile at my question. "She'll stay with my mom, but she'll want to visit after school, spend time here. Is that okay?"

The question is directed at all of us, but she's looking at me. "Of course. She's part of this now. Part of us."

"There are going to be practical considerations," Keric cuts in. "Food, clothing, security protocols. We'll need to establish routines that keep everyone safe."

"And media management," Jonus adds grimly. "This story isn't going away anytime soon. The whole world is watching the video of the two of you in front of the school. It's the top news story and top search on the internet, everywhere."

CHAPTER 21
Ellie

I JUST TOLD Garlen that I'm moving in with him, his cousins and his uncle, Dane.

Am I crazy?

Maybe.

But I think I'm crazy like a fox.

Yes, this means I'm going to be living in a house with the orc I'm falling in love with and his four relatives. But this isn't so bad, it's not really like I'm moving in with strangers. I've known Garlen's cousins and his uncle for two weeks already, and I'm ninety-nine percent certain his uncle Dane is most likely going to end up being my mom's new husband. It's probably good if I get to know all of them better anyway.

When I entered their home with Garlen and sat down in the living area, I was focused on our talk. But now, I can see that this is an open room. From where I sit, I can see the entire living area, the long dining room table and most of the brand-new kitchen. It's very nice and surprisingly clean, considering a bunch of single males live here. Living here will be no hardship.

All four of his relatives are now crowded near the window, deep in conversation about what to do with all the journalists outside.

Meanwhile, my mind drifts towards my six-year-old daughter who won't understand why her mom is suddenly moving next door without her. I bite at my lip. Of course, I want nothing more than to sleep beside Garlen each night. It's what I've wanted for the last two weeks. Butterflies take flight in my stomach when I think of the both of us snuggling into bed together, preferably naked.

But my want and need to be closer to Garlen clashes with my need to be with my little girl. I haven't spent a single night away from her since I brought her home from the hospital. How can I be separated from my Zoe, even if she's only next door? I love that Garlen asked about Zoe, before I even could. That's good news that he's putting her first in his head, just as I would. But…

"Are you worried about Zoe not being here in this house with us at night?"

Garlen is still sitting right by my side, holding my hand.

I look into his dark gaze, with those impossibly long eyelashes. Is he reading my mind? "It's hard for me," I admit. "I know when you asked about her a minute ago, I said it would be easy for Zoe to come and go, but now, the more I think about it, my heart is telling me it won't be easy. This doesn't mean I'm not moving in here, because I am, it just means I have to figure out a way to see my baby girl as much as my heart needs. She's everything to me."

Garlen's features soften. "This is only natural."

I swallow hard and look away. My words are also for the benefit of the other orcs in the room, who've now turned and are looking at me with concern. "I'll still want to know everything that's going on with her. What did she eat for breakfast, for lunch and dinner? What did she wear to school? What's in her backpack? Her hair has to be just right. And…I'm better at Zoe's hair than my mom."

Garlen points at my phone. "You can call or FaceTime with her whenever you like. She can eat dinner here with us each night. You can FaceTime your mother too. They can always come between both houses and visit as long as you want."

My brow furrows. "But all the reporters outside would see us. We don't have any privacy. I feel like we're housebound."

He shrugs those massive shoulders. "For me, this is an improvement. Prior to this I was chained in a cage in the basement. Now I'm still chained but I'll be in my bedroom, with you."

I can't help but scoot closer and lean into him. Garlen puts an arm across my shoulders and pulls me in tight next to him. I inhale his woodsy scent, which I love, and suddenly I'm a thousand times calmer. Roadblocks to this situation suddenly turn into mere bumps in the road. This will all work out.

Jonus moves a curtain aside, exposing himself to the gaze of the media. There's immediately a wave of muffled shouts and the flash of lights. He shakes his head, closes the fabric and steps back. "You have a valid concern. It's getting worse out there. I've already warned them to stay off our property, but the new arrivals are bold. We will work together with them to come to some sort of truce that works for everyone."

I let out a breath. "Thank you, all of you, for helping me think of work-arounds. I'll figure out what to do about Zoe later tonight. First, I need to call the principal back and then get in contact with Anna. I feel like I can't relax until I know how tomorrow is going to go."

"Anna?" Keric questions. "Is that Ms. Kim?"

"Yes, you may have already met her at the school. Anna Kim is the head of the English department. She's basically my best friend on campus. She's already said before to reach out to her if I needed help in any way. Also, I should check in with her and make sure she's okay. She was right next to me when Garlen rushed up to us at the school. The last I saw of her, she was scared and anxious. I need to make sure she's okay."

"I was behind the both of you when Garlen arrived on campus," Keric says. "I heard what you said to her and pulled her back into the hallway. I spoke to her for a moment and made sure she was all right, then I went out to meet up with the others."

"Oh, thank you. I appreciate you for checking on her like that." I look at Garlen. "Talking to Anna and VanWagoner means they will get things set up so that you and I can both teach remotely."

Garlen nods in agreement. "The both of us teaching remotely is a good solution."

He still wears his shredded pants that hang on him like super-long, fringed shorts, but his voice sounds normal, similar to how it sounded when he was teaching. "Are you ready for me to call? Do you feel you are able to speak to them too?"

"Yes. We can both speak."

I pull out my phone and scroll to Principal VanWagoner's contact. "I'm calling the principal first. I should call him back now, while we're all here to discuss logistics."

"Put it on speaker," Aldar suggests. "We all need to hear how the school administration is handling this."

"Um, before I call…is there anything that you don't want me to say? Anything off limits?"

"Say the truth," Dane offers.

I nod and tap the speaker icon before hitting call. The phone rings twice before a familiar voice answers. "Ellie Willis? Thank goodness you're calling back. Are you all right?"

"I'm fine, Mr. VanWagoner. I'm here with Professor Irontree and his family. We're working out the details for continuing our teaching program. I think it would be best if I taught remotely, alongside Professor Irontree."

"Good, good. I have to say, that footage of you two…well, it's certainly made an impression. My phone hasn't stopped ringing all afternoon. We've got interview requests from CNN, *The Today Show*, and about fifteen educational journals."

I exchange glances with Garlen. "Is that…good or bad?"

"Honestly? It's the best publicity Black Oak could ask for.

The way you handled that situation, stepping forward instead of running, calming Professor Irontree with such composure. That's exactly the kind of integration success story we hoped for."

Garlen leans forward toward the phone. "Mr. VanWagoner, this is Garlen Irontree. I want to apologize for the disruption I caused at your school."

I can't help but smile. His deep voice, talking in this formal and professional manner is so freaking sexy. I feel small and in fact petite next to him on the couch. He still holds my hand as he talks and I'm having trouble keeping my eyes off those powerful, green muscles and that wide chest.

"Professor Irontree, no apology is necessary. From what I understand, you were the victim of some kind of attack? The police mentioned something about a chemical device?"

"Yes. A scent bomb designed to trigger orc winter instincts. It was an act of sabotage by those opposed to our integration efforts."

"Despicable," VanWagoner says firmly. "I want you to know that Black Oak Academy stands firmly behind both of you. Which brings me to tomorrow's classes…can you both continue teaching remotely as soon as tomorrow?"

I look at Garlen and smile. He smiles back, and my belly flutters again, wanting to kiss those lips. "Absolutely," I say, forcing myself to focus on the matter at hand. "We've already discussed it. Professor Irontree and I will both teach remotely from his home until spring break."

"Actually," Garlen adds, "I believe our remote teaching arrangement might be even more effective now. Ms. Willis and I have had time to perfect our collaborative method."

Oh my, how does he manage to sound this professional when he was basically Hulk-smash just an hour ago? My mind flashes to images of working together with this orc, in this house for the next two months, and it sounds like the best teaching arrangement ever invented. I look down at his rough, green hands and I want them on my naked body.

"Excellent. And Ms. Willis, you're comfortable with this arrangement? The media is portraying this as quite the... romantic development."

My cheeks heat up, but I keep my voice steady. "I'm very comfortable with this arrangement, Mr. VanWagoner." And then I look at Garlen and over at the rest of the family and add, "Garlen and I were originally co-teachers but as you can tell our relationship has grown into something more. We work well together, and I believe our students will continue to receive the highest quality education."

"That's what I like to hear. Now, I'll need you both available for a brief video conference with the school board tomorrow morning at seven o'clock, before classes begin. Just to discuss logistics and address any concerns."

Garlen nods toward the phone. "Of course. We'll be ready."

"Perfect. Oh, and Professor Irontree? That first lesson you two taught together...I've had three parents call asking if their children can transfer into your class. You're quite the natural teacher."

A genuine smile spreads across Garlen's face, exposing more tusk. "Thank you. That means a great deal."

"Well, I'll let you both get settled. Take care, and I'll see you both on screen tomorrow morning."

"Thank you, Mr. VanWagoner," I say. "We'll talk tomorrow."

I end the call and immediately scroll to Anna's number. "Now I'm going to check on Anna."

"Yes," a deep voice says. "She needs to be reassured." I look up and see that Keric has moved and stands above me.

I hit her contact and put it on speaker again.

"Ellie," Anna's kind voice comes through immediately. "I'm happy you're calling. Oh my gosh, are you okay? I've been worried sick."

"I'm fine, Anna. I'm sorry I didn't call sooner. Things have been intense."

"Intense is one word for it. That footage is everywhere. The way you just walked up to him like that. At first, I thought you'd lost your mind."

Are Garlen's cheeks getting red?

I can't help but smile. "Anna, you need to know I'm here with Professor Irontree. You're on speaker. In fact, all his relatives are here too. We just called VanWagoner and now we're calling you next."

"What? Oh gosh, um, hello everyone. I'm Anna Kim, from the English department."

"Ms. Kim," Garlen's voice is warm and professional. "I apologize for the disruption today, when I stormed onto the campus. Please know that I was the victim of a scent bomb I inhaled, which caused me to change and behave that way. Now that I'm back to normal, I want to make sure that you are all right. In fact, I suspect it will take time for me to apologize to everyone I affected today. I hope you weren't too shaken by the incident."

I look over at him again with wide eyes. Damn, this man could be a public speaker. He's that good at this. I'm definitely letting him take lead tomorrow morning when dealing with the school board. What a relief.

"Thank you for saying that, and I'm sorry that happened to you. Actually," Anna replies, "one of your family members— Keric, I think?—made sure I got safely back inside the building. He was very protective of me and took the time to talk me down, which I appreciate."

Keric's expression is unreadable.

I pause a beat, giving room for him to reply if he wants, but he remains quiet. "That's...that's good to hear," I quickly add. "I'm happy he was there for you. Anna, I'm calling too because I want you to know that I'm going to be staying, um, living, with Garlen at his home I'm certain at least until spring break."

"Oh *really*?" she comments.

"Yes," I chuckle. "And this also means we're both going to be teaching remotely together from his home. We've learned that after the lingering effects of that scent bomb, it's best if I stay close to him. It helps Garlen to keep his equilibrium."

"That actually makes sense," Anna says thoughtfully. "After today's excitement, both of you remote teaching might be the safest option. Plus, you two work so well together. I already told you this earlier, but Professor Irontree needs to know too that the buzz around campus is that the students absolutely love having you as their teacher and they loved the lesson and are hungry for more. You're a popular guy on campus right now."

I swear he's beaming with pride. "Thank you," Garlen coughs. "That's very encouraging to hear."

"Will you need help setting up anything technical on the school end?" Anna asks. "I'm pretty good with all the equipment. Your first class is during my break so I could go in there and double-check that everything is set up, for VanWagoner."

"Do you think he's going to call in a sub for me, to get each class going and be the teacher in the room?"

"No, I'm ninety-nine percent certain, at least at first, that he's going to be in that room himself. This is because that's how many eyes are on this now and he'll want it to go perfect."

"True," I reply. "We'll need someone to manage the classroom while we're teaching remotely, might as well be the principal. Thank you for offering to help."

"No problem. And Ellie? I'm glad you're safe. I have to admit, when I first saw Professor Garlen in that state, charging across the parking lot..." She trails off.

"He was never going to hurt me," I say softly, looking at Garlen. "The scent bomb had scrambled his brain and he thought I was in danger. He was coming to protect me. All I did was let him know I was safe and that I was staying with him."

"Well," Anna says with a slightly breathless laugh, "it's certainly the most romantic rescue I've ever witnessed. You two are going to be famous."

I blink with surprise.

"They are both already famous," Jonus mutters from across

the room. "The internet is calling them the new Beauty and the Beast."

"Is that good or bad?" I ask nervously.

"Definitely good," Anna assures me. "It's all over the news and social media. The comments and videos I'm seeing are overwhelmingly positive. People are calling you brave, calling it true love, saying it's proof that despite the odds, integration can work."

Relief floods through me. "That's...actually really wonderful to hear."

"Right? Get some rest," Anna says. "You sound tired. I'll handle everything on the school end tomorrow. You two just focus on the lesson and we'll do the rest."

"Thank you, Anna. You're the best."

"You know it," she laughs. "And one more thing. The media is hounding me already, trying to get me to talk about what happened. What should I do? Do you want me to keep quiet? Or is there something you do want me to say if I'm asked? Just let me know."

"Say the truth," Keric answers.

I smile up at him. "Yes, just say what feels comfortable to you. We have nothing to hide."

"Oh, okay. I'll do that then."

We exchange a few more quick words and then I end the call and look around the room at all the orcs watching us. "Well, that went better than expected."

CHAPTER 22

Garlen

MINUTES later they bring out the chains and click them on my wrists.

My female looks horrified. "I haven't seen you like this since I saw them tackle you on my front yard that first day. Are you sure about this? Those are so heavy. I mean, I understand you needing to be handcuffed but are all those chains around your waist really necessary?"

"Yes," my relatives answer in unison.

"Well, then."

"Ellie, these might not even be enough. But at least they will slow me down until the others can come and sedate me." I look at Dane. "If these don't work and you have to restrain me to keep Ellie safe, then you have my permission to separate me from her permanently and keep me caged again."

"Agreed," he answers.

My female places her hands on her hips. "Garlen, that won't happen."

"You don't know that."

She exhales, and then a yawn escapes her lovely lips.

"My bride needs food and a nap," I announce.

Ellie bites her lip, her cheeks turning pink. "It's true. At this time of day I usually change into my flop clothes and have a snack and sometimes even take a quick nap in the recliner. But after all that's happened today, I think I'm fading fast. I was so excited about our first day co-teaching I didn't sleep well last night, and then we had to walk all the way home." She meets my gaze. "You've got to feel tired too."

"I do," I agree. "And I'd like a chance to change out of these rags."

"Yes," she chuckles. "You're half-naked. Not that I mind but I bet you'd like to wear proper clothes again."

"Take her upstairs," Aldar says. "We will bring up a tray for both of you. What type of food do you prefer, Ellie? Do you like meat and orc ale?"

"I like meat, but I don't think I could handle your ale right now."

They all let out deep laughs.

"I will do my best to bring up some human-style food for you too."

"Thank you."

"And the media?" I question, lifting my chin towards the front windows.

A deep growl rumbles in Jonus's chest. "We will make sure they remain off our property and yours and that they respect our privacy."

"Give me your car keys," Dane announces to Ellie. "We'll go and get your car from the school and bring it back."

She quickly pulls her keys out of her purse and hands them over to my uncle. "Thank you."

I take her hand and pull Ellie up with me and we both leave the front room behind. "That is the door to the basement and that's the door to the garage," I tell her as I give an impromptu tour. "There are three bedrooms down here and two upstairs. My bedroom is upstairs." I climb the stairs slowly, so she has time to grow accustomed to the shift of my chains.

Upstairs there's a lofted living space and short hallway. I

open my bedroom door and my bride steps inside and looks around, wide-eyed. "Oh wow," she gasps. "I had no idea you lived in such splendor."

I crook an eyebrow.

She shakes her head. "I'm sorry, of course I knew this home is nice, because of how the outside looks, but I guess I didn't think you'd have all the furniture and décor so quickly since you moved in only two weeks ago and spent most of that time caged."

I watch as Ellie moves about the room, touching the dark bedding of the king-sized bed. Over the last two weeks I fantasized about this moment, when I would be able to bring her into my domicile and show my bride the room that I hoped we would share. It is a large space with a balcony that overlooks the backyard, a sitting area with a couch and a fireplace. There's also an enormous closet and a large bathroom. I shrug. "We hired human movers and a decorator."

"I don't even remember seeing you move in."

"We happened to arrive late at night and got it all in at once. Since then, my relatives have been working on any unpacking that was left. It's now all done and we're moved in."

She walks around the bed and stops in front of the gas fireplace. "This room is all yours? You don't share it with anyone else?"

"This home has five bedrooms so we each have our own room. I have the primary bedroom. I was planning on living here for the next six months and then hopefully I would be asked back for next year and many years after that. I wanted to live here and work, even before I met you."

"That's good to hear," Ellie says. "I was hoping the same thing, that you'd say you liked Truckee enough to stay. I really believe that if we can get past this part, what you are wishing will really happen."

"I appreciate you taking a chance with me."

She gives me a wide smile. "Don't worry about what

happened today. The last man I was with started off by showing his fake, too-nice part of himself to me. He basically faked being a good guy. Then much later I found out that he wasn't a good guy. I find it comforting that I've already seen your worst parts. And we've already overcome those parts. Even though we've only known each other for what, two weeks now, I feel I know you. And I hope you feel you know me."

I take a step closer. "I hope I will not frighten you away and you will want to remain with me after spring break ends this frenzy. We met through those letters but now we can spend private time together."

"I want the same."

I blow out the breath I didn't know I'd been holding. "I'm going to go change out of these rags and into fresh clothes, I'll be right back."

Ellie waves a hand and walks toward the glass door that leads to the balcony. "No worries, I like the idea of having a moment to look around the place I'll be calling home for at least the next two months."

A smile widens across my face at that thought. I move into the walk-in closet and quickly remember that changing clothes while handcuffed, with chains around my waist, is difficult. Normally, Keric helps me with my buckle. I'm seconds from having to embarrass myself and ask for help when the shredded pants finally drop to the floor. I manage to pull on a pair of black pajama pants. The difference is that I don't also have the previous shackles on my ankles and the chains that linked my legs to my waist. The handcuffs that keep my hands in front of me and the accompanying chains leave a small amount of flexibility to put on my own clothes.

I exit the closet, feeling better about my appearance and the fact that my shaft is no longer obscenely tented.

My female has removed her coat, boots, scarf and gloves. She's even taken off her black blazer and wears a long-sleeved white, silky shirt and grey pants. "Oh, I'm jealous," she says. "I wish I had my loungewear here to change into."

"We can get those for you right now."

"That might take awhile to get from next door, first I want to eat…" she drifts around the room and sits on the couch, changing the subject. "The good news is that all the lesson plans for tomorrow are already done. It's a good thing we are a week ahead in lesson planning."

A heavy knock interrupts our conversation. "Come in," I call.

Aldar enters carrying a large wooden tray loaded with food. "An early dinner for two," he announces, walking into the room and placing it on the small table in the sitting area. "Seared meat, roasted vegetables, fresh bread, and some of those human crackers Ellie might prefer."

"Thank you for all of this," my female says, standing to examine the offerings. "This looks wonderful. And it's so nice of you to bring this food upstairs for us. I feel spoiled, like we're at a fancy hotel."

"We want you to feel at home here. All of us are truly grateful that you are staying with us and calming this raging beast. We hated having to tend to his every need in the basement." He looks over at me. "You can take your own showers now."

I grunt in response.

"There's also a pitcher of water and some of that herbal tea Dane found at the human market," Aldar adds before departing.

Ellie pulls out her phone. "I should call Zoe before I eat. Do you mind?"

"Not at all, as long as you don't mind if I eat while you talk."

She picks up a cracker, pops it into her mouth and gives me a wide smile in return.

This is my cue and I begin eating ferociously, because my body is truly depleted after my transformation.

Ellie sends a text to her mother and soon my female is able to FaceTime with her daughter. I watch with growing warmth as my future stepdaughter's small human face fills the screen. She does look very much like her mother, with the same type of glorious golden-red hair and that same spark of genuine friendliness that I sense from her mother towards most humans, as well as orcs.

"Hey Zoe, how are you doing?"

"Mommy, are you having a sleepover with Garlen?"

Ellie looks over at me and then back to her daughter and laughs. "Something like that, baby girl." She tilts the screen for a moment so that Zoe can have a view of me devouring a large meat stick. I lift my chin and continue eating. "First, we're eating though because we're starved. Are you being good for Grandma?"

"Yes. We made another hat for Scarlett. Grandma said you're helping Garlen feel better."

"That's right. Garlen was sick and he feels better if I'm close to him and he can inhale my scent. This means I won't be there in the house with you in the morning while you're getting ready, but I'll see you tomorrow after school, okay?"

"Can I visit Garlen too?"

Ellie glances at me.

I nod.

"Of course you can visit. We'll figure all of that out later."

Ellie talks to her daughter for a while longer and then speaks to her mother briefly to coordinate tomorrow's schedule. Laurie lets her know that she's packing clothing and something called "toiletries" and my uncle will bring her luggage.

I'm struck by how naturally she includes me in these family conversations, as if I already belong.

Finally, the communication is complete.

Ellie holds up a remote. "Do you mind if I turn on the fireplace?"

I nod in agreement and watch as she smiles in delight as she fiddles with the different settings.

"I should probably change before I eat this food," Ellie announces, looking down at her work clothes. "I'm worried I'll get this silk shirt stained. These aren't exactly comfortable for sleeping. My mom is sending my stuff over but that will take awhile…"

I gesture toward my dresser. "You can borrow anything you need. My shirts will be large on you, but they're clean."

Ellie opens drawers and looks through my clothes with curiosity and selects a soft gray t-shirt. Then my female disappears into the bathroom and reappears only wearing my shirt that falls to her mid-thighs. The sight of her in my clothing sends a possessive thrill I have to carefully control.

She bites her lip and twirls her hair. "Does this look okay?"

My gaze travels from the heft of her breasts to the flare of her hips and down to her perfect little toes. "You are the sexiest female I have ever encountered," I growl.

She laughs. "I bet you say that to all the girls."

Ellie bounces over and sits down next to me again on the couch. Soon she has a plate of food on her lap. We continue to eat and talk. "Did you buy this house because you knew I lived next door?" she questions.

"No, that was simply a happy coincidence."

"Do you own this house, or is it co-owned by all of you?"

"I own this domicile, but I made sure the house I purchased would be large enough to accommodate all my relatives. I like the idea of them having a home base, a sort of mini commune within the larger human world. They can come and go as they please but have a place to stay. All of us are interested in moving out of our communes and living amongst humans, but I was the first to have a job to try out. Any of us could have purchased this home, but I was the one to have it in my name because it was more likely that I would stay and possibly make it a real home."

We're both quiet for a moment as we eat, and then Ellie says something surprising. "I want you to know I'm not one of those women who chases after orcs because they hate human men. It doesn't matter to me that much if you were orc or human, what matters most is that I like you."

I laugh. "But if you did feel that way, it would be entirely understandable."

She grins over at me. "Do orcs believe they are better than human men?"

"Yes."

She crooks an eyebrow. "In all ways?"

I nod. "You are with me because orcs do it better."

"Orcs do what better?"

"Everything."

She rolls her eyes.

I shrug. "We do."

"Um, quick reminder that for millennia your species used to regularly kidnap women off the street and take them to your cave, or commune, and that woman would never be seen or heard from again."

I open my mouth to remind her that modern orcs don't kidnap but then I look down at my handcuffs.

She leans into my side. "But I do have to admit, I wouldn't mind finding out if what you say is true."

"Finish your food," I grumble.

CHAPTER 23
Garlen

EVENTUALLY, I've eaten every scrap of food on the tray that wasn't eaten by my bride. I carefully balance the empty tray in one hand and manage to open the door with the other, then place the tray in the hallway.

Moving awkwardly like this in front of Ellie is not the best circumstance. Half the chains are removed which is good, but the restraints that remain still cause great difficulty. Yes, this was my idea to keep the chains and I don't regret it, it's still necessary to keep Ellie safe from me. But that doesn't mean I have to enjoy the restraints.

"Sleep," I order.

She gives me a fake military salute. "Yes, sir."

My lips twitch. My female is obviously becoming more comfortable around me. It pleases me that she isn't frightened of me in the least, despite how I've behaved.

Soon we are in bed together, ready to sleep. It's odd being in bed so early, but this time of year the sun sets early and it's already dark outside. Both of us are under the covers and I'm certainly pleased to be back in my own bed and not in the narrow cot downstairs. This bed is extra-long, able to accommodate my horns and still leave room for my feet. And I'm happy to have Ellie beside me. "I've always slept alone," I comment.

She looks over at me. "Can you sleep with me here, in this bed with you? Are you trying to say you want me to take the couch?"

"Why would I say that? If anything, I want you closer." Confusion crosses her soft features, so I force myself to explain further. "Orcs speak very abrupt and plain to each other. We are direct. Humans speak in a much more convoluted way, with double meanings and emotions that we do not quite understand. One of the reasons why I was chosen for this teaching assignment is because of my speaking skills, which I can modify to sound more human. Jonus is good at this too. But when I'm tired, I might sound more orc-like than usual."

"I understand. Thank you for explaining. And there's something I need to explain too." Ellie turns on her side, facing me. "First, I want you to know this bed is freakishly comfortable and I love this bedding. I thought I would miss my own bed and pillows, but I don't, at all. I like this better. And second, I was trying to say earlier that I'm with you not because you're an orc but because of you. Who you are. Your personality. I think we have a lot in common."

"You only like my personality?"

Her eyes linger on my bare chest and the outline of my erection that is still visible under the covers. "Well, of course I'm attracted to you."

I inhale deep. "Yes, I can scent your arousal."

Her brow furrows. "You can smell that on me that I...I want to kiss you and touch you all over?"

Should I tell her that I've scented her arousal since that first moment on her front yard? Maybe not. Too soon. "I know that you want me to bring you relief and I want to give you that relief."

She bites her lip. "What exactly do you mean when you're

talking about bringing me relief? Are we both thinking the same…?"

"I want my face between your thighs, licking and sucking until you scream out your release and come on my tongue."

Her eyes widen. "Oh my." Ellie shifts, obviously trying to get comfortable. I can also scent a new wave of arousal. She looks down at my chains. "I want you to do that and you want that, but can you touch me right now? I thought the whole point of the chains was that there would be no touching. This is why I was sad to see you like that. To me, it was a barrier. I know we need to remain close but I thought not too close. I felt lucky to simply be invited to sleep next to you on this big bed. But I thought there would be no kissing or any snuggling, just us side by side and maybe some hand holding."

I take a deep, calming breath. "I thought the boundaries would be the same as you described but now that we've spent more time together this evening, just the two of us in this room, I believe I can tend to you while retaining my composure."

She moves closer. "I would love for you to tend to me."

"But first, we need rules."

"Yes, tell me."

"If I ask you to stop touching me a certain way, you must stop, only because I like it too much and I'm losing control."

"I can do that."

"And don't touch my cock. I'm not ready for that yet."

Her eyes dart to my tented erection and then back to my face.

"If I start to behave in a way that makes you uncomfortable, you must yell out for the others. Don't wait too long, because I might get to a state where these chains won't keep me from you."

"How would they hear me if most of their rooms are downstairs?"

"Orcs have excellent hearing."

"Can they hear what I'm saying right now?"

"Possibly."

Her eyes linger on my lips. "Well, then they'll know how much I want to kiss you. Is kissing okay?"

This confession breaks what little restraint I have left. "Come here," I growl. "Take what you want."

She moves even closer and her lips are now so close to mine. I want my arms around her, to pull her in tight, but this is Ellie's choice and I will wait as patiently as possible for my first kiss from my bride.

Her lips capture mine, careful of my tusks. We both moan as desire flares between us. The kiss starts out sweet and then morphs into steamy. Ellie's hands come up to frame my face, fingers tracing the edge of my horns. The chains around my wrists clink as I struggle not to grab her and pull her closer.

"Don't touch my horns," I rasp against her lips. "I won't be able to control myself if you do that again."

She nods in understanding but doesn't stop kissing me. Our mouths move together. She tastes amazing, like the herbal tea I tasted earlier. Does she realize this is my first kiss? The scent of her arousal grows stronger and the sweet scent makes my cock throb. Kissing Ellie feels right. Natural. I want my arms around her, but that will have to wait. Her tongue brushes against mine and I want more, so much more.

When we finally break apart, we're both breathing hard.

"I should let you rest," I murmur, though every fiber of my being wants to continue.

"Do you still want to bring me…relief?"

My cock leaks at her words. "I cannot give you relief in exactly the way I want, just yet. But, if you allow, I can put my hand between your thighs and bring you to orgasm."

"Please."

"You are going to have to sit on my stomach, basically on top of the tips of my hands so I can touch you with my fingers."

"Ooh. Should I take off my underwear?" she boldly questions.

"No," I groan. "I'm not ready for that yet."

In moments Ellie pushes the covers back, shifts and sits up right, trying to move a leg over me. I'm allowed an erotic flash of her white underwear between her thick thighs. I want to help her, position her right where I can reach her pussy, but my cuffs only allow slight movement. Finally, she shifts until her knees are on either side of my stomach.

I look up at my beautiful female, wearing my shirt, taking in the magnificent sight of her up so close. That hair spread out over her shoulders, her lips swollen from my kisses and her eyes bright with desire.

"Move closer," I say, trying to stay calm at not being able to touch her as I want, which causes agitation. "Closer."

She is just above my hard cock and her warm pussy rests on the tips of my fingers, as asked, and I know that I can move my hands enough to easily finger her clit.

"Garlen, are you sure I'm not...too heavy for you, sitting on top of you like this?"

"No," I chuckle. "You are light as air. I could've easily moved you with my arms, but my cuffs won't allow it. In the future you'll see how easily I can move you about."

"Okay," she smiles.

"Can I put my hand in your underwear and play with your clit?"

"Please."

"This time I will only touch you here, but in the future I will put my fingers in your channel too. And I might want to suck or pinch your nipples while kissing you."

"And I would want to hold onto your horns while I come."

A moan escapes my lips.

"Do you want me to take off my shirt and bra?"

I love this female. She has no idea how magnificent she truly is. "No, viewing your perfect breasts will cause me to lose control. I will have to wait."

"Then we'll wait."

My hands move aside her underwear and I'm right there,

feeling her wet pussy. "You're so wet," I rasp, working to remain sane.

"For you. Only you."

And then I have a finger against her clit and I move it and check for her response.

I continue to stroke that spot that I know brings a female relief. I might be a virgin, but I also have done my research on how to pleasure a female, in case I ever did find my bride. My studies have finally come in handy, allowing me to touch her just as she likes. I study her face, the way her body moves and the quickening of her breaths. I learn she likes it best when I don't touch her clit directly but have my thick finger right next to it.

"Oh yes, right there." She leans forward and drops her head, bracing onto my forearms. I work her faster, giving her exactly what she needs. Her hips undulate, trying to push harder against my hand. She's so damn hot and wet. My cock throbs in my pants.

The cuffs make this an awkward angle, but I continue to move my finger faster against her hard clit, keeping up a steady pace of what she likes.

"Oh Garlen," Ellie cries out. And then she freezes above me for a moment and then cries out, her nails digging into my skin. Her body shudders and there is a gush of warm moisture on my fingertips.

I slowly pull my hand out of her underwear. She watches in wonder as I lick her juices off my finger. My eyes close as I take in her scent, her taste and the intensity of a bride's satisfaction.

"Can I kiss you again?"

"Please."

She leans down and gives me a passionate kiss, filled with all the desire of a bride in need of a rough fucking from her orc. One day, I will fill this female with my seed and see her swollen with our orc son. Soon. Soon.

The kiss ends and I remain still as she moves off me. Ellie glances again at my tented erection. "Are you sure…?"

"I'm sure. I might want you underneath me, fucking you hard, but that will have to wait."

"Are you going to be able to sleep?"

"Yes," I lie.

She curls up against my side, her head on my chest. "This feels perfect," she whispers. "I've been wanting to sleep next to you since the night you sent that first letter."

I kiss the top of her head. "I've been wanting you in my bed like this since I first saw you in your yard and inhaled your compatible scent."

There's a scratch at the door.

"What's that?"

"Just a moment, I forgot someone."

Ellie moves back and I get out of bed and let the dog inside. Loki gives me a stubborn look, letting me know he's highly disappointed in me for leaving him out of the room.

I return to the bed. This time Ellie has turned, offering her back to me and she sleeps on her side. I spoon her from behind with my chained hands and erection trapped between our bodies. This proves surprisingly comfortable. My chin on the top of her head and her satisfied scent in my lungs has an enormous calming effect. Within minutes, Ellie is asleep in my arms.

My dog sleeps in his own bed near the fireplace.

I remain awake long into the night, watching over my female, memorizing the feel of her warm body against mine, and fighting the constant urge to wake her with the slide of my cock inside of her wet channel.

CHAPTER 24
Ellie

THE NEXT MORNING, I look out the front windows of Garlen's home, with the sun barely rising. It's shadowy outside but I sip at my coffee, and notice that all the media out front is gone. I turn around with a wide smile on my face. "It's so quiet outside."

Dane snorts. "They all learned they must remain out of our neighborhood and can only enter at the front gate if allowed by one of us. And if we see a single drone or helicopter overhead there will be consequences."

"What front gate?"

"We worked together with the neighborhood watch and the newly formed homeowner's association and donated enough money for a gate to be installed."

I blink up at him. "This happened overnight? While I was sleeping, a brand-new gate to our neighborhood was installed?"

Aldar pours me another cup of coffee. "We offered generous bonuses to the human workers and their employer for getting it done within a tight time frame."

I look around at the five orcs assembled at the dining room table. "You paid extra for that gate to be built and installed overnight?"

Dane shrugs. "Yes."

I cross my arms. "How rich are you guys?"

"We have a lot of gold leftover from previous centuries of gold mining," Keric says.

My mouth drops open.

Garlen drags his chains close and explains. "North American orcs lived in caves in ancient times and in more recent centuries some of us have moved onto communes in the forests, closer to humans. We brought our gold and jewels with us when we moved from the cave to the commune. We've never had much need to spend it, but we keep it stored in case we need to negotiate or purchase items from humans."

"Like buying privacy gates overnight," I murmur as I return to my seat next to Garlen, the sexy orc who lit up my world last night. I had no idea Professor Irontree would be so diligent at providing me with orgasmic "relief" in his king-sized bed. And I also had no idea he and the other Irontrees were so damn wealthy they could toss money at last minute, local building projects.

All in all, neither are bad revelations.

I take another sip of my coffee, trying to hide my smile.

Jonus looks up from his massive plate of eggs and bacon. "Speaking of media, they desperately want to be in contact with you both. I've been fielding calls and emails since yesterday."

"They've never called me or even emailed directly," I say, confused.

"Since the moment this all began I've let them know that I am their contact. I tell them I'm your agent," Jonus grins, clearly pleased with himself.

"You did?"

"Yes, and the good news is all the media believe this and they contact me all the time, and I put them off with various excuses. I did send them pictures of Garlen's former cage and pictures of Loki with an explanation of that particular breed. This has kept them busy with content. But I believe they will never go away until you and Garlen both give them a proper interview."

Garlen leans back in his chair, chains clinking, his dog in his lap. "What kind of interview are they requesting?"

"Joint interview. Something like Good Morning America or 60 Minutes. They want the full story. They want to know how you two met, the details of orc winter biology, the integration program, the present status of your relationship." Jonus scrolls through his phone. "Actually, the offers are quite lucrative. Some are offering payment."

"We should probably do it," I say thoughtfully. "Get our correct version of the story out there instead of letting people make things up."

"I agree," Garlen nods. "But not until we've had more time to settle into our routine."

"I'll tell them maybe next week. Keep them interested but not pushy."

"I don't care about being paid at all," I say. "And I only want to give this interview to Oprah Winfrey."

"Who?" Garlen questions. "Is that a famous human journalist?"

"Yes. She's very famous and basically the only person I'd feel comfortable and safe with as our interviewer. You'll like her a lot. She's well-known for being easy to get along with."

"Okay," Jonus says. "Good to know. I'll string the others along and play them against each other and in the end only pick this Oprah Winfrey you speak of."

Aldar checks his watch. "You two have that school board call in twenty minutes."

I wrinkle my nose. "Right. The seven o'clock video conference."

Garlen reaches over and takes my hand, his chains dragging across the table. "We'll do fine."

"I agree, but only because you'll be there with me." I squeeze his hand, the one that was touching me so intimately last night. I look into those gorgeous eyes, trying to focus on work and not on his sexy body. "Okay, let's get ready."

We head upstairs for our first official remote teaching day. Loki, the adorable corgi, follows us up, wanting to be part of the show.

The sitting area in Garlen's bedroom has been turned into a setup that looks very much like an actual broadcast studio. There's a backdrop, professional lighting, microphones and a nice camera mounted on the coffee table.

It's amazing.

If it were up to me all we'd have was a laptop and maybe we'd each have a pair of ear buds.

Early this morning Dane arrived at our room with two suitcases stuffed with all my clothes and toiletries, packed by my mother. She'd even sent a travel steamer and my favorite shampoo. Jonus arrived a few minutes later to bring in and set up the fancy equipment for the remote teaching.

Garlen took a quick shower first, because he'd be faster than me. Then he got dressed and went downstairs. I showered and got ready and also spent a little bit of time unpacking and placing my things in the bathroom and in the closet. That part was exciting. I'm loving the idea of playing house with Garlen. We're essentially having a trial run for an actual marriage.

And now, as I look around the closet, with my clothes on one side and his on the other, I'm loving the idea of a real marriage.

"Can you help me button up and tuck in this shirt?"

I grin and step close. "Sure." My mind floats back again to last night and how it felt to kiss Garlen and have his hands in my underwear. Is he going to do that again tonight? Will I get this type of attention each night and maybe, each morning too? When will I be able to touch him that way in response? Will I have to really wait all the way until spring break to see him fully naked?

"Ellie?"

"Hmm?"

"Can you button my shirt and tuck in my pants so we can get to work?"

"Oh, yes. Sorry."

I fix his shirt and then he uses his hands to lift my chin. I gaze up at his dark, sparkling eyes. "I want you too," he says. "All I can think about too is last night and how I'd love to throw you on the bed and let you have your way with me, but…"

"We've got work to do."

"Yes."

I give him a quick kiss on the lips and then walk with him out of the closet and back to our little makeshift studio.

Minutes later we're both seated together on the couch with the laptop open and all the equipment and software properly turned on.

"Ready?" Garlen asks, adjusting his position so the chains aren't visible on camera.

I smooth my navy-blue, double-breasted blazer and nod. "Ready. But I want you to know that I'm going to let you do all the talking."

Garlen looks at me with surprise.

I wink at him in return.

The video call connects and Principal VanWagoner appears on screen along with three school board members. "Good morning, Professor Irontree, Ms. Willis. Thank you for making time for this call."

"Of course," Garlen responds professionally. "We're both here because we are committed to maintaining the highest educational standards despite our remote arrangement."

"That's exactly what we want to hear," says Mrs. Xiong. "Yesterday's incident has brought unprecedented attention to Black Oak Academy. We want to ensure we're handling this properly."

"I know you've been inundated with response from the media, but has there been any negative reactions from parents?" Garlen asks.

"Quite the opposite," VanWagoner responds. "We've had twelve more new enrollment inquiries since yesterday. Parents are specifically requesting your joint classes. We've now had to start a waiting list."

"That's wonderful news," I say, relief flooding through me.

"Now, about the logistics," continues Mrs. Xiong. "You'll both be teaching remotely for how long?"

"Until spring break," Garlen answers. "The winter season affects my... biology in ways that make close proximity to humans inadvisable."

"We understand. And Ms. Willis, you're comfortable with this arrangement?"

"Completely comfortable. Professor Irontree and I have developed not only a close relationship but an excellent teaching partnership. I believe our remote collaboration will be even more effective now, with me here beside him instead of how it was before, with us apart."

The call continues for another twenty minutes, allowing introductions and questions from all the board members present, covering technical details and scheduling. Unfortunately, I do end up having to answer one more question, but other than that I'm happy to remain silent. When we finally disconnect, I slump back in my chair.

"That went well," Garlen observes dryly.

I slap him on his considerable shoulder. "You did great."

Suddenly there's a knock on the bedroom door and it swings open to reveal my baby girl in the doorway, holding Dane's hand.

"Mommy?"

"Zoe," I cry out. I hop up and rush over to give her a big hug. "I missed you baby. I'm happy you're here."

Dane hands me a small bag that includes my favorite brush and hair ties. "Laurie sent me. She said you were supposed to do Zoe's hair and then send her back to finish her breakfast."

I hug the bag close to my chest.

Zoe looks in wonder at the large bedroom, her eyes lingering on the bed, the fireplace and the sitting area with all the equipment. Suddenly I'm happy that I took a moment to remake the bed before I left the room earlier.

Loki runs up for a pet from his favorite person. Garlen says good morning from the couch, trying to hide the chains. I lead her away because there's no time for niceties. "Come on Zoe, we've got to get you back with plenty of time before the bus arrives."

"Mom," Zoe whispers when we're alone in the fancy bathroom, "these orcs have a big house."

I start brushing her hair. "Right? I was surprised too at how fancy this place is and how it's got so many rooms. All of Garlen's relatives each have their own bedroom."

"Do you live here now?"

"Well, I think I might be moving here," I admit.

"Am I going to live here with you too?"

"If I do end up moving here, then of course you're coming here too, because I don't go anywhere without my Zoe."

She remains strangely silent, with no response.

"Do you want to move into this house with me?"

She shrugs.

I think about it more, then I say, "Would you want to live here if you could still see grandma all the time? What if you moved into this house with me someday, but grandma was still next door and she could still take care of you when you went to school and got home? And you could still see Scarlett as much as you see Loki. Would that be okay?"

She nods vigorously.

I laugh. "I'll work on it, honey. I'll make sure that no matter what the grownups end up deciding that things won't change much for you and you get to take your regular bus and see grandma all you want."

She smiles wide.

I put in the last clip. "Okay, I'm all done. Your hair looks cute. Time for school."

Our first remote lesson of the day begins at 8:30. Loki curls up in his dog bed near the fireplace. And we get to work.

Garlen transforms into the natural teacher I witnessed yesterday, his expertise and charisma shining through the screen. The students are engaged and asking thoughtful questions. I find myself falling a little more in love with him as I watch him work.

I'm basically his glorified assistant which is fine with me. I've had many, many years of everything being on me and I'm happy to take a break and let him do most of the actual teaching and I do the background work—the grading, lesson planning, messaging with VanWagoner, emailing the other history teachers, replies to parent messages.

And a very awesome thing about working from home is that I can use our bathroom, eat lunch right here and best of all, there's no commute. I could get used to this.

"Professor Irontree," one student in second period asks, "what's the biggest misconception humans have about orcs?"

Garlen considers this carefully. "Probably that we're beasts that are incapable of change or growth. Humans often see us as either savage primitives or noble warriors, but rarely as individuals capable of education, career ambitions, or…" He looks over at me. "Modern relationships."

I think this orc might be falling in love with me too.

A student who is notorious for always asking the cheeky question, raises her hand. "Is that why integration is important to you personally? Because of your relationship with Ms. Willis?"

There are twitters and gasps of surprise at the question, but Garlen allows it and gives her a thoughtful response.

"Yes, it is important to me personally. Ms. Willis and I are demonstrating that our two species can work together as equals."

I catch his eye and smile.

By the time our third and final class ends at three o'clock in the afternoon, we're both exhausted but exhilarated.

"That went great," I say, closing my laptop. "The students were so engaged today."

"We work well together."

"We do indeed."

I scoot closer, because I've got to give this orc a passionate kiss.

But then a text from my mom interrupts the moment.

Zoe's bus arrives in ten minutes. Should we come over for dinner?

I show Garlen the message. "What do you think? Ready for a family dinner tonight?"

"I'm always ready to eat."

CHAPTER 25
Ellie

THREE HOURS LATER, the dining room table is crowded with all five Irontree orcs plus the three Willis women. Zoe chatters excitedly about her day at school while Loki roams about underneath, begging for scraps.

I'm thankfully changed into my favorite matching loungewear outfit and my comfy, fuzzy slippers.

Aldar and I proved to be a good team in the kitchen. He made the food that the orcs would like best and I was able to cook Zoe's favorite foods and provide a few human side dishes I knew the orcs would like to try. The kitchen itself was wonderful and the cookware that they used was top notch, basically the sets I've always dreamed of owning. All the while, Garlen remained close, watching and chatting with his cousins as we cooked.

And now Mom sits next to Dane and I'm across from the both of them, next to Garlen. Zoe sits between Garlen and Jonus. Aldar and Keric are across the table from her. She looks like she's having a great time being the center of attention amongst all these interesting orcs.

"Garlen, do you like mac and cheese?" Zoe asks, offering him a spoonful from her bowl.

"I've never tried it before, but I'd be honored to taste something you recommend."

She beams as he samples it. "Do you like it?"

"I do. Would you like a bite of my meat?"

Zoe wrinkles her nose and shakes her head. "Yuck."

Garlen lets out a hearty laugh. Despite his handcuffs, he is in the best mood I've seen so far. I suspect that having me nearby isn't the only change. He's out of the basement and able to sleep in his own bed. The teaching is going well. And now he's here with me and my mom and Zoe, being accepted. I think it's sweet that he wants so much to become a part of my little family. What he doesn't know is that I have all the exact same feelings. I've worried that I won't fit in amongst the orcs who are the most important to him too. But so far, I like all his cousins and his uncle. They have been nothing but nice to me. And I believe they like me too. We get along.

And most importantly, Zoe gets along well with Garlen.

I watch this interaction with growing warmth. Marcus never showed interest in Zoe's preferences or opinions. I don't remember seeing them laugh together. Seeing Garlen engage with my daughter so naturally feels like a missing puzzle piece clicking into place.

"Mom," Zoe asks, "can I sleep over here tomorrow night? Like a real sleepover?"

Before I can answer, Laurie jumps in. "We'll see, sweetheart. Let's see how this week goes first."

Dane and my mother exchange a look that doesn't go unnoticed by anyone. Jonus grins into his tankard.

"Dane," Zoe asks suddenly, "are you going to marry Grandma?"

The table goes completely silent. I drop my face in my hands, ready to die from embarrassment. That girl, always digging into other people's business. I have a feeling she's going to grow up and become a match maker. "Zoe..." I start, but mom holds up a hand.

"It's a fair question," she says calmly. "Zoe, to answer your question…Dane and I are getting to know each other better and I'd say we are definitely boyfriend and girlfriend. We'll see what happens next."

I glance over at Dane and note the smile that exposes more tusk.

"I hope you do," Zoe declares. "Then Garlen would be my stepdad and Dane would be my step-grandpa, and I'd have orc uncles." The happiness in her voice makes everyone at the table smile.

"That sounds like a good idea," Garlen says seriously. "If one day, your mother and I decide to get married—and if it would be okay with you and your mom—I'd be happy to be your stepdad."

"When are you getting married?" Zoe asks with six-year-old directness.

"Well," Garlen glances at me, "your mom and I need to date like humans do, for a while first. We need to get to know each other better."

"But you're already living together," she points out.

"She's got a point," Aldar mutters, earning chuckles from around the table.

Garlen leans into Zoe and lifts his cuffed wrists. "Also, we have to wait until I don't need to wear handcuffs anymore. I don't think your mom would like it if she was marrying a chained orc."

Zoe giggles.

After dinner, Zoe insists on showing Garlen her homework while the adults clean up. I watch them together at the kitchen counter, Garlen's massive frame hunched over her tiny worksheet, patiently helping my daughter with an addition facts coloring sheet.

"He's good with her," Mom observes quietly. "I think he's genuinely happy to spend time with our Zoe."

"Yeah, he really does."

"And you? How are you feeling about all this?"

"Twenty-four hours ago, I was a single mom living with my mother, teaching at a new school. Now I'm living with an orc, our relationship is international news, and my daughter is already planning our wedding. Strangely, I'm doing really good. Like this is exactly where I'm supposed to be."

"Are you sure you want to live here, with him, when he's chained? You don't have to do this. Dane told me that you were here of your own free will with zero coercion. I'm just asking to double-check he's right."

"He's right, I want to be here to help Garlen remain sane so he can complete this teaching assignment with me, but also because…" I shrug, suddenly too shy to say more.

"Dane also said all you have to do is tell him, or any of Garlen's relatives, that you want to go home and they will make sure you can immediately leave without having to worry about Garlen chasing you down. They will do that for you, at a moment's notice."

"I know. Aldar pulled me aside early this morning to tell me this. I appreciate them all looking out for me like that. Garlen is the one who insisted on remaining chained so that he wouldn't ever do anything he'd later regret. And also, he let them know that if he starts to ever act like he's starting to go wild again they are to sedate him and separate us. At that point I assume he'll have to be banished to the commune. But I really don't think any of that will be necessary. As you can see, when I'm here with him and he can see that I'm safe, it keeps him calm. My scent in his lungs is like an antidote. And I like that I'm having a chance to get to know the real Garlen. And the real Garlen is…well, he's a hardworking man of honor."

Mom nods approvingly. "Your father would have liked him."

The observation brings tears to my eyes. "You think so?"

"Definitely. Any man who treats you and Zoe with such obvious care and respect would have earned his approval immediately."

. . .

Two hours later my mother and daughter head home with promises to return tomorrow. This set up doesn't bother me so much, because it almost feels like I'm living at home with them still and all that's happened is we're going our separate ways to bed. The good news is that dinner together at the Irontree residence is now going to become a nightly occurrence.

I feel bad that my mom has to take on more when it comes to Zoe though, but I suspect she doesn't mind. It's for a good reason and is only temporary. I'm usually the one who gives Zoe her bath at night, gets her dressed in her pajamas and makes sure she brushes her teeth. I used to read a book to her in bed but lately she'd rather play a game or read on her kid tablet.

I follow Garlen up to our bedroom. My eyes linger on his perfect ass. I want to bite it like an apple. After a whole night of watching this man act so kind and genuine towards my daughter, as well as my mother, I'm finding him sexier than ever, and sad that he's chained and unable to have hot sex because he might do something both of us would later regret.

"Thank you," I say as we both head into the walk-in closet to change into our pajamas. Garlen often needs my help to remove his clothes, especially when he's wearing a belt. This is no hardship.

"For what?"

"The way you were with Zoe tonight. You didn't have to be so patient and sweet with her."

He lets out a deep snort. "Ellie, I already explained this in my letters to you. Remember my gift where I carved the mother fox and the kit? If you become my mate, Zoe becomes my daughter. Of course I want to build a relationship with her."

The certainty in his voice makes my heart flutter. "I know, but are you still certain that's what you want? Now that this is real and you've actually met Zoe and my mother, can you see having not only me, but them in your life too?"

His chains clink as he reaches for my hand. "Now that you've spent more time with my relatives. Could you see yourself wanting them in your life too?"

"Yes, of course. I like all of them."

"Even Keric?"

"Yes," I laugh. "I even like Keric."

"I feel the same towards your family."

It's almost scary how close I feel towards Garlen. We're two different species. He's orc and I'm human. He was raised on a commune in Maine and I was raised in southern California. And yet, I've never felt this close to anyone before. Certainly not with Marcus. And not with anyone else I dated. And over these last few months it's not even the fact that I'm so off the charts, deeply, deeply attracted to this guy, it's that I consider him my best friend.

Not only have I fallen in love with an orc, but I want to marry him too. But I have to admit there's a small part of me that wonders if for him, this is still only a biological imperative. He wants me, because his body is making him want me. But does that mean he loves me too? Sometimes I'm certain that he is falling in love with me and other times not certain at all.

"And are you still certain about wanting a permanent relationship with me?" he questions.

Instead of answering directly, I start unbuckling his belt. Because I'm too chicken to tell him yet about all the love that is growing in my heart, so I try for a distraction that we will both enjoy. "I have an idea."

"What kind of idea?"

"You mentioned earlier about wanting to take a shower before bed. What if... what if we took one together?"

His voice deepens. "Ellie, I don't think—"

"Just a shower. You stay chained, I help you wash your back. Nothing more than that."

He looks down at his feet then back up at me, adorable with the weight of his uncertainty. "We'll both be naked. I am not sure

I can control myself if your beautiful body is exposed to me this way."

"My beautiful body?" I let out a snort. "You are so sweet. Mainly I'm nervous about you seeing me naked and not liking what you see."

I finally get his belt off and the black pants slide down his green, muscular thighs, leaving the outline of his epic erection visible underneath his black underwear.

He gestures toward his crotch. "I am bigger and longer than the average human male. What if you see all of this and are scared away?"

I lick my lips. "Garlen, it's already been established that nothing about you can scare me away."

His gaze lingers on my chest then back to my lips. "I feel the same about you."

I take one of his hands in mine because holding hands is always safe between us. "Last night you said for me not to touch you anywhere except for kisses on the lips. I will respect those boundaries. And I'd love to take a shower with you, but if that's too soon and you think it might cause you to revert to your beast mode, then of course we don't have to do this. It was just a suggestion and it can wait until spring."

"I want this." He inhales. "The more I'm around you and the longer I have your calming scent in my lungs, the more I believe I can touch you, or you can touch me. Last night was proof of how far I've come."

"Well, okay. All that's happening is naked times and back washing. And possibly a kiss or two. Does that sound like it will work?"

He stares at me for a long moment, then slowly nods. "Yes. But even if we aren't touching and I'm under that water and simply reacting from the situation and if I seem like I'm losing control—"

"I'll stop and step away immediately. Shower over."

His wide smile exposes large amounts of white tusk and is

equal parts nervous and anticipatory. "Then yes. Let's take a shower together."

"Can I take off my clothes right now, down to my underwear, like you are? I think it would be a good idea to practice how this works, before we go into the bathroom. Baby steps."

"Yes," he growls. "That is a good idea. We can check how I react to this and then go forward from there."

I kick off my slippers, take a deep breath and start pulling off my top. Underneath I'm wearing my cute but comfortable, matching bra and panties. I pause when I hear a growl rumble in his chest. "Are you sure this is okay? It looks like you're already straining against the chains."

"Slowly. Take your clothes off slowly."

This is basically unbelievable, that this orc is so turned on by the thought of viewing my half naked body, he's having a difficult time restraining himself. Since when did my size eighteen body cause a man to behave this way? Never.

I smile and pull my shirt slowly off my head and toss it aside. Then I lift my chin and look over at him. My best feature is my torso and my second best features I'd say are my hair and teeth. So at least he's seeing this first. It's the moment after I take off this supportive bra that I'm worried about.

"More," he snarls.

So, I take off more.

I slowly, slowly move my wide leg stretch pants down my hips and past my thighs and let them puddle on the floor, then kick them away. And I stand before him in only a matching pink bra and panties. My stomach has a roll in the front and there's that back roll that never seems to go away. Light stretch marks line my hips from carrying Zoe. And there's that pesky cellulite on my thighs.

He closes his eyes, takes a deep breath and opens them again. "You are the sexiest female I've ever seen."

CHAPTER 26
Garlen

IF THIS WERE any other season besides winter, I would already have torn off the rest of Ellie's clothes and her back would be pressed against the wall as I placed her on my dick.

But that will have to wait for another time.

I will remain in control and refrain from roughly taking my female in ways that are beyond her consent.

She wants to take a shower with me.

I want to take a shower with her.

But I also want to make sure I don't turn into a snarling beast, causing all four of my relatives to charge into the bathroom to sedate me.

"I can't get over how nice this shower is," my innocent female chats as we step into our bathroom.

She wears nothing but a bra and panties. I'm a predator, watching its prey.

"The primary bathroom in my house next door is of course very nice, but that's my mom's bathroom. I share the secondary bathroom with my daughter. I've never seen a bathroom this nice in real life, outside of a hotel."

It pleases me that she likes it. I'd purchased this newly built home sight unseen, originally viewing this bedroom online, with its large seating area, walk-in closet and restroom as space not just for me, but for a future mate. I was born and raised on the commune, attending high school at the nearby human school. I lived with my parents while growing up and then for several years with my uncle in his cabin, until I began working at the university. For my first ever purchase of a human-style domicile, I'd allowed myself the brief fantasy that while I was teaching amongst so many humans, I might possibly meet one who connected with me and would become my mate. This was never my primary objective for this teaching assignment, because I could've possibly met my mate at any time in my life, even while in high school. But for some reason, it seemed that it could happen.

These thoughts crowd my mind, leaving me unable to speak. It takes all my energies to not break these chains and lick her all over.

Her female beauty products are everywhere, proving she's moved in and shares this bathroom with me. Ellie's clothes and shoes line one side of the closet and fill the previously empty drawers of the dresser.

I've dreamt of the day when I'd meet my female and wondered if I'd be lucky enough to entice her to stay. Orcs are notorious for being unlucky in love. In ancient times our tendency to kidnap meant that the many of the females never remained behind with their mate after giving birth to their orc son.

Nowadays most females choose to stay because orcs have learned how to treat women with respect. Modern women often have little need for human men or orcs to take care of them financially or even serve as protectors because they can take care of themselves. This means to keep Ellie at my side I must convince her that I'm a value add. A male who will not burden her with unnecessary tasks as if I'm a child in need of caring. I must be a true partner who gives her love, respect and companionship, as well as provide countless orgasms. She's already told me that I must also become a genuine father to her existing human child.

All these requirements I can happily and naturally provide.

First, I must get past this first winter.

I love this human more than life itself. She has no idea what I'd do for her. Ellie, her daughter and any future sons we have together. They will be everything to me and will always come first.

"I know I've brought a lot of products but I'm actually low maintenance compared to other women," she continues to chat. "If I'm going to blow out my hair then okay, I need about an hour or so to get ready, but otherwise I can get ready pretty quickly."

"You will have to help me remove my underwear," I remind her.

"Oh, okay," she smiles. "I can stand in front this time?"

I take a deep breath. "Yes."

My bride loves helping me get dressed. She puts out my underwear so I can slip them on after she steps out of the closet. And later she pulls them down for me, while standing behind me. It's an odd set up, but it works. I've noticed her gaze often lingers on my chest and the bulge of my cock underneath my pants. I want to give it to her, but this will have to wait.

She pulls down my underwear. My throbbing green erection bobs in front of her. A choking sound emanates from her throat.

"Ellie? What is wrong?"

She meets my gaze. "Is that going to fit?"

"When we get to that point, I'll make sure you are ready for me. Do not worry, you will be able to take all of me."

She blows out a breath, reaches over toward the shower, as if she's about to turn on the water and then pauses and turns back to me. "I feel nervous taking off the rest of my clothes. You'd think I wouldn't be, considering I've been overweight like this for most of my adult life and I was married before, but that's not something I look back at fondly. I consider the whole first year of my relationship with my ex to be a lie. It was all a show he was putting on to entrap me. And I was an easy target, I believe, because of my self-doubt caused by my weight."

I reach out and tug her closer, because I sense she has much she wants to say.

Her eyes meet mine. "I'm attracted to you because of your essential goodness. You're a good guy. Also, you may think you have a lot of baggage, but I have a lot of baggage too. When we met, you did lose your mind with that orc winter frenzy, but just prior to that you were performing a citizen's arrest of my ex-husband, who was breaking his restraining order. And, he's still basically stalking me and has banded with a local orc gang. Not many men would want to deal with all of that, not to mention I'm a single mom."

"I'm not a human male, I'm an orc."

She smiles. "I happen to think that's a good thing." Ellie looks away, takes a deep breath and then looks at me again. "You need to know that I've come to realize I never loved him."

"You don't have to tell me this. It doesn't matter one way or the other. I understand that humans are different. You can have many different mates. You can even have pleasure mates before you find your life-long mate."

"I guess I need to say this out loud for my benefit as much as yours. Being with you, getting to know you, has caused me to reevaluate my first marriage even more. Which is amazing considering I went to a whole year of twice-a-month therapy just to get over what happened. I thought I'd loved him, because why else would I marry him? Even after the therapy I thought I'd loved him, but he'd changed and broken my trust with the addiction he couldn't kick and the revelation of his narcissism, which changed him drastically. He's now a criminal. I couldn't be with someone like that anymore and that was why I'd fallen out of love with him. I really tried to be there for him, to help him out of the addiction, but he became more and more verbally abusive, and I was worried he'd become physically abusive too.

And then he was also turning that negative behavior towards Zoe and I had to leave. Luckily, I had the ability to leave. I packed up and went to live with my parents. But what I've now figured out is that I was with him originally because I was settling. I'd told myself that I was lucky to have someone like him—a handsome man who was going places—because normally I'd never have anyone, I'd be alone, because…because I was fat."

A growl rumbles in my chest.

"I first met Marcus twelve years ago, when I was in college. I was the same weight then as I am now. And I was in college in a new town and hadn't made many friends. I'd gone away to college thinking it was going to be this great experience, but it wasn't as great as I'd thought. Marcus was a popular guy on campus and I'd seen him from afar with a variety of gorgeous, thin girls on his arm. He was always at parties and belonged to one of the big fraternities, essentially a frat boy. I was quiet and never partied, but I suppose I secretly wanted that in my life. It was like a secret club I could never become a part of. I wasn't even part of a sorority. This is how introverted I was back then."

While she's talking, I start working on pushing down her panties.

"Well, at the end of the last year in our university," she continues, "Marcus was accused of something, which was never proven, but which caused him to be cancelled socially. So for the last two semesters he was basically alone and not the big guy on campus anymore and during that time is when he asked me out. I basically thought I was getting him on sale. Like I'd gotten a Chanel bag for a screaming deal."

I gently turn her around and lift my cuffs to unclasp her bra.

"During the last six months of our marriage, before I got up the nerve to kick him out and get the divorce and restraining order, he'd started telling me that because I was 'fat' I was lucky to have him. That he couldn't believe he'd settled for someone as ugly as me, that he used to have the most gorgeous rich girls on campus and now he had to take me to work parties when all the other wives were thin. I've never told anyone this stuff, not even the therapist. We mainly talked about his addictions and creating boundaries and keeping my life safe for Zoe. I married Marcus because I thought I was lucky, considering I was overweight, to get a guy like him and I'd never be able to do better than that. I guess I also believed at the beginning that he was seeing beyond the weight too. He used to really tell me that I was beautiful and that he loved me. But then at the end of our marriage he threw that all in my face and told me that he'd just been saying that to get me to marry him. He'd gotten a job with a conservative company who wanted all the executives to be happily married. And also, my dad was a mover and shaker in his field so he thought by being married to his daughter it would help his career, considering he's never actually finished his degree. Marrying me was simply a career move for that time in his life."

All her clothes are removed and now my female stands in all her naked glory. I feel light-headed, stunned at the ability to see every bit of her skin and the curve of her breasts. The tuft of golden hair between her thighs is the most erotic sight of my life.

"What's sad is that at the beginning, I thought for a minute he wanted me exactly as I was."

I step closer and press my erection against her, letting her feel how the sight of her naked body causes by own body to react. "And I was always worried a human female would never want me because of how I look. I am large for an orc. My nose is crooked and my tusks are not perfectly white. I have a cock she might think is too thick. I have tall horns and I talk very loud. What if I accidentally hurt her with my strength?"

"I think you are sexy exactly as you are. I'd never want you to change."

"And I feel the same about you, Ellie. I do not understand how a female of your worth could want an orc as a mate. You could have anyone and you choose me? Are you certain you could make this choice for life?"

She grins. "Wait, wait. Is this the same male who was boasting to me that orcs do it better?"

"We do everything better. But you are such a worthy female, you could choose any human male, or any orc. Why choose this orc?"

"Because, as I said before, not only do I find you sexy, but your essential kindness is a huge turn on."

"That unworthy human male was lucky to have had a female as amazing as you and he threw it all away. I will never make that mistake."

"I took my vows very seriously."

"I'm sure you did."

"I'm telling you this because I know that orcs mate for life."

"This is true. There is no divorce in my species."

"I want to reassure you I can make a lifelong vow. I think I was susceptible to Marcus's attention because I had a lot of self-doubt, because of my size. But just because I was in a marriage that failed, this does not mean that I won't be able to commit to you in the way that you'll need."

She has mentioned her weight many times and I remain confused. "What is wrong with your size?"

She gestures down at herself. "You know, I'm…I'm overweight. I was very self-conscious about it and…and I thought I wasn't good enough and that no man would think I was sexy with all this weight. And then this guy, who'd I'd been crushing on, suddenly asks me out. He seemed so out of my league. I was really swept off my feet by this guy who treated me so well at first and… but I'm not like that anymore. What I'm trying to say is I can't go back to that in my life again. I need to be with someone who wants me just as I am, not wanting me to change."

"Ellie, as I said before, I think you are the sexiest female I've ever seen and I want you exactly the way you are. I love every dip, curve and roll in your desirable little body. Especially that bright golden triangle between your thighs. This will not change. I will feel the same about you one year from now, five years from now, ten years from now. Forever. I won't ever want you to change. Do you expect me to change?"

"No, I don't. I like you exactly as you are."

"Good."

Ellie licks her lips. "How am I supposed to get into the shower with you and ignore that magnificent cock?"

"How am I supposed to get into the shower with you and ignore your tits?"

She smiles. "You don't have to."

"I still don't understand this whole concept of you thinking you were unworthy. Ellie, I am so very lucky that you have decided to give me a chance. You are smart and beautiful, loyal and brave."

"You are so sweet." She turns on the water and checks the temperature. "I have to ask you something though that I can't get out of my head. I wonder sometimes, am I the person you really want, or is your body making you want me."

I nod in understanding. "I understand how this could be confusing to a human. Amongst orcs it's true that our mating urge can occasionally prove wrong. In the past especially, it used to happen often that a male orc would want a female and kidnap her and often that would go wrong for all the reasons you would suspect. But even in instances where there was mutual attraction and it seemed that the female wanted to start something with the male, it was often instead a female pleasure mating and she was horrified to discover she was pregnant with an orc. Females have historically hidden out in communes to give birth to orc sons, then leave their child and mate behind to never return. This proves that not all mating instincts are correct. But there is always something there, that could flourish if given the opportunity."

She pulls me into the shower with her. The water sprays down on the both of us.

"I masturbated here each morning, thinking of you," I admit.

"While you were handcuffed?"

"It was difficult," I chuckle. "But I was always so enflamed that I could've simply rubbed against fabric and found release. I didn't need much to set me off."

"Does that mean you masturbated in your cot in the cage too?"

"Yes, every night and every morning, and that was so I could stay sane."

"Do you need to continue that? I can help."

I take a deep breath, assessing my level of winter madness and I'm pleased to note that I remain steady, which causes me to seriously consider letting her touch me more than I'd originally planned.

"There is no penetration," I remind her, "because I want to wait for that until after spring break, when I can be trusted to take you without needing chains or nearby sedatives. When I can act sane."

"I understand...Can I wash your back?"

"Yes."

She washes my back and I wash her back in return, the best I can with my hands cuffed together. She laughs, teasing me at my lack of movement.

"Sometimes it's easy to forget that we haven't known each other for that long because we fit so well into each other's lives," Ellie comments. "It seems as if I've known you all along."

"I agree. Are you looking at my ass?" I question.

"Yes, I can't help myself. You're so big and strong. I swear you look like a Greek sculpture, but bigger. I feel small next to you."

"I like your size too. If you were smaller, I'd be concerned that you couldn't withstand my orc lust."

"You're right. I can handle all of you...*all* of you," she emphasizes.

I take my aching shaft in hand and give it a few rough strokes so she can see its full length. "This is for you," I tell her because I know how much she loves my cock.

She bounces up on her toes and gives me a kiss on the lips. "Are you trying to tell me something?"

"I want you to touch my cock."

"Oooh, can I use my mouth?"

I close my eyes and take another calming breath. Then I look down at my sexy female who looks glorious with water running down her tempting nipples. "Yes, please. The chains will be my boundaries. I can do this and treat you with respect. Having my female give me the same daily release I required before will keep me steady."

She grabs a towel, puts it on the hard tile floor of the shower and drops to her knees in front of me.

How did I get this lucky?

Ellie moves close and reaches for my thick erection. Seeing her on her knees, naked and boldly taking me in her hand makes me sway with desire. My bride can't take all of me with her small human mouth, but she tries and it is enough. Her blunt teeth make it easier to slide back and forth in her hot mouth. She starts with the crown and I love watching it disappear past her lush lips.

Soon she hums with happiness because she has one small hand on the base of my green shaft and her mouth is moving up and down on the top, busy working my cock just the way she likes. It's the best feeling of my life. Her mouth on my shaft is tight and hot, much better than all those times I awkwardly touched myself these last two weeks.

She doesn't have to do much before I gasp at that familiar tingle. And now I'm so close to jetting my seed in her mouth. "Ellie," I shout, "I'm about to..." And then it hits me hard, the best orgasm of my life. It starts in my spine and rushes through my balls, that tighten and stream out all my seed in her mouth. I roar out my release, shaking as it hits, wave after wave. Then I slump to the side, finally spent.

Ellie takes me like a champion, swallowing all I have to offer again and again. There is so much, it dribbles down the side of her mouth. She pulls back and looks up at me and wipes what's left off her lips and the side of her mouth with a mischievous grin.

"I need to feel your release too," I growl. Then I pull her up and my hand is between her legs feeling all her juicy wetness, wishing I could sink inside of her, or at least pump my fingers inside of her channel. But I feel on edge, despite the release. So I finger her clit instead, just how I know she likes.

"Oh Garlen," she gasps, leaning into me.

I hold her tight as the warm water continues to spray down on us.

She holds onto my neck and kisses me hard as her own orgasm rushes through her body, gushing on my finger.

CHAPTER 27

Ellie

TWO WEEKS LATER...

I wake up to the familiar sound of Garlen's chains.

They clink softly as he shifts beside me and yet they do nothing to decrease his sex appeal.

Poor guy. It must be difficult living with his hands cuffed and literal chains around his waist, linking those cuffs, so that he cannot raise his arms. But then, prior to this he was in a cage and his legs were also chained and cuffed and he was even chained to the wall.

So, as he's told me before, this is an upgrade.

He does this for me, so I can't possibly complain. He thinks he needs the chains, so I suppose he still does. Garlen knows where he's at in his winter rage level and so do his relatives, much better than I do and I trust their judgement.

We've been living together for two weeks now and everything feels different between us. More intimate. More real. We take showers together and sleep together each night. The memory of his hands on my body, the way he looks at me like I'm the most beautiful thing he's ever seen, sends heat through me all over again.

Garlen's kisses remain the stuff of legend. And those tusks are surprisingly sexy. They don't really get in the way of the kisses and I love the feel of them sometimes rubbing against my lips.

Garlen is unbelievably sexy.

After that first evening where he allowed a shower between us, which turned into everything but the actual penetration sex, we've been all over each other. Each night, something else comes online. One night I discovered he was able to suck and pinch on my nipples without losing his mind. Another night he kissed me all over, except between my thighs. I was able to give him a back massage the next evening, which I loved.

I'm really, really enjoying spending these last two weeks with him, talking about work, about life, the universe and everything. And then falling into bed, working around the chains to bring each other satisfaction.

This man heals my heart as well as my mind. And I hope I am providing the same support for him, despite the fact that I cannot take his luscious green cock inside of me, because he says he'll lose control and bad things will happen to good orcs.

Also, he wants to wait until we can fully be together without the chains.

This makes sense, but is such a hard rule to follow, but I do this out of respect. My consent is important to him and conversely his consent is important to me too. But I can hardly wait for spring break to end this torture wherein I can freely touch the orc that I love.

"Good morning," I murmur, turning to face him.

His dark eyes are already open, watching me with that intense gaze that makes my stomach flutter. "Good morning, my bride."

The way he says it, so certain and possessive, makes me want to kiss him again, despite my morning breath. And those darn *rules*. It would be lovely to initiate some morning sex, feeling him slide that enormous green cock inside of me. But I refrain. Instead, I stretch and check the time on my phone. "I need to brush my teeth and take a shower. And we need to get ready for the day."

"Mmm." He leans over and kisses my forehead. "I could stay in this bed with you all day."

"Don't tempt me." I laugh and start to get up, but he catches my hand with his chained ones.

"Ellie." His voice is serious now. "About last night..."

"What about it?" I ask, suddenly nervous. We'd had yet another session where I slid on top of him so he could give me yet another mind-blowing orgasm. Everything was perfect last night but old worries resurface. Did I do something wrong? Was I too forward? Was he secretly turned off by my rolls and bumps of cellulite?

"It was perfect. You are perfect." The sincerity in his voice makes my chest tight with emotion. "I just want you to know that I—"

A loud banging on our bedroom door interrupts whatever he was about to say.

"Garlen. Ellie," Dane's voice booms through the wood.

Garlen immediately sits up, chains rattling. "Come in."

The door bursts open and Dane strides in, his face grim. Behind him are Aldar and Keric, both looking equally serious.

Uh oh. "What's wrong?" I ask, pulling the covers up to my chin.

"It's about Marcus," Dane says simply. "He violated his bail conditions. He's been missing for twenty-four hours."

"Missing?" I squeak. "What do you mean missing?"

"The FBI contacted us because we're listed as your emergency contacts," Dane explains, moving closer to the bed. "Marcus hasn't checked in with his probation officer, hasn't been at his motel, hasn't used his credit cards. He's completely off grid."

"Shit," I breathe, my mind immediately going to Zoe. "Do they think he's coming here?"

"We intercepted some Crimson Tusk communications," Aldar says from the doorway. "They're losing patience with Marcus. He needs to prove his worth or face consequences."

Garlen's entire body tenses beside me. "What kind of consequences?"

"The kind that involve eliminating failed assets," Keric answers grimly.

I feel sick. "So, he's desperate."

"Desperate humans do desperate things," Dane confirms. "The FBI believes he might try something drastic to prove his value to Crimson Tusk."

"Like what?" I ask.

"Since he can't get to you directly," Dane says carefully, "we believe he might try to target Zoe and use her as a way to cause compliance."

The words hit me like a physical blow. I'm grabbing for my robe. "I need to call my mom. I need to make sure Zoe is safe."

"Already done," Dane assures me. "We've contacted the school. Security has been increased around Zoe specifically. Your mother has been informed and is taking extra precautions."

Garlen struggles to get out of bed with his chains, his face dark with fury. He looks so angry he's even scaring me. "I should be protecting them myself."

"You can't," Dane says firmly. "And we've got it covered. There is no dishonor in leaning on your family line in a time like this. As I've always told you, we will look after them because they are our family too. Keric and Aldar will be positioned at the school during pickup. Jonus is monitoring all communications. I'm coordinating with local law enforcement."

I pace in front of the gas fireplace I haven't even had a chance to light yet, biting at my nails.

"Ellie." Garlen's deep voice stops me. "Look at me." He's out of bed too, still in his typical black pajamas. His familiar features and the sound of his voice are comforting. He steps forward and takes my hands in his. "This is not your fault. Marcus is the one who chose this path."

"I can't help but feel…"

"You have five orcs who will die before they let anything happen to you, your mother or Zoe. I am trusting my family in this and you need to trust them too."

The certainty in his voice steadies me slightly. I take a deep breath. "Okay." I look at the others. "What do we do to keep Zoe safe?"

"We stick to our routine," Aldar responds. "Teach your classes, act normal. The moment anything changes, we'll know."

"Shouldn't we keep her home today?"

"No," Keric says, "we need to flush him out and catch him in the act. We can finish this today, instead letting him rule your lives for any longer."

I nod in agreement. "It's just…I don't know how I'm supposed to teach when my daughter might be in danger."

"Because showing fear gives Marcus power," Garlen says. "And we will not let him win."

Two hours later, I'm sitting next to Garlen in front of our cameras and screens, trying to appear normal for first period. Inside, I'm a mess of anxiety and worry, but I force myself to smile at the students.

"Good morning, class," I say, hoping my voice sounds steadier than I feel. "Today we're continuing our discussion of orc communal governance systems."

Garlen takes over, and I'm amazed at how calm and professional he sounds despite everything. His voice remains steady as he explains the complex hierarchy of orc communes, occasionally glancing at me with reassuring looks. VanWagoner, I'm certain, has no idea that anything is amiss.

"Ms. Willis?" One of the students raises her hand. "You seem kind of tense today. Is everything okay?"

Oh shoot. Heat floods my cheeks. So much for appearing normal. "I'm fine, just didn't sleep well last night because I had a stomach bug." And now I'm lying. Jeez, things are going from bad to worse.

Garlen smoothly redirects. "Let's focus on the reading assignment. Who can tell me about the role of orc elders in dispute resolution?"

Somehow, we make it through the first class, then the second. During our lunch break, my phone pings constantly with updates. Mom checking in. Keric and Aldar who are on campus assuring me of Zoe's safety. FBI agents confirming Marcus is still missing.

"I can't focus," I tell Garlen as we prepare for our final class of the day. "My brain keeps imagining worst-case scenarios."

"Breathe. Zoe is in her classroom, surrounded by teachers with my cousins in the hallway and working the perimeter. She had no idea today is any different than any other day. Keric texted ten minutes ago confirming visual contact."

I give him a big smile. Garlen smells so good. I love looking at his strong, green hands on my thigh, which feel warm and protective even over my clothes. "I just want this day to be over."

"One more class. We can do this."

But I can barely concentrate during the third lesson. Every notification on my phone makes me jump. Every pause in conversation makes me worry. I find myself staring at the clock, counting down the minutes until Zoe's school day ends. I don't want anything to happen to my baby girl today, but on the other hand what if this drags on for days on end and we live our lives in constant worry?

The students finish their group work and VanWagoner graciously takes over the very end of class for us. Garlen and I use a tablet to watch the school security cameras. The parking lot looks normal. Parents gather for pickup. Buses line up. It's ten minutes before school starts letting out in a staggered release schedule. Zoe should be walking with her class to the pickup area any minute. Kindergarten releases first, then first through sixth grade, then seventh through seniors are released last.

My phone buzzes with a text from Mom:

> In position at home. Bus should arrive in fifteen minutes.

I feel slightly better knowing Zoe will be on the bus with other kids and the driver, not walking through a parking lot where Marcus could grab her.

The bell rings for Kindergarten and the classes start to exit their rooms. On the security feed, I watch children stream out of the building.

Then I see him.

"Oh my God," I gasp, pointing at my phone screen. "Garlen, look."

Marcus walks toward the school office, carrying what looks like official paperwork. He's cleaned up since I last saw him. His hair is combed and he's wearing a collared shirt and looks almost respectable.

"Is he bringing fake identification?" Garlen demands, leaning over to see the screen.

I'm already calling the school, talking to the secretary at the front attendance desk. "Hi Janice, this is Ellie Willis. Remember how I'm not on campus because I'm teaching remotely?"

"Oh, hi Ellie. Yes, of course I remember," she laughs. "It's good to hear from you."

"It's good to talk to you too. I'm calling about my daughter, Zoe Willis. Her father, my ex, Marcus Adams is on campus and he's not supposed to be there. He has a restraining order and is *not* authorized to pick her up. I'm worried he's going to try and talk his way into picking her up before she can get on the bus home."

"Oh, no. That sounds like something I need to alert the principal about. Let me transfer you—"

"Janice, there's no time," I exclaim. "He's walking into the office right now."

"Uh oh, um, the problem is I'm answering this phone from the workroom. There's a sub at the front desk because Hilary is out sick today. The sub shouldn't let him take Zoe because she'll check Zoe's emergency card and see he isn't authorized. But I'm walking over there right now to double-check." She hangs up.

I whimper into the phone.

On the screen, I watch as Marcus approaches the school secretary I don't recognize. I can't hear what he's saying, but he's showing her his paperwork and pointing toward the hallway where the classrooms are.

The secretary seems to accept whatever he's showing her as proper documentation and starts typing on her computer.

"She's going to call Zoe to the office," I whisper in horror. "She doesn't know he's not supposed to be here. What the heck is he showing her?"

"I just sent a text to Aldar and Keric. They already knew he was there and are on their way."

Two familiar figures move across the parking lot. Keric and Aldar, both walk with purpose toward the school entrance. Keric enters the office just as the secretary reaches for her phone. Even through the security camera, I can see his commanding presence as he speaks to her. Marcus's head snaps up, his face going pale when he recognizes Keric.

"What is Keric saying?" I wonder aloud.

Whatever it is, it's effective. The secretary puts down her phone and starts shaking her head at Marcus. Marcus's calm facade cracks, and I can see him getting agitated. Principal VanWagoner and Janice both appear, followed closely by Aldar. Marcus is now surrounded by orcs and school administration, his fake paperwork apparently not working as planned.

"Is that the FBI?" Garlen points to new figures appearing on the screen.

Two people in dark suits walk rapidly toward the school entrance. Marcus sees them too and starts backing toward the exit, but there's nowhere to go.

"They were already en route," Garlen explains. "The FBI were arriving because of the bail violation, which put him on their radar again."

Marcus is handcuffed in the school office, his desperate attempt to get to Zoe thwarted before it even really began. Through it all, I notice that children are still boarding buses in the pickup area, completely unaware of the drama unfolding in the school office.

Zoe never knew he was there. She never saw him, never felt scared or threatened. The protection worked exactly as it was supposed to.

My phone rings and I answer right away. "Ellie? Its Principal VanWagoner. Everything is secure here. The situation has been resolved."

"Is Zoe—"

"Zoe is fine. She's on her bus as we speak, heading home to your mother. She has no idea anything happened."

I sink back into my chair, shaking with relief. Tears well up in my eyes. "Thank you. Thank you so much. Please tell Janice and the other secretary that I say thank you too."

"The FBI wants to speak with you, but they said it can wait until this evening."

An hour later, Zoe and Mom arrive for our usual dinner, both completely normal and happy. Zoe chatters about her day at school, oblivious to the danger that had been circling. I watch her animated face and feel overwhelming gratitude for the orc family and caring school staff that surrounded us with protection.

. . .

Later, after Zoe and Mom have gone home, Garlen and I are alone in our bedroom when FBI Agent Lopez calls to debrief us on what happened.

"We've added this newest arrest to what we already have and we've taken this over from the local police. Marcus had fake custody paperwork," she explains. "Not very good fakes but convincing enough to get him a visitor's pass. He was planning to claim he had emergency custody rights and take Zoe from the school."

"What would've happened if he'd succeeded?" I ask, though I'm not sure I want to know.

"Based on communications we intercepted, he was going to use Zoe as leverage to force Professor Irontree to publicly renounce the integration program. He told Crimson Tusk that threatening Zoe would make the both of you give up teaching."

Garlen's chains rattle as his fists clench. "Endangering a child is against the Orc Code of Ethics. Our elders will have to be informed."

"Crimson Tusk does many things that are illegal in the western states and cover their tracks well, but as far as we know they've never trafficked in drugs and I've never seen them harm women or children. This case is unusual, them meddling like this so closely in what happens at a school. They also underestimated Marcus," Agent Lopez continues. "During questioning, he broke down and admitted he never actually cared about Zoe. He just needed money from the Bloodtrees to pay off gambling debts. Apparently, he owes some very dangerous people and was getting desperate."

The words hit me like a slap. I knew Marcus was a bad father but hearing him admit he never cared about Zoe still hurts.

"He said, and I quote, 'I never wanted that kid anyway. She was just a means to an end.'" Agent Lopez's voice is disgusted. "Even his contact who I'm certain was Crimson Tusk was appalled by that. The orc was angry, claiming they never authorized him to target a child."

"So what happens now?" I ask.

"Marcus is back in custody, this time with no possibility of bail. Between the bail violation, the attempted kidnapping, and the wire fraud investigation that is complete and committed at his last job, he's looking at serious federal time. You won't have to worry about him again. We are only here to arrest Marcus Adams and give you this information and that's the end of it on our end. We are not getting involved in the dealings between the Irontrees and Crimson Tusk. That's orc business and has nothing to do with the FBI. I've also told all of this to Dane Irontree who is your emissary between the elders, your orc congressmen and your senator?"

"Yes, he is. Thank you."

After the call ends, I sit in silence for a long moment, processing everything. "It's really over," I finally say. "I don't have to worry about him reappearing and meddling in our lives anymore. I used to feel a tiny bit bad for not trying harder to keep a relationship between Zoe and her father, but now that he's told the agents that he didn't care about Zoe, that he was going to use her to get to me and then get paid…that's it. In my mind she doesn't have a biological father to reach out to. That's all done in my mind. In the end, he wasn't the type who really wanted a family."

"He never could have hurt you or Zoe," Garlen says firmly. "Not with all of us protecting you."

"I know. But it feels different now. Final." I look at this incredible orc who's become my anchor. "When I saw Marcus on that security feed, my first thought was anger. How dare he try to hurt my daughter? How dare he threaten our family?"

"*Our* family," Garlen repeats, his voice warm.

I lean against his solid chest, feeling safe and protected and loved. "Marcus chose working for Crimson Tusk and criminal money over his own daughter."

"No matter what happens, Zoe will always be protected by not only me, but the other Irontrees too."

That night I lie next to Garlen in bed, not thinking about Marcus or Crimson Tusk. I think instead about spring and our future. Tomorrow, we'll probably have to deal with more fallout from today's events. But tonight, we're safe, we're together, and the man who tried to use my daughter as a weapon will never be able to hurt us again.

I snuggle deeper against Garlen's snoring form, inhale his pleasant scent and finally fall asleep.

CHAPTER 28

Garlen

HEAVY FOOTSTEPS STOMP on the front porch, followed by three deliberate knocks that echo throughout the entire house. Not the light, casual rap of a weaker human neighbor or the hurried knock of a delivery driver. This is formal, and in fact... ceremonial?

My eyes blink open.

Crimson Tusk, or really their official clan, the Bloodtrees, are leaving a challenge scroll on our porch.

There goes my relaxing Saturday morning with my bride and our families.

My jaw clenches and I wonder how long it will take for this news to echo throughout the orc communes of North America. In fact, the story of this epic debate will most likely spread to orcs world-wide.

Ellie stirs beside me. "What time is it?" she rasps, pushing her red-gold hair away from her face.

That familiar tightening in my cock occurs at the sound of her lovely voice. Somehow, despite the handcuffs and chains, each night I sleep reasonably well, with her scent and touch nearby. And the fact that she knows exactly how I like to be touched is an extra bonus.

I lean forward and kiss her smooth forehead. My innocent bride has no idea that the Irontrees have received a scroll. She's human and cannot hear what happened. I will always protect her with my enhanced orc hearing and vision.

"Too early for anything good," I mutter, listening as more footsteps pound through the house below. My cousins are already awake and responding.

Familiar sets of heavy footsteps climb the stairs. Dane throws open the door, without knocking. He knows I heard everything. His face is grim as he holds up an ornate wooden box that will hold the parchment scroll bound with leather cord and sealed with red wax.

"What is that?" Ellie asks, sitting up and pulling the covers around herself.

"A formal challenge," I answer because I recognize the elaborate woodwork, the ancient symbols carved into the handles of the box. "From the Bloodtree clan."

"We were all supposed to have pancakes today," she whines. "And mimosas. That isn't happening, is it?"

"I don't think it is. We'll have to reschedule for another time." Dane steps forward and hands me the box. He opens it for me. "It arrived by messenger five minutes ago. The seal on the scroll inside is intact." Keric, Jonus and Aldar are behind him.

I take the box with my chained hands, feeling the weight of centuries-old tradition in the carved wood. The wax seal of the scroll bears the Bloodtree clan symbol, a crimson tree with twisted branches.

I get out of the bed and walk over to the couch. Ellie puts on her robe and uses the remote to start the fireplace. In moments we're all seated.

"What does this mean?" she asks.

"Crimson Tusk is invoking ancient orc law to challenge our integration program," I explain, breaking the wax and unrolling the heavy parchment. "A formal debate to settle the dispute.

Nothing else they have done has worked and now they are using this as a last resort."

"We brought this for Garlen to read aloud because he's the best at reading our new written language," Jonus explains.

The scroll is indeed written in the newly established orc script, flowing and elaborate. Formal debate challenges used to be oral and face to face, and the accompanying scroll bore illustrations of wrongs to be righted. Nowadays these symbols include this new formal language I suspect written by an elder with ties to Tusk.

"What does it say?" Keric demands.

I clear my throat and begin. "To Garlen Irontree of the Northern Maine Commune, teacher of humans and violator of sacred traditions. The Bloodtree clan, speaking for Crimson Tusk and all orcs who value our heritage, hereby invoke the right of Great Debate."

Ellie frowns. "Great Debate?"

"Ancient orc law," Dane explains. "When clans have fundamental disagreements, they can demand a formal debate instead of violence."

I continue reading. "We challenge your position that orc knowledge should be shared with humans. We demand cessation of all orc-human educational programs."

"Can they do that?" Ellie asks, alarmed.

"If they win the debate, yes," I answer grimly. "The elders will consider this outcome law and we will have to follow this decision. The challenge will be held at the new Redwood Brewery, tomorrow at sunset. Orc breweries are always considered neutral territory. Both parties will present their arguments before witnesses from all major orc clans. The arbiter will be a representative from Senator Overthrow's office."

"Tomorrow?" Aldar says. "That's not much notice."

"Ancient law requires the challenge be answered within forty-eight hours," Dane explains. "It's designed to prevent either side from preparing too extensively or gathering unfair advantage."

I finish rereading the formal language and set the scroll aside. "I have to accept. If I refuse, they win by default."

"But if you lose?" Ellie asks quietly.

"Then I'm banned from teaching humans, Black Oak's integration program ends, and any other schools considering hiring orcs will abandon their plans." I meet her worried gaze. "Everything we've worked for dies."

Ellie stands up, her eyes flashing with defiance. "Then we have to make sure we don't lose."

"We?"

"You think I'm sitting this out?" She tosses her glorious hair over her shoulder. "I'm going as Black Oak Academy's official representative. This affects my school, my students, my career. I'm coming with you."

"This is an orc dispute," Keric says. "Humans are not allowed into a Great Debate, not even mates or mothers."

"Well, that doesn't sound right. They will have to make an exception. I can't be separated from Garlen. If they want to challenge him and have him speak in a sane manner then I have to be by his side. And while I'm there I'd like to be able to speak up a little bit, if I can."

"Ellie, this isn't a human courtroom," my uncle comments. "Ancient orc law can be... unpredictable."

"Good thing I have Garlen, and all of you, to explain it to me." She sits on the couch again and takes my chained hands in hers. "We're in this together, remember? All the way."

Two hours later, our dining room table has been transformed into a war room. Maps, legal documents, student testimonials, and printouts of parent emails cover every surface. All five Irontrees crowd around the table while Ellie paces, occasionally pausing to add notes to the growing list of arguments.

"Is Crimson Tusk actually just another name for the Blood-tree clan?"

"No, I believe most of Crimson Tusk are Bloodtrees, but they also pull from other clans too. The leader of Tusk does happen to be a Bloodtree."

"Tell me more about this Bloodtree clan," she says, pen poised over her notepad. "Who are we facing?"

"Dylan Bloodtree is their current leader," Dane answers. "He's younger and unmated. Intelligent but rigid in his thinking. He genuinely believes orc culture is under threat. He thinks that citizenship means orcs will one day behave just like humans."

"Rhys Bloodtree is their speaker," I add. "I've met him before, when I was working with a team of orcs towards convincing the government to allow orc citizenship. He'll make compelling arguments. Don't underestimate him."

"Dylan Bloodtree is challenging you, but Rhys will do the speaking? Does that mean you won't speak for yourself either?"

"We can choose who will speak for us. I assume Dylan will choose Rhys and I will choose myself."

"Owen and Gareth Bloodtree are the muscle and members of Crimson Tusk," Keric contributes. "They won't speak much, but their presence is meant to intimidate. I've seen these two many times over the last month."

"They also have a clan historian," Aldar adds. "He'll have statistics, examples of other cultures that were lost through integration, evidence to support their position."

Ellie stops pacing. "Do you guys believe they have legitimate concerns?"

"They do have legitimate concerns, that all orcs have struggled with, which makes them more dangerous," I agree. "If they were simply out to randomly thwart humans and hated the idea of orcs and humans together, we could dismiss their arguments. But they raise real questions about cultural preservation."

"Then we better have real answers." Ellie returns to her notepad. "What's our strongest argument?"

"That isolation leads to irrelevance," I say immediately. "Orc culture survives by adapting, not by hiding."

"Our students will be good examples," Ellie adds, writing rapidly. "The way they respond to your teaching. Their genuine respect and curiosity."

"Economic benefits," Jonus suggests. "Integration creates opportunities for orcs in human society."

"Building allies instead of remaining strangers," Aldar contributes.

We spend the morning preparing, but my mind keeps drifting to a larger concern. "There's something else," I finally say. "They'll have to address Marcus."

The room goes quiet.

"He was their asset," I continue. "Their plan to discredit us through him backfired spectacularly. They'll have to explain that failure."

"Could work in our favor," Dane muses. "Hard to claim moral superiority when your human ally was a male who tried to kidnap a child."

"Or they'll throw him under the bus and claim they were deceived," Ellie counters. "Distance themselves from his actions."

"Either way, it's a weakness in their position," I decide. "We'll be ready for it."

An hour before we need to leave, Dane unlocks my chains for the first time in over a month. The weight lifts from my wrists and waist, and I nearly stumble from the sudden freedom.

"Ancient protocol," he explains as I flex my fingers. "Formal challenges require both parties to be unrestrained."

Ellie steps forward and takes my hand. I lean in and inhale her scent, allowing those luscious pheromones to clear my mind. "I'm here," she says, squeezing my hand. "I'll be close the whole time. If you struggle at all, just look at me and know that I'm close and I'm safe."

"Yes." I nod. "Yes." Then I take her in my arms, giving my

bride a hug for the very first time. She steps closer, in the circle of my arms, her cheek resting against my chest. The both of us sigh with relief, loving the feel of so much closeness.

"Let's go," my uncle chuckles.

CHAPTER 29

Garlen

THE ABSENCE of chains feels strange, almost wrong after so long.

But there's also relief, and a growing sense of anticipation. Tonight, I'll stand as an equal, not a caged Irontree beast, with my bride at my side.

Redwood Brewery is a massive log building that serves as neutral ground. As we drive up, I see orcs from various clans gathering in the parking lot. Word has spread quickly through the orc community.

"How many are there?" Ellie asks, staring through the window at the crowd.

"Looks like elders from at least eight clans," Dane observes. "This is bigger than I expected."

"Good or bad?"

"Depends on how well we argue," I answer honestly.

We park and walk inside. The brewery has been arranged for the formal debate. A large circle of chairs surrounds a central area where the speakers will stand. The air smells of warm ale and wood smoke. Ancient orc weapons hang on the walls.

The Bloodtree clan is already here, clustered near the bar. Dylan Bloodtree stands at their center, a tall orc with intelligent eyes. When he sees us enter, he nods once in an acknowledgment, not a greeting.

"Professor Irontree," a voice calls from across the room. Senator Overthrow's representative approaches. He is a middle-aged orc dressed in a custom-made human-style business suit, who looks completely out of place in the rustic brewery. "I'm Councilor Mort. I'll be arbitrating tonight's debate."

"Thank you for coming," I reply, shaking his hand. "This is Ellie Willis, representing Black Oak Academy."

Councilor Mort studies Ellie with interest. "The first human to attend a Great Debate in over fifty years. This is indeed historic."

The ceremony begins with the sharing of ale. Dylan Bloodtree and I meet in the center of the circle, each carrying a tankard of the brewery's strongest orc ale. Neither of us is allowed to bring our own commune's ale, but instead we must drink to the neutral brewmaster. It's a ritual older than written history, orc disputes negotiated over the sharing of drink before we share words.

"To an honorable debate," Dylan says, raising his tankard.

"To words spoken in place of battle," I respond.

We drink and the warm ale burns down my throat. Dylan's eyes never leave mine as we drain our tankards. When we're finished, we return to our respective sides.

"Let the Great Debate begin," Councilor Mort announces.

Rhys Bloodtree steps forward first. He's older than Dylan, with deep green skin, a bald head and abnormally large black horns. His charismatic presence commands attention. When he speaks, his deep voice carries clearly through the room. "Fellow orcs," he begins, "we gather tonight to decide the future of our species. Will we remain orcs, proud and distinct? Or will we dissolve into the human masses, our culture diluted until it disappears entirely?"

Murmurs ripple through the crowd. He's starting strong.

"For thousands of years, we have survived by keeping our

knowledge sacred, our traditions pure. The humans who once hunted us with torches and pitchforks now claim they want to live with us and learn from us. But what they truly want is to possess our secrets, to strip-mine our culture for their own benefit."

He gestures toward me. "Professor Irontree believes he is building bridges. But bridges allow traffic to flow both ways. For every human student who learns respect for orc culture, how many orcs will abandon their heritage for human conveniences?"

The crowd is engaged now, nodding along with his arguments. Rhys has a gift for speaking, and his passion is genuine.

He pulls out a tablet, displaying statistics. "In communes where orcs go to school alongside humans, they learn human languages and forty percent never learn how to write and read the orc language. In communes near human cities traditional hunts and skills are being abandoned and orcs leave to find jobs in human cities. Integration isn't preservation, it's voluntary extinction."

When Rhys finishes, the applause is substantial. He's made a compelling case, and I can see doubt in some faces around the room.

Now it's my turn.

I stand and walk to the center of the circle, looking around at the assembled orcs, ready to convince them that my vision serves them better than isolation. "Rhys speaks of preservation," I begin, "but I ask you, what good is preserving something if it becomes irrelevant? If our culture survives only in hidden communes, speaking only to ourselves, what have we truly saved?"

I pause, letting the question settle. "Until recently, humans still feared us. They saw us as monsters, relics of a barbaric past. That fear bred hatred, and hatred bred violence. How many of you have lost ancestors to human mobs? How many have been denied jobs, basic rights because of that fear? We aren't even allowed guns or any weapons beyond our own traditional orc weaponry, because orc bodies are legally considered deadly weapons in comparisons to humans. This is why we are at a disadvantage."

Several orcs nod grimly. Everyone here has experienced discrimination.

"But when humans learn about us directly, when they see our intelligence, our art, our complex social structures, that fear transforms into respect. When they understand that orcs are now citizens who can work amongst them, my students don't see me as a monster. They see me as a teacher, a scholar…an equal."

I gesture toward Ellie. "Ms. Willis didn't fall in love with an orc because she was desperate or curious. She fell in love with me because she saw who I truly am. That's the power of integration; it reveals the equality between our species."

I surprise her with this declaration. Neither of us has mentioned love, but it's there, with every word we say and touch we've given each other.

The crowd stirs at the mention of love. Relationships between our two species always capture attention.

"Rhys worries about cultural erosion," I continue, "but isolation is the true threat. Cultures that don't adapt, don't grow, don't engage with the wider world become museum pieces. Dead things preserved in amber. And we need to remember that there are many more humans than orcs on this planet. Thousands of years ago there were as many orcs on Earth as humans, nowadays their population has exploded and they out number us by billions. Humans not only have the population advantage but the technological advantage too. It doesn't matter how much we resist, they can annihilate us with a touch of a button. I'm not saying that we should bow to the humans because of their might. I'm saying that the data shows us that the smart move is to join our former adversary. Humans used to be distant and removed but now they are everywhere. And we have to stop viewing them as our enemy.

We are citizens now and they are instead our neighbors. Even orcs who live in the farthest communes in Siberia know worthy humans. Remember that humans are also our mothers and our brides. They are the women we love and procreate with."

"Human males hate us," someone shouts.

I nod in agreement. This is a fair challenge. "This will change with time," I respond. "We've already vowed as a species that we would stop kidnapping. As each generation of humans is raised amongst orcs and befriend us and work with us side by side, the future will bring less and less hate and more friendship."

I pull out my own evidence, student and parent testimonials, emails from other schools asking about integration programs. "These human students are learning our history from our perspective for the first time in their lives. They're asking questions their textbooks never raised. They're developing respect for orc weaponry, orc craftsmanship, orc values."

I can see I'm gaining ground, but I need to drive the point home.

"And let's address the real reason we're here tonight," I say, my voice hardening. "This challenge isn't really about cultural preservation. It's about a failed plan to discredit integration through sabotage."

The room goes dead silent. Dylan's face remains impassive, but I see other Bloodtree clan members shifting uncomfortably.

"Marcus Adams," I announce, "was a human asset recruited by Crimson Tusk to infiltrate Black Oak Academy through my relationship with Ms. Willis. This criminal was supposed to manipulate and blackmail a teacher but instead violated restraining orders and yesterday attempted to kidnap a six-year-old child."

Dylan stands slowly. Formal protocol requires him to respond to direct accusations. "Marcus Adams was a mistake," he admits, his voice carrying across the suddenly quiet room.

"This human was supposed to be an asset. Instead, he proved to be a liability."

"A liability you recruited," I press. "A human who told the FBI he never cared about his own daughter, that she was just 'a means to an end.'"

Rhys looks disgusted. "We have standards," he says quickly. "All orcs fight amongst adult orcs or adult human males; we never mistreat women and children. This is a main difference between humans and orcs. Even when we kidnapped females, we never meant to hurt them and they were always allowed to leave our communes after giving birth. And in modern times we've even disavowed this practice, forcing our bodies to work against this biological imperative. Marcus Adams violated every principle we hold sacred. We formally disavow any connection to him."

"But the fact still remains that you used him," Ellie speaks for the first time, standing up in the circle.

I can't help but gaze in wonder at my brave, gorgeous female. She strides forward, ready to speak. This is the second time she has publicly stood up for me and the Irontrees. She is fantastic.

"You used a human with an alcoholic disease, causing him to try to sabotage my school and my relationship with Garlen because you couldn't win this argument through honest debate. Marcus was my ex-husband who I was trying to escape because of his verbal abuse and criminality. You hired him and directed him to use me as a way to thwart the integration. Because of your actions he threatened me and tried to kidnap my daughter."

The crowd murmurs angrily. Using an unworthy human to attack a respected female or mistreat a child is a serious violation of orc honor codes.

"Which raises the question," I continue, "if your position is so strong, why resort to dishonorable sabotage? Why not simply request this debate months ago?"

Dylan looks genuinely uncomfortable now. The moral high ground has shifted, and everyone in the room can feel it.

Councilor Mort steps forward. "The accusation of dishonorable sabotage is serious. Does the Bloodtree clan wish to respond?"

Dylan exchanges glances with his clan members before answering. "Our methods were... questionable. We believed the cause justified extreme measures."

"But the cause was wrong," I say firmly. "You assumed Ms. Willis was ignorant, exploitative, temporary. You never considered that she might genuinely care about orc culture, about the orc species, about me." I turn to address the entire gathering. "This is what orc integration really offers. Not the erasure of our culture, but the chance to share it with worthy humans. Not the loss of our identity, but the opportunity to build alliances with humans who can help us thrive."

The room is silent as the implications sink in.

Finally, Dylan stands again. "Perhaps," he says slowly, "we have been too rigid in our thinking."

Rhys looks shocked. "Dylan, we agreed—"

"We agreed to preserve orc culture," Dylan cuts him off. "But preservation through isolation isn't preservation, as Garlen pointed out, it's a slow death. You were the one who hired Marcus Adams."

Rhys growls, steps back and takes a seat.

Dylan looks directly at me. "Your students respect you?"

"They do."

"They're learning accurate orc history?"

"From primary sources. From oral traditions. From perspectives no human textbook has ever included. For the first time ever, our story will be told accurately."

Dylan nods slowly. "Then perhaps...perhaps there is a middle path."

Councilor Mort seizes the opening. "Are both parties willing to negotiate a resolution?"

Dylan nods in agreement.

I step forward and put out a hand, Dylan takes my hand and we shake on it.

What follows is two hours of intense discussion. Not the formal speeches of debate, but genuine conversation about how to protect orc culture while allowing for integration. Ellie contributes insights about educational safeguards. Rhys suggests a cultural review board. Dylan proposes limits on what aspects of orc tradition can be shared publicly.

Slowly, carefully, we craft what becomes known as the Blackwood Accords. A framework for monitored school integration that respects both orc heritage and the potential for human partnership.

When Councilor Mort finally calls for a vote, the result is overwhelming: the Accords pass with support from seven of the nine elders present.

As orcs begin filing out of the brewery, Dylan approaches me one final time. "You argued well," he admits. "And your human female... she has spine."

"She does," I agree.

"Perhaps worthy humans, beyond our own mothers and brides do exist," he muses. "Marcus Adams was an aberration, not a representative."

"Just as truly violent orcs who harm our own are aberrations," I reply. "Most of us, and most of them, simply want to live peacefully."

Dylan extends his hand again. "To peaceful coexistence, then."

"To mutual respect," I agree, shaking it.

Outside the brewery, Ellie and I walk to our car under a star-filled sky. The other Irontrees follow behind, saying their good-byes to orcs from other clans. The weight of what we've accomplished is just beginning to sink in.

"Did we just save Black Oak Academy's integration program?" she asks.

"We did more than that," I tell her, putting my arm around her shoulders. "We laid the foundation for the future. Other schools will follow Black Oak's lead. Other orcs will become teachers. Other humans will view orcs as their teachers or as fellow students in a classroom being a common occurrence."

Ellie laughs. "Perfect. The whole world is going to know how orcs really do it better."

"In every way that matters," I agree. "Oh, and one more thing," I add as we reach the car. "Jonus managed to schedule our interview with Oprah Winfrey next week. Apparently, she's fascinated by the Accords and wants to hear our story."

"And us? What about our future?"

I turn to face her. "Spring is less than a month away. I can touch you without restraint." I don't want to tell her that I want to not only have a sex marathon during the entire week of spring break, but I'd also love to perform a surprise human wedding ceremony to cement our mating. Because I'm also planning on filling her with my orc son and seeing her swollen with our first-born by this summer.

Her smile is radiant. "Yes, Garlen Irontree, this sounds like a great idea."

Heat radiates through my entire body and my tusks begin to lengthen. A thunderous roar fills my lungs...

Ellie's eyes widen. "Uh oh."

"Chains," Keric shouts.

In moments they have me handcuffed again, a chain around my waist and are dragging me to the car.

I breathe a sigh of relief.

I wasn't ready.

CHAPTER 30

Ellie

TODAY IS the first day of spring break and yet again, my love of sleep is thwarted by well-meaning Irontrees.

I wake to the sound of hushed voices and movement in the hallway outside our room. For a moment, I'm disoriented because it's still dark outside, barely dawn. Garlen breathes deep and even beside me.

Wait. Why are orcs moving around at this hour? This is early, even for these orcs. I've come to understand that is literally the worst house to live in for someone like me, who enjoys sleeping in. These crazy Irontrees go to bed early and rise at dawn. Even on the weekends.

And then I hear the tinkle of female laughter.

I blink and rub at my eyes. "Garlen," I whisper, shaking his shoulder gently. "We have visitors."

His dark eyes open immediately and he turns to look at me, but instead of alarm, I see something else there. Anticipation? Nervousness?

He shifts his magnificent bare chest, moving chains to a more comfortable position. "It's okay," he grins, instantly turning bright-eyed and fully awake. "Today is a special day."

Before I can ask what he means, more heavy footsteps pound up the stairs. The bedroom door swings open without a knock.

The way they barely knock and just randomly enter our bedroom at the crack of dawn to tell us something that they think is time sensitive but isn't and could've easily been said downstairs, never ceases to amaze me. I've grown used to this behavior, to the point where it's literally expected. I just automatically reach for the robe I keep nearby, slip my arms inside and tie it around my waist.

Dane strides inside our bedroom carrying what looks like an ornate wooden box and some kind of ceremonial tools.

"What's happening?" I sit up, pulling the covers around myself. "Why is everyone here so early? Are we being summoned to another Great Debate?" I narrow my eyes at Garlen. "What have you done this time?"

Garlen chuckles and leads me to the couch.

Behind Dane are Aldar, Keric, and Jonus. The other Irontrees file into our bedroom, all of them dressed in formal suits despite the early hour. It's odd seeing these males with actual shirts on that are buttoned up and wearing blazers on top of that. They look serious but excited, like they're barely containing some kind of secret.

Aldar carries a tray of coffee and hands me a steaming mug. Bless his heart.

"Today is the spring equinox," Dane announces solemnly. "March twentieth. The official end of winter."

My heart jumps. "Oh thank god. I was hoping you'd say that."

After three months of chains and careful boundaries, winter is finally over. But something about the way everyone is acting tells me there's more to this morning than just Garlen's freedom.

"Ancient orc tradition requires that winter chains be removed for the final time, ceremonially at sunrise," Dane continues, opening the wooden box to reveal specialized tools. "On the exact moment winter ends."

Garlen sits up beside me, and I can feel the tension radiating from his body. Not the dangerous tension of winter urges, but something else entirely. Excitement. Pure, barely contained excitement.

I tilt my head. "Do you really feel different?"

"I do," he says. "I feel all the same feelings, but they aren't irrational. My skin isn't as hot and my focus is better."

"We need to do this on the balcony," Aldar says, gesturing toward the doors that lead outside. "Sunrise ceremony."

"All four of you are dressed so nice. I feel like I'm not dressed right. Do I need to go get ready first?"

"No, there is no need for you to change your appearance. This has special meaning to the Irontrees. Garlen is the first of us to have this happen. Many orcs in the past have needed to be chained and restrained in the dark of winter. There hasn't been an Irontree restraint in over a hundred years. We are here to mark this moment, when Garlen Irontree is finally able to walk free."

I take another sip of coffee, tuck my feet into my favorite warm slippers and move with them toward the balcony doors. Garlen slides them open and I step outside into the freezing ice cold morning air. I gasp so loudly that several birds take flight from nearby trees, dislodging clumps of snow.

The backyard has been completely transformed.

A huge white tent has been erected, the type that is set up for an elaborate party.

"What is all that?" I whisper, my voice barely audible.

Garlen moves to stand behind me, his chained hands settling on one shoulder. When he speaks, his voice is deep and warm. "Ellie, orcs love a good surprise. And I know you do too."

I turn to face him, my heart pounding. His dark eyes are intense, focused completely on me, and there's something in his expression that makes my breath catch.

"I want to solidify our relationship with a human-style

mating ceremony," he says, taking my hands in his. "A wedding. Today."

I put a hand over my heart. "Today? Right now? This morning?"

"Yes." His thumbs stroke across my knuckles. "We're doing two things at once today, celebrating my freedom from winter madness and chains and performing our wedding ceremony." He leans down and whispers in my ear. "Because I plan on filling you with our first orc son right away."

I lean back and stare at him, then at the elaborate setup below, then back at his nervous, hopeful face. "A surprise wedding?"

He nods, watching my reaction carefully.

Laughter bubbles up from somewhere deep in my chest. "I love surprises too. But... are you sure? I mean, we never really talked about—"

"The rest of us have been planning this for weeks," he interrupts gently. "Your mother helped. My family helped. Everyone you love and know is coming to the house today."

"My mother knew?"

"She's been the mastermind," Dane says with a chuckle. "We just provided the funding."

"So," Garlen's voice draws my attention back to him, "will you marry me today, Ellie Willis? I know we've already been living as if we're married, but will you let me surprise you with the human-style mating ceremony you deserve?"

I look at this incredible orc who charged into my life three months ago and turned everything upside down. Who was chained in a basement cage because he couldn't control himself when I was near. Who taught alongside me when the world was watching. Who faced down his own species to keep our shared dream of orc integration alive.

"Yes," I breathe. "Yes, absolutely yes."

Garlen's features transform with relief and joy.

Dane steps forward with his ceremonial tools. "Then let's

make this official. Garlen Irontree, you have survived the dark of winter while maintaining your honor and control. By ancient law and modern choice, I now release you from winter's bonds."

The chain removal is surprisingly moving. Dane speaks additional words in the old orc language while carefully unlocking each piece of Garlen's restraints. The handcuffs. The chains around his waist. The connecting links that have defined our relationship for three months. As each piece falls away, Garlen seems to grow taller, more confident. When the last chain hits the balcony floor with a final clink, he flexes his fingers and rolls his shoulders like he's remembering what freedom feels like.

"How does it feel?" I ask softly.

"Like coming back to life," he answers, then pulls me against him for a kiss that's deeper and more passionate than any we've shared. Without the chains limiting his movement, he can hold me properly, his large hands framing my face as he kisses me like he's been waiting his whole life for this moment. And of course I love the brush of those tusks at either side of my mouth.

When we break apart, I'm breathless and dizzy and more in love than I thought possible.

"Now," Dane says with a grin, "let's get you two married."

My mother appears in the bedroom doorway wearing an elegant navy dress I've never seen before. Her eyes are bright with tears and barely contained excitement. "Out. Out. Girls only now," she calls to the lingering orcs.

They retreat with good-natured grumbling.

I wave goodbye to Garlen who gives me a wink before he shuts the bedroom door closed behind him.

"Happy wedding day, sweetheart. Surprise."

"Mom." I throw my arms around her. "You knew? How long have you been planning this?"

"Since Valentine's Day," she admits, hugging me tight. "Dane and I have been coordinating everything."

The door opens again and Anna appears in the doorway next, carrying what looks like a professional makeup kit and several hair styling tools. "I've been in on this secret for two weeks," she announces. "I couldn't look you in the eye during faculty meetings because I was afraid I'd give it away."

"Anna. You too?" I laugh and cry at the same time. "How did you all keep this from me?"

"It wasn't easy," Mom says, pulling a garment bag from behind the bedroom door. "Especially when you kept talking about wanting to plan your wedding someday. The only thing that made it work was that we weren't living in the same house anymore. Are you ready to see your wedding dress?"

Most women would be horrified at the thought of their mother picking out their wedding dress, but instead I'm excited. Laurie Willis has impeccable taste and knows what I like and don't like and best of all she knows my size and understands what looks good on my shape.

Anna stands next to me. We wait with bated breath as she unzips the bag.

"Oh my gosh," Anna sighs.

The most beautiful white wedding dress I've ever seen hangs in front of me. It's elegant but not too formal, with delicate lace sleeves and a flowing skirt that will be perfect for an early spring ceremony. I can see just from looking at it that it'll show off my torso and hint at cleavage. It's basically the dress of my dreams.

"Mom. It's gorgeous."

"The orcs are very generous with their gold, honey. Money was no object, so I was able to get you something that hinted at a royal wedding but was pared down to a backyard event in Truckee, California." She wipes at her eyes. "I wanted you to have everything perfect. Last time you had a quickie Vegas ceremony and no one was with you. I wanted this time to be different for you."

I give her another tight hug in response.

Zoe comes bouncing into the room wearing an adorable

white dress with a flower crown in her hair. "Mommy I'm the flower girl. And Loki's the ring bearer."

"You are?" I scoop her up for a hug. "Did you know about this surprise too?"

"Grandma told me. I got to practice walking with the flowers and everything." She wiggles down and runs to show me a small white basket filled with rose petals. "And look, Loki has a special bow tie."

Sure enough, Loki trots into the room wearing a special harness with tiny bow tie with small white ribbons attached. When I look closer, I can see a small box tied to the harness.

"The ring," I gasp.

Mom and Anna exchange a look.

"About that," Mom says carefully. "Garlen has had a ring for you for weeks. But..."

I reach into the pocket of my robe and pull out the small velvet box I've been carrying around for over a month. "I have one for him too."

"You do?" Anna squeals. "Oh my God, that's so romantic. Do you realize this means the two of you have been wanting to marry each other for the last two months."

"I bought it right after the Great Debate," I admit. "I kept waiting for the right moment to ask him, but I was too nervous."

"Well, today's definitely the right moment," Mom says, her eyes looking suspiciously wet. "Come on, let's get you into the shower so we can get you ready. We have a wedding to pull off."

"Thank you for doing all of this for me, mom. How funny, all that time we were commenting on who was remodeling and building this huge McMansion next door. And it turns out I'm the one who is living here."

"And I'm taking over the house next door. Dane has officially moved out of this house and moved in with me. We are sharing that primary bedroom that was always a little big for me anyways."

I give her yet another big hug. "That's wonderful."

"I think so too. Now get in that shower. This wedding won't wait forever."

The next hour passes in a whirlwind of activity. Anna works magic with my hair, creating an elegant updo with soft curls framing my face. Mom helps me into the dress, which fits perfectly.

Through the bedroom windows, I see more and more guests arriving. They walk into the backyard and enter the tent. Principal VanWagoner wears a formal suit and carries what looks like an official folder. Several orcs I recognize from the brewery debate arrive.

"Is that Dylan and Owen Bloodtree?" I ask, pointing to two familiar figures.

"Garlen invited representatives from several clans," Anna explains while applying my makeup. "Apparently word of that speech you told me you gave at Redwood brewery has spread throughout the orc community."

"And there are some other special guests too," Mom adds mysteriously.

"Who are they?"

Mom's smile is radiant. "Oh, I can't keep the secret any longer. It's Garlen's parents. They flew down from Maine last night."

My stomach flips. "His parents are here? I'm meeting Garlen's parents at our surprise wedding?"

"His mother is so excited to meet you," Anna says, putting finishing touches on my lipstick. "She completely understands what you're going through."

"You're sure?" Relief floods through me. "Garlen has told me all about his parents and I know he sends text messages to them often, but I haven't seen or spoken to them yet. I supposed he wanted to wait for that until the chains were off."

"Oh really? I've been talking to Lori Irontree for months now.

She told me last night that when Dane told her about you, she cried happy tears."

"Okay, all done," Anna announces. "Time for a final check before we get this party started."

There's a knock on the door. I look up to see a woman arrive with a camera around her neck. "Hi," she greets. "I'm Alma, your wedding photographer. I've been downstairs making sure to take pictures of your guests' arrival. Is it alright if I capture pictures up here, of you dressed? I know there isn't time for formal pictures, but I'll do my best to take photos that you'll enjoy later. And I'll just follow along afterwards and get pictures of the ceremony itself. I'll be at the reception too."

"Thank you, it's nice to meet you. And yes, I'd love for you to take pictures."

I slip into my high heels and look at myself in the full-length mirror. The woman looking back hardly seems like me. I turn back and forth, admiring the views from every angle. The dress is perfect, my hair and makeup are flawless, and despite my nerves, I'm glowing with happiness. "I can't believe this is really happening," I whisper.

"Believe it," Zoe announces, practicing her flower girl walk across the bedroom. "You're marrying Garlen and he's going to be my real daddy."

My heart melts. "Is that okay with you, baby girl? Are you happy about that?"

"The happiest," she declares. "Can I call him Daddy now instead of Garlen?"

"I think he'd love that."

Anna steps back to admire her work. "You look absolutely beautiful, Ellie."

Mom hands me a simple bouquet of white roses. "Ready?"

I take a deep breath, touch the ring box in my dress pocket one more time, and nod. "Let's go get me married."

. . .

We make our way downstairs and through the house toward the back doors. I can hear music playing outside. A live string quartet that definitely wasn't in our budget before the orcs got involved.

"Wait," Mom stops me just before we reach the back doors. "There's one more surprise."

The doors open, and Garlen's parents step inside. His mother is beautiful, with graying brown hair and kind eyes that remind me immediately of Garlen's. His father is a distinguished-looking orc with silver-streaked hair and a warm smile.

"Ellie," his mother says, stepping forward with tears in her eyes. "I'm Lori, and this is my husband, Thorin. We are so happy to finally meet you."

She pulls me in for a brief hug. "Finally, another human woman in the family," she whispers in my ear. "I've been waiting so long for this day."

"Thank you for coming all this way," I manage, overwhelmed by their immediate acceptance. "I'm sorry we're meeting under such crazy circumstances."

"Are you kidding?" Lori laughs. "A surprise wedding? This is exactly the kind of grand gesture my son would plan. He gets that romantic streak from me."

Thorin steps forward and takes my hands gently in his large ones. "My son chose well," he says in a deep voice similar to Garlen's. "Welcome to the Irontree family, daughter."

Oh gosh, these two need to stop or they're going to make me cry.

Lori and Thorin wave goodbye and disappear through the doors and inside the tent. I walk out into the cold air and peek inside the tent to see the ceremony space in full daylight now. It's even more beautiful than I imagined. Nearly one hundred people are seated in the white chairs, all turned expectantly toward an enormous flower arch. I recognize neighbors, school staff, several orcs from various clans, and even some extended family members I haven't seen in years.

"How did you manage all this overnight?" I ask Mom in wonder.

"Turns out when you have unlimited funds and very motivated orcs, you can accomplish anything," she says with a grin. "The wedding planner I hired has never had a bigger budget to work with. We have a huge amount of staff who are ready, right after the vows to transform this in record time into your reception, complete with food and DJ."

Principal VanWagoner approaches, looking official but excited. "Are you ready, Ellie? I got ordained online specifically for this ceremony."

A squeal of delight escapes my lips. "You're officiating?"

"Garlen asked me personally. Said it would mean a lot to have the principal who believed in your integration program be the one to marry you."

I'm crying again, but Anna quickly touches up my makeup.

"Okay, positions everyone," Mom directs. "Zoe, remember to walk slowly and scatter the petals gently. Loki, stay with Zoe." Then she looks at me again. "Are you okay, walking alone?" Mom suddenly asks.

I stare at her blinking. "Yes."

She grabs my hand and squeezes. "Remember, your Dad would be thrilled to know you were marrying Garlen. It's as if he's here with you."

"Please stop making Ellie cry," Anna begs.

"Is Garlen out there?" I ask, suddenly nervous.

"Oh honey," Mom says, peeking inside, "you should see him. That orc is practically vibrating with excitement."

The music shifts to the wedding march, and suddenly this is really happening.

Mom and Anna disappear.

Keric suddenly shows up, still dressed formally. He opens the tent for Zoe and she goes first, walking carefully down the aisle and dropping rose petals with serious concentration. Loki trots beside her, his bow tie slightly askew but the ring is still secure. The guests "aww" and chuckle at the adorable procession.

Then it's my turn.

Keric opens the tent for me again and immediately I see Garlen waiting for me at the floral arch. He's wearing a perfectly tailored black suit that emphasizes his broad shoulders and tall frame. His dark hair is styled and his tusks gleam white in the morning sun. But it's his expression that takes my breath away, pure love and awe as he watches me walk toward him.

The guests stand as I carefully make my way down the aisle, but I barely notice them. My entire focus is on the orc waiting for me, the one who's about to become my husband.

When I reach him, he takes my hands and leans down to whisper, "You are the most beautiful sight I have ever seen."

"You clean up pretty well yourself," I whisper back, making him grin.

The music ends and Principal VanWagoner begins the ceremony with words about love transcending boundaries and differences. But honestly, I'm so focused on Garlen that I barely hear the opening remarks.

Then Garlen takes the small microphone and gets down on one knee in front of everyone, just like in my dreams.

"Ellie Willis," he begins, his deep voice carrying clearly across the tent, "two months ago you saw a wild orc charging across a parking lot and instead of running, you stepped forward. You chose to trust me when I couldn't trust myself. You moved into my home when I was chained like a beast. You taught alongside me when the world was watching. You defended our love to anyone who would listen. And you made me believe I could be the male you deserve."

Loki hops up close and I watch as Garlen unties the box from his harness and opens the small black box. "I've been carrying this since January, waiting for spring to set us both free."

The ring inside is stunning. It's a princess-cut diamond surrounded by smaller stones that catch the light like tiny stars.

"Will you marry me, Ellie? Will you be my mate, my partner, and the mother of future Irontrees?"

I'm crying openly now, but I manage to reach into my dress pocket and pull out my own ring box.

I take the microphone from his hands. "I've been carrying this too," I say, my voice shaking with emotion. "Yes to everything you just asked. But I have a question for you too."

His eyes widen in surprise as I get down on my knees as well, facing him.

"Garlen Irontree, you saved me from my ex-husband, then saved me from believing I wasn't worthy of true love. You've been patient and honorable and protective. You've made my daughter feel loved and important, and you get along well with my mother. You've brought joy and laughter into our lives. Will you marry me? Will you be my husband, my best friend, my partner in all things?"

"Yes," he says immediately, his voice thick with emotion. "Yes to everything."

We slip rings onto each other's fingers at the same time, both of us laughing and crying. Then he stands and pulls me up with him, and we're kissing while the crowd cheers and applauds.

The kiss is everything, it's both sweet and full of promise and desire. When we finally break apart, Zoe shouts from the front row, "Now you're really my daddy."

"That's right Zoe," Garlen calls back to her. "I'm your daddy now."

Loki barks his approval, his bow tie now completely sideways.

Principal VanWagoner pronounces us husband and wife. The crowd erupts with clapping and whistles of appreciation. But even as people surge forward to congratulate us, Garlen pulls me aside.

"I need my mate," he groans, his voice low and urgent. "Now."

I glance down and see that his crotch is yet again obscenely tented. A snort-laugh escapes my lips.

We are supposed to walk back down the aisle and the reception is supposed to start, but I can see in his eyes that waiting isn't an option. Three months of careful boundaries and restrained touching have led to this moment, and we're both ready to finally be together completely.

"Take me upstairs," I whisper.

He sweeps me up in his arms without warning, lifting me easily against his chest. The crowd cheers and whistles as he carries me down the aisle, toward the house. I'm in amazement, giggling with delight because never in my life have I been carried in someone's arms as if I'm light as air.

"Take the whole week," Dane yells after us.

"The whole week?" I ask as Garlen exits the tent.

"My cousins have moved out," he explains. "Dane is staying next door with your mother and Zoe. Even Loki is staying with them for the week."

"So we're completely alone?"

"Completely alone." He carries me through the house and up the stairs, taking two steps at a time.

CHAPTER 31

Garlen

I CARRY my bride through the cheering crowd, her laughter bright in my ear and her arms around my neck. Thankfully, the fabric of the wedding dress covers my obvious erection.

"You're so strong," Ellie murmurs, pressing a kiss to my neck.

"I've been wanting to do this since the day I met you," I admit, shouldering open our bedroom door. "To carry you away and have you to myself." I set her down gently in the center of our room. "But this time, it's so we can simply be alone in our own bedroom and not in my lair in the mountains."

The sound of the wedding and eventual reception continue unabated outside our windows. Music and laughter, as our friends and family celebrate in the tent without us.

"They won't miss us," I say, turning the lock on our bedroom door.

Ellie's eyes sparkle with mischief and desire. She moves forward to close the black out curtains, then uses the remote to turn on the gas fireplace. "Good. I've been waiting for this moment for months too and I can't wait a moment longer."

We stand facing each other and suddenly the magnitude of this moment hits me. This is really happening. After months of measured touches, we're finally free to be together completely. I don't have to angle my hands and fingers so I can touch her, hold myself back so I don't have to be sedated.

My hands shake slightly as I reach up to cup her beautiful face. After months of chains, controlling every impulse and wanting her so desperately I thought I might go mad, now Ellie is mine and there are no more barriers between us.

"No more chains," she whispers, her fingers tracing the line of my tusks with gentle reverence. "No more boundaries."

"I dreamt of this moment every night in that cage and also in that bed," I confess, my voice rougher than intended. "Of touching you freely and sinking inside of you."

Her hands slide up to frame my face. "I've been dreaming of it too."

Warmth blossoms in my chest. Ellie will be my first and only and I will fill her with my seed and our son. This is the moment all orcs wait their whole lives for and it's finally happening. And I'm luckier than most, because my bride is truly my bride. She loves me and wants to stay and become a family. She's declared her love for me in front of everyone we know.

My hands, free for the first time in months, roam down her sides to her waist. "I can't believe you're really mine," I murmur against her hair.

She tilts her head back to look up at me. And I capture her lips again. My fingers tangle in her hair causing it to loosen from the knot at the back of her head. Ellie's arms go around my neck and we kiss like it's our last moments on earth.

When we finally break apart, we're both breathing hard.

"That dress," I say, running my hands over the elegant fabric, "you look like something out of a dream."

"My mother picked it out," she says, smoothing her hands over my formal jacket. "You look very handsome in this suit, but I have to admit I prefer you shirtless."

I laugh, already reaching for my tie. "That can be arranged."

Then I pause and take her small, delicate hands in mine. "I need you to understand something important."

Her eyes search mine. "What?"

My voice comes out as a growl. "Orcs are very potent and human birth control doesn't work with orcs. I can scent that you are ready to accept my seed and create our son. You will become pregnant this evening. Are you ready for this to happen now?"

"Oh, Garlen." Happy tears sparkle in her eyes. "I would love to be a mother again. I've wanted more children for so long, but I never thought I'd find the right partner. Zoe would love to be an older sister." She grins up at me. "A few children, I think. And my mom would love more grandchildren to spoil."

"A large family," I say with satisfaction. "I like the sound of that."

"Then let's start making our first son tonight," she says, pulling me down for another kiss.

This time when our lips meet, it's with the knowledge that we're choosing this together.

My hands find the zipper of her wedding dress, and I lower it with reverent care. This dress that made her look like a queen, that marked the moment she became mine; this dress deserves to be treated like precious fabric.

The dress pools at her feet and she steps out of the circle of fabric. Heats spreads through my entire body as I see Ellie in the matching white lingerie and high heels. Her generous breasts are lifted by scraps of fabric that beg to be removed. She bends down, showing me her magnificent ass, as she gently picks the gown off the floor and carefully spreads it across the couch to save for later.

The she turns back, her hands on her wide hips. "Your turn."

"I can do this myself now."

"I know, but sometimes I might like to still help you undress." Ellie helps me out of my jacket and starts working on the buttons of my shirt. "Your chest is a work of art," she says, running her hands over my green skin as she reveals it. "Now I can touch all I want." Her exploration of my unchained body sends fire through my veins. Her hands roam over my arms, my chest, my back. "I've wanted to touch you like this since that first day in the snow," she confesses, her fingers tracing the lines of muscle down my torso.

I lean down to gently score my tusks against her neck, kissing down her throat. "And I've wanted to worship every inch of your body since the moment I caught your scent."

"It's a good thing I've taken my clothes off many times for our showers. At least I'm not shy being naked in front of you." She reaches back and unclasps the bra and it drops to the ground. I let out a growl of pure appreciation. Ellie has large breasts with small, pink nipples that I love to suck and pinch.

"Beautiful. Perfect. Mine."

"Yours," she agrees, her voice breathless with desire. "Always yours."

The removal of both of our final fabric barriers becomes a slow, deliberate dance. My hands shake slightly as I reveal more of her skin, months of fantasies finally becoming reality. "I have a confession," I murmur against her ear as I help her to lower her underwear and reveal her mound. "Every morning I was alone in that shower, every night in the cage, when I touched myself, I was thinking of this moment. Thinking of you."

"I have a confession too," she says as her cheeks flush. "For those two weeks when we couldn't meet but were only exchanging letters, I did the same thing, knowing you were just next door but I was unable to touch you the way I wanted."

Our confessions fuel the fire building between us.

And then we are both naked, with my erection bobbing in front of me, aching with need. I look at Ellie from head to toe, loving the sight of her dips and curves.

"Leave the heels on your feet."

She grins. "No problem. I like them too."

When I lift her and place her on our bed, the reality of our situation hits me again. She's here, she's mine, and I can claim her completely. But even with my freedom, I find myself holding back slightly. Three months of careful control are hard to shake.

"Garlen," she says, reading my hesitation perfectly. "I'm not fragile. I want all of you."

I give a curt nod. "I need to get you ready for me."

She splays her legs, putting those white heels perfectly on display. Ellie offers herself to me. Her hand with the sparkling ring moves down, near her mound to widen her pussy lips so I can see all she has to offer.

Her encouragement breaks through my restraint. I settle between her thick thighs and taste her properly for the first time, months of dreaming about this moment finally becoming reality. I've wanted this ability to stop at simply fingering my female to completion, and instead taste her, as she's tasted me. And then afterwards, sink inside of her wet channel.

Ellie is always so wet for me.

Her response to my tusks, my tongue, my complete focus on her pleasure is everything I hoped for. I start licking and sucking on her clit. These last two months of fingering her to completion have come in handy because I already know exactly how Ellie likes to be touched. This time I replace finger with tongue and enjoy the added benefit of her taste and juices on my face and mouth. This is the most erotic moment of my life.

She arches beneath me, pushing her hips closer to my face. Her hands fist in my hair as I work her with single-minded determination.

"Garlen," she cries out, her voice echoing freely through our bedroom. No need to muffle her sounds, no fear of being over-heard by family members downstairs. I love hearing my name on her lips. She grabs onto my horns and holds on tight.

I continue to lick and suck right where she needs me.

When her first orgasm crashes over her, she screams without restraint, her body clamping down as waves of pleasure course through her.

As Ellie recovers, I press gentle kisses to her inner thighs, savoring the satisfaction of pleasuring my mate without any limitations. I sit up and look down at her and use the back of my hand to wipe her juices off my face.

"That was..." she pants, then laughs breathlessly. "I want you inside me. Now."

"Are you sure?" I ask, though my cock throbs with desperate need.

"I've never been more sure of anything in my life. I need you. Now."

I position myself over her, my hands braced on either side of her head. Despite my desperation at losing my virginity to Ellie Irontree, I vow to go slowly. My female has never taken an orc into her body and I am indeed larger than a human male. She's had plenty of time to get used to my size in her hands and in her mouth, but this will be different. I've gotten her wet and ready, but I will take this slow. I notch the head of my cock at her entrance and slide only the crown in carefully, watching her face for any sign of discomfort. The slit at the tip continues to leak seed, causing the easy slide inside of her body.

"Keep going," she begs.

So I continue.

Ellie's nails scratch my back and she cries out as I fill her up. I lift one of her thighs with my hand so I can bottom out all the way. She chokes as I sink fully inside her.

I pause, allowing myself to take a moment to wonder at the feel of her hot channel enveloping my shaft. The sensation is exquisite. Eventually I'll want my seed in her mouth, on her face and even rubbed onto her breasts. Ellie covered in my scent is my daily goal. But my overriding goal right now is to get her pregnant. I need to breed this female.

She whimpers in distress. "Why have you stopped?"

"I love you," I growl against her neck.

"I love you too," she responds, her legs wrapping around my hips. "Faster," she orders.

I grin then I'm kissing her. I thread her fingers in mine and hold onto her tight as I fuck her hard on our bed. The bed squeaks as I move in and out, loving the feel of the slide in her tight channel around my cock for the first time. "This time will be fast," I warn her. "It's my first."

Her order to go faster quickly pushes me closer to the edge. But because I'm determined to give her everything, I reach between us to stroke her clit as I move inside her, and her response is immediate and explosive.

My female cries out as her second orgasm crashes through her and I feel her channel clamping down on my shaft.

I throw my head back and roar out my own release, months of need finally satisfied as I begin to fill her with my seed. The moment feels monumental, claiming my mate, potentially creating our first child, finally consummating the bond that started in the snow three months ago.

My own release hits me hard.

I lift up and look down at where we are joined and watch as my cock throbs inside of her with my release. I'm filling her up and at the same time the pleasure is so intense it's hard to remain upright. "I love you, my bride," I rasp.

Finally, I pull out, trying my best to keep all my seed inside of her. The feeling of being with my bride completely, with no barriers and no fear, overwhelms me.

We stay connected afterward, both of us overwhelmed by the emotional intensity of what just happened. I gather her close, pressing kisses to her hair as we catch our breath.

"Was it worth the wait?" she asks eventually, her voice teasing but her eyes serious.

"Worth every day in chains," I answer honestly. "Worth every moment of restraint."

We lie together while the sound of our reception continues faintly outside. Her head rests on my chest as she traces lazy patterns on my skin.

"We have all week," I murmur, my hands already roaming freely over her curves. "Seven days with just us, in this house. I plan to keep you in this bed," I add, already stirring with renewed desire. "We have months to make up for," I explain, rolling her beneath me again. "And now that I'm free to touch you, to claim you, to love you properly, I plan to make the most of every moment." I slide inside of her wet channel.

Her smile is radiant as she pulls me down for another kiss. "That sounds like a great plan."

Epilogue

Anna

I SIT at one of the long, white-draped tables, watching the wedding reception continue in the tent, despite the fact that the bride and groom disappeared over an hour ago. When Garlen swept Ellie off her feet and carried her into the house, everyone cheered and whistled.

Now the guests make jokes about how the newlyweds "couldn't even wait for cake."

"Twenty bucks says no one sees them until school starts again," Principal VanWagoner announces, obviously tipsy from the orc ale. Several orcs from various clans chuckle and raise their tankards in agreement.

Everyone happily enjoys the food, the music and the orc ale.

I smile at the scene but that familiar hint of sadness returns. That feeling of being on the outside looking in. I'm thrilled that my friend has found the love of her life. I'm equally thrilled for Garlen that he found a woman who was brave enough to put up with him turning into a wild beast each time she was near. And they really do seem right for each other. I'm happy for them. But a part of me is jealous, because I've always wanted that for myself…marriage and a family.

The way my life is right now, that fantasy seems farther away than ever.

Zoe runs around with Loki, collecting flower petals and probably getting grass stains on her white dress. There are lots of people, mingling with orcs and everyone looks so happy, so carefree, so genuinely joyful to be celebrating love.

Dane and Laurie sway together on the makeshift dance floor. She looks so beautiful, wearing high heels and a sexy, mother of the bride dress that shows off her figure.

I used to be like that once. I was confident. Outgoing. The kind of woman who drew attention without trying. I had long black hair that flowed past my shoulders and wore form-fitting, plus size outfits that made me feel beautiful and powerful at the same time. I taught college literature courses and loved every minute of it. I was still the same size as I am now, still short and thick, but I carried myself differently. I believed I deserved good things.

Now I dress in neutral colors and slightly baggy, conservative clothes. My hair is cut into a severe bob and I wear minimal makeup. Not because I think I'm unattractive, but because standing out feels dangerous. What I told Ellie is true, I do think that being overweight means less eyes on me, but in the past I never let it bother me so much. I was in the same frame of mind as Ellie, strutting my stuff in stylish clothes. Despite the weight I always thought I looked damn good. I was asked out often, I believe, because I exuded confidence.

But nowadays being noticed feels like a threat. A year ago, my life changed drastically to the point where I had to go into hiding and start all over with a new name. This changed my relationship with my own confidence.

My gaze drifts across the assembled party and lands on Keric Irontree. He stands near the buffet table, talking to an orc I've learned is named Owen Bloodtree. They are deep in conversation. Even in his formal suit, there's something undeniably commanding about Keric's presence. Broad shoulders, confident posture, those intelligent dark eyes that seem to notice everything. And a very fine ass.

I know orcs appreciate women of all sizes. Ellie's taught me that much through her relationship with Garlen. But there's a difference between being appreciated and being desired, and I've spent so long trying to be invisible that I'm not sure I remember how to be seen.

Keric is almost as tall as Garlen and his features are a tiny bit terrifying. His black horns are tall and twisted, his tusks seem thicker and his nose is crooked. Women whisper that he's the "scary Irontree." I've noticed over these last few months that everyone approaches Jonus if they need to talk to an Irontree, or maybe they go to Dane or Aldar, but they entirely avoid Keric.

I don't feel that way at all. Yes, he's quiet but I've always liked the dark, brooding type. The type who would save his best words for me.

My mind immediately goes back to that terrifying day at Black Oak when Garlen lost control. I was leaving the building with Ellie when we heard the commotion in the parking lot. Parents were screaming, students were running, and there was this massive orc charging toward the school like something out of a nightmare.

Back then, I didn't personally know Garlen and I was simply terrified of this raging beast that looked like it was going to attack us. I tried to get Ellie to run away with me, but she stood strong, boldly, telling me to go and that she would take care of it.

I was confused for a moment, unsure of what to do.

Then suddenly, Keric was there. Strong hands gripping my shoulders, pulling me back, his body shielding mine from whatever danger might be coming. I remember the scent of his skin, something warm and clean and utterly masculine. I felt protected for the first time in years, wrapped in the safety of his large body.

"Stay here," he'd murmured in my ear once we'd reached the hallway, his voice calm despite the chaos around us. "I've got you."

I'd wanted him to keep holding me even after the danger passed.

And ever since, I've been harboring this secret attraction towards Keric, but how could I possibly admit it to anyone? Especially Ellie, who's so happy with her own orc romance. How do I tell my best friend that I'm hopelessly attracted to her husband's cousin when he was obviously just doing his job that day? He protects everyone, that's what he does. It wasn't personal.

Maybe orcs only like confident women like Ellie? I'm still working on remembering who I used to be, let alone figuring out who I want to become.

I catch Keric looking in my direction and feel that familiar jolt of electricity. Our eyes meet across the space for a moment, long enough for my heart to start racing, before we both look away. He's probably just keeping an eye on everyone, making sure all the guests are safe and comfortable. It doesn't mean anything.

Does it?

I'm lost in my own thoughts when a shadow falls across my table. I look up to find Keric standing there with two plates of food from the buffet, looking slightly uncertain.

"Is it appropriate for me to sit here, next to you?" he asks, gesturing to the empty chair beside me. "Everywhere else seems to be taken."

I glance around the tables and notice at least a dozen empty chairs scattered throughout the space.

"Of course," I manage, hoping my voice sounds steady.

Keric settles his large body into the chair next to me, close enough that I can smell that same warm, clean scent from the day he protected me. My entire body heats up again because I swear I'm even more attracted to him than I was before.

"I noticed you weren't eating yet so I brought you a plate," he says, sliding one of the dishes toward me. "Wasn't sure what you liked, so I got a little of everything."

"Thank you." I stare down at the food, noticing the perfectly arranged samples of everything from the elaborate buffet. "That's nice of you. I was waiting for the line to die down and I was about to get up soon and go over there. I appreciate you thinking of me."

He gives me a smile that looks more like a grimace.

We eat in companionable but slightly awkward silence. I overthink every bite, worried about chewing too loudly or getting food stuck in my teeth. Keric seems relaxed, but I catch him stealing glances at me when he thinks I'm not looking.

This is ridiculous. I'm a grown woman. Having dinner conversation with a perfectly nice orc shouldn't be this hard.

"Anna. Keric." Zoe's voice breaks through the tension as she plops down in the chair across from us. Loki, her constant companion, immediately positions himself under the table for optimal begging opportunities.

"Are you having fun at Mommy's wedding?" she asks, reaching down to pet Loki's head.

"It was a beautiful ceremony," I tell her honestly. "Your mommy looked like a princess."

"She did," Zoe agrees enthusiastically. "And Garlen looked like a prince, even with his big teeth."

Are Keric's lips twitching?

"And you and Loki did a great job, going down the aisle and giving Garlen the ring."

She smiles wide, loving the praise. Then Zoe looks over at Keric. "Uncle Keric, why are you always at the school?"

"It's my job to make sure everyone stays safe."

She tilts her head. "Do you like being a bodyguard?"

Keric reflects on her question for a moment before answering.

"I've never thought of myself as a bodyguard, but it's true that I like protecting people who are important to me."

Zoe turns to me with innocent, six-year-old directness. "Do you like Keric, Anna? He looks scary but he's really nice and he's not married."

Heat floods my cheeks. "Zoe, that's not... we're just..."

"I think Anna's very nice too," Keric answers smoothly. There's something in his tone that makes my stomach flutter. "She's an excellent teacher."

"How do you know?" Zoe asks.

"I've been paying attention."

The way he says it, looking directly at me, makes my breath catch. He's been paying attention? To me?

"Loki wants some chicken," Zoe announces, apparently bored with adult conversation. She tears off a small piece from her plate and feeds it to the eager corgi.

"Is that okay for him to eat?" I ask, grateful for the distraction.

"Everything in moderation," Keric says. "Though I think Loki's definition of moderation is different from ours."

Zoe wanders away, and Keric and I fall into easy conversation. We talk about the wedding, the school, and where he's going to live now that Ellie and Garlen are officially married and most likely starting a family at this very moment. I wouldn't be surprised if Ellie ends up needing to go on maternity leave for the second half of next school year.

Keric asks thoughtful questions about my classes and my students, like he's genuinely interested in my thoughts and opinions, which is super sweet.

I reach for a napkin and Keric happens to be doing the same thing, which causes our hands to brush together for a moment. The contact sends electricity shooting up my arm, and from the way Keric's eyes widen slightly, I think he feels it too.

"I should probably get your number," he says suddenly, then seems to realize how abrupt that sounds. "For school security updates, I mean. In case anything else happens that might affect faculty safety."

I adore his flimsy excuse.

"Of course," I say, pulling out my phone with slightly shaky hands. "That makes sense."

We exchange numbers, and I try not to read too much into the way he smiles when he saves my contact information.

I look around and notice that we must've been talking for much longer than I'd thought, because the music has stopped and it looks like people are leaving. "I should probably head home," I say reluctantly, even though I don't want this conversation to end. "It's been a long day."

"It has," he agrees, standing at the same time as I do. "Anna?"

"Yes?"

"I'd like to text you. If that's okay. Not just about security updates."

My heart does a little flip. "I'd like that too."

And then a group of rowdy orcs arrives, sweeping Keric along with them "to the brewery."

I laugh and wave goodbye to the orc I'm crushing hard on.

After making my goodbyes to everyone else still there, I finally walk to my car feeling lighter than I have in years. I check my phone every few seconds even though I know it's too soon for him to have texted. For the first time since I entered witness protection, I feel like maybe, just maybe, I could have something good in my life again.

My apartment complex is quiet when I arrive home. I'm still thinking about Keric's proud profile, about the way he said he'd been paying attention and I can't get over the power of his muscular arms.

Then I notice a package sitting outside my door. And it's not a delivery. It's a plain brown box with my name written on the front in block letters. No return address, no delivery service sticker.

Dammit.

Nothing good will come from this. I wasn't expecting anything, and packages don't usually get left in the hallway without building management signing for them.

I carry it inside with a heavy heart and set it on my coffee table, staring at it like it might explode. With trembling fingers, I open the box and start pulling out the contents one by one.

A picture of my original driver's license with my real name and a photo from my old life. Another picture of my faculty ID from the university where I used to teach. And then, underneath those painful reminders of who I used to be, I find the recent surveillance photos.

Me walking into Black Oak Academy.

Me having coffee with Ellie at the faculty lounge.

Me laughing at something Principal VanWagoner said during a staff meeting.

And the final photo, clearly taken just hours ago of me sitting at the wedding reception, talking to Keric. Who at the reception could've taken this? Everyone there should've been friends or family of Ellie and the Irontrees.

At the bottom of the box is a simple white note card with a message written in the same block letters as my name on the package:

We've found you Dr. Kim. You have 24 hours. Give us the information we require and no one will be hurt.

The note falls from my numb fingers as the full impact hits me. They found me. After years of hiding, of carefully building this new identity, of finally starting to feel safe again, they found me.

And they've been watching. For how long? Weeks? Months? They know about my job, my friendship with Ellie, and now they know about Keric.

I sink to the floor, surrounded by the evidence of my shattered security. My hands now shake so badly I can barely hold the surveillance photo of Keric and me. We look happy in it, relaxed, like we might've had a future together.

But there can't be a future. Not now. Not when being near me puts him in danger, puts all of them in danger.

I look at my phone, at Keric's number that I entered less than an hour ago with such hope and excitement. I think about his smile and those shiny tusks, about the way he said he'd been paying attention, about the possibility of something real and good finally coming into my life.

"I'm so sorry," I whisper to the photo, heat stinging behind my eyes.

I have to disappear again. I must protect everyone I've grown to care about, even if it means breaking my own heart in the process.

The cruel irony of this moment isn't lost on me. For the first time in years, I felt a genuine connection with someone. I thought maybe I could have a normal life, maybe even find love.

But my past has finally caught up with me, and the price of staying is too high.

About the Author

Michele Mills lives in California and leads a life of quiet, G rated desperation with her husband and two sons. In an attempt at a fulfilling, R rated inner life that does not include Disney movies and Nickelodeon; Michele reads and writes filthy romance and, well...filthy romance. And she wouldn't have it any other way.

For more books and updates:
authormichelemills.com

www.ingramcontent.com/pod-product-compliance
Lightning Source LLC
Chambersburg PA
CBHW010726310726
48971CB00009B/2747